A MISBEGOTTEN MATCH

RITA BOUCHER

AVON BOOKS NEW YORK

A MISBEGOTTEN MATCH is an original publication of Avon Books. This work has never before appeared in book form. This work is a novel. Any similarity to actual persons or events is purely coincidental.

AVON BOOKS
A division of
The Hearst Corporation
1350 Avenue of the Americas
New York, New York 10019

First Avon Books Printing: November 1994

AVON TRADEMARK REG. U.S. PAT. OFF. AND IN OTHER COUNTRIES, MARCA REGISTRADA, HECHO EN U.S.A.

Printed in the U.S.A.

RA   10 9 8 7 6 5 4 3 2 1

"You seem very anxious to be rid of me and I find myself wondering why."

"I should think it would be obvious. 'Tis your irresistible charm," Amanda said, her tone sarcastic but her heart knowing that she spoke far more honestly than she wished to admit.

To her surprise, Sebastian laughed. It was a delightfully deep and resonant sound, sending a delicious shiver down to her toes.

"Oh that hurts," he said, a devilish gleam lighting his eyes.

"The truth usually does, Mr. Armitage."

———— ∞∞∞ ————

To Binnie,
the labor coach in the birth of this book
and to Sann L.B.C.L.

PROLOGUE

CHESHIRE, ENGLAND, 1805

Lady Claire had always numbered "if only" among the saddest phrases in the English tongue, as well as the most useless. Yet, she could not help but castigate herself with it. If only she had not gone to London for the Season. If only she had not suggested that her dear friends, the Reverend and Mrs. Armitage, borrow her carriage for a holiday in Bath. If only she had gotten the message regarding the fatal roadway accident sooner, the boy need not have mourned alone.

But all the wishes in the world could not undo the whims of fate. In her nearly threescore years, Lady Claire had learned that much. Nonetheless, as Sebastian Armitage entered the room, she could not help but mourn the carefree child who had waved away her traveling coach only a month before. Disaster had conferred its own dark dignity and it was now plain to see that her godson had passed from that downy-cheeked youthful state of grace into the harsh reality of manhood. The black crepe band around his arm was entirely superfluous. One had only to look at that bleak face, that aspect of utter despair, to know the true meaning of sorrow.

"Lady Claire," he bowed formally as the butler closed the door behind him. "I presume that you have heard."

She wanted to rush forward, to hug the boy close, to comfort and be comforted for the loss that they shared. A month ago, it would have been so, but now those azure eyes regarded her with terrible wisdom more fitting to a man of sixty than a mere stripling of sixteen. "Sebastian," she said,

1

infusing the name with every ounce of her sorrow and sympathy. "I . . . I . . ."

Sebastian watched his godmother, listening as she struggled to pull forth the words from the depths of her heart, but he could not help her by joining his sorrow to hers. His own emotions were barely under control. A part of him wanted to throw himself in her arms, to bawl like a baby, but he was determined never to cry again. He would have to tell her, of course. As his godmother, she had the right to the truth. Yet, even though he had known this diminutive woman all of his life, he suddenly felt very much a stranger to her. And to himself.

Deliberately, he put himself at a distance, his eyes without tears, his voice without tone, as he gave her what little consolation he could. "They died quickly, Lady Claire," Sebastian said stiffly. "The magistrate said that they scarcely knew what hit them."

"And the drunken lout whose phaeton swiped them off the road?" Lady Claire asked.

"Dead as well," Sebastian answered.

"Good." Lady Claire gave a nod of satisfaction as she wiped away a tear. "Then there is some justice to be found in this world. Although I suspect that your dear papa would have styled that a vengeful thought."

"The Reverend was a saintly man," Sebastian said, his nails biting into his palms. How was he to begin? he wondered. He could scarcely believe the fact himself much less bear it. Lady Claire would be dreadfully hurt when she found out that Nathan and Celia Armitage had deceived her for all those years.

"You will move in here with me, of course, my boy," Lady Claire said, giving him the freedom of her mansion with a sweep of her arms. "Consider the Mills your home until you return to school."

"I am not going back to school, Lady Claire," Sebastian said softly, looking down at his muddy boots.

"Not now, naturally," Lady Claire said, her voice deep with sympathy as she drew closer to him. "It is too soon, I know. But next term . . ."

"I am not going back," he repeated.

"But it was what your father would have wished," Lady

Claire said in growing puzzlement. The boy was not acting himself. Of course, that was to be expected, given the fact that he had buried his parents barely a month before, but he was avoiding her eyes.

"What the Reverend wanted is no longer of any importance," Sebastian said, his teeth clenching despite himself. "I am not the stuff of which good clerics are made, Lady Claire. One must have faith to serve in the church, and I have quite lost mine."

"Oh, my dear boy," Lady Claire said gently, coming to his side and placing a hand on his shoulder. " 'Tis quite natural at times to doubt, to misplace faith temporarily if you will, but to lose it entirely? Why your father . . ."

"Nathan Armitage was not my father!" Sebastian exploded, shrugging her hand away. "And Celia Armitage was not my mother!" He met Lady Claire's eyes at last, seeking expectantly for some sign of indignation, of shock, but all he saw was pity and sadness. "You *knew,*" he whispered, his stomach roiling at the sudden realization. "You knew that I was a foundling child."

"Yes, I knew," Lady Claire replied hoarsely, his look of betrayal striking anguish into her very marrow. "How did you find out?"

Sebastian nodded, his eyes storm-laden. "My erstwhile *uncle* was *kind* enough to offer me a ride in his carriage on the way home from the cemetery. I was somewhat surprised, since he and . . . his sister . . . had never quite gotten along."

"He had never approved of Celia's marriage to a penniless cleric," Lady Claire said.

Sebastian swallowed, recalling his humiliation. "He only wished to make certain that I had no foolish ideas. He made it quite clear that there was no familial obligation to some whore's misbegotten whelp left on the church altar."

"Dear heaven," Lady Claire whispered, a tide of outrage swelling within her. There had been no need for such cruelty. . . . If only . . .

Sebastian's eyes darkened as he continued, "I watched him as he went through the Vicarage, touching their things, cursing his foolish brother-in-law for dying with no more than thirty pounds to his name. He took everything of value . . . *everything.*"

Lady Claire closed her eyes, feeling the anguished echo of Sebastian's tormented voice vibrating in the air. She had feared this moment might come eventually, discussed the possibility with Nathan and Celia. But they had never anticipated quite these circumstances, this welter of anger and emotion. Sense would not prevail and there was no balm that she could offer to soothe this raw pain.

"Who else other than you and my 'uncle' know of my origins?" Sebastian demanded from between clenched teeth. "Was *I* the only one kept in the dark?"

"Other than myself, as your godmother, your parents told no one," Lady Claire hastened to reassure him. "Your father left an excellent living in Kent so that you would be fully accepted as their son here in Cheshire. Nathan had no relations that I know of. Only your un . . . Celia's brother was aware of the truth."

"The truth . . ." Sebastian echoed, bitterly. "That the woman who bore me was likely some harlot who threw me away, a bit of useless trash."

"No . . . Sebastian," Lady Claire said, taking a step toward him, but his cold glare warned her away. It was clear that he would accept nothing from her, not even comfort. Taking a deep breath, she realized that reason was the only available course. Although she doubted he could be brought to see it, she had to try. "If you do not intend to return to your studies, what do you wish to do?"

"It is my intention to enlist in the army," he said, his chin thrust out in defiance.

"As a common soldier?" The plumes on Lady Claire's turban waved in indignation. "I can only conclude you to be mad with sorrow. Or do you wish yourself to Hell so quickly? You were meant for a cleric, not cannon fodder. You are my godson, boy," Lady Claire said, trying to reach beyond his grief and rage. "I took that responsibility freely and I will fulfill that obligation. Your father—"

"He was not my father!" Sebastian exclaimed. "It was a lie. *All of you* lied to me."

"You were his son, in all ways that mattered," Lady Claire said, desperation seeping into her voice. "They loved you. If you do not wish to live with me, the Vicarage can remain your home. I will let you stay for as long as you wish."

"I cannot remain here," Sebastian said, turning away, refusing to be moved by her plea. "Can you not see that? When the villagers give me their condolences upon my *father and mother,* 'tis all I can do not to scream like a madman. Ever since I can remember, I have been Sebastian Armitage, the vicar's son. The cloth of my dreams, my expectations were shaped by that simple fact. But all that has changed. In the space of a few days, nothing is true, not even my own name. I could be anyone's son, a sweep or a lord, a beggar or a dustman, but someone's bastard just the same. I must go, Lady Claire."

"Yes," she said sadly. "I can see that. But if it is the army that you choose, let me buy you colors at the least and frank you until you are on your feet."

"Fulfilling your godmother's obligation?" he asked with a humorless laugh. "Very well. I may be a bastard, but I am not a fool. I fully intend to pay you back, in full; I swear it."

" 'Tis not obligation," Lady Claire said, "but a gift of love. I want no payment."

"Then I want none of your charity or your lies," Sebastian retorted. "Take my oath or I shall take nothing from you."

"Very well, Sebastian," she said, turning away from the force of his scorn. It was almost unbearable to look at him. "But you must believe—"

"Do not tell me what I ought to believe," he said, his voice close to breaking. "I have been a believer all my life. From now on, I have only myself to believe in. Only myself to depend on . . ."

Tears slipped silently down Lady Claire's cheek. "Remember, Sebastian, you can always come back to me," she said, but she was never quite sure if he had heard her. For when she turned round to face him once again, she was alone.

1

LONDON, 1821

Amanda Westford stepped uncertainly from the entryway into the elegant interior of Madame Robarde's salon. The glances of the shopgirls were scornful as they apparently dismissed her as unworthy of their attention; for the first time in years, Amanda was conscious of the sorry state of her clothing.

"Do you have an appointment?" one of them inquired in a tone that put the question beyond the realm of impossibility.

"I . . . I . . ." Amanda had never thought of herself as vulnerable to intimidation. Yet she now found herself feeling almost cowed by those disdainful eyes. In fact, the young woman might very well have retreated if not for the small, bony hand that reached up to clamp with bracing firmness on her arm.

"You are obviously new here, gel," Lady Claire said, popping out like a jack-in-the-box from behind Amanda. *"I* have *never* required an appointment." The elderly spinster's red-plumed turban bobbed like a cock's comb as she hobbled into the salon, her ivory-headed cane thumping an angry rhythm.

Amanda followed reluctantly behind and helped the old woman settle into one of the plush, gilt-armed chairs at the center of the shop. "Please, Lady Claire, you really ought to rest," she whispered.

"Nonsense!" Lady Claire hissed. "I have waited years for this day and you shall not cheat me of it." She scowled forbiddingly, as if daring Amanda to speak another word. "Tell Natalie Robarde that Lady Claire has arrived," she commanded the shopgirls, brandishing her cane like the scepter of a miniature potentate, "and if she wishes to sell her ridiculously priced garments, she had best make a quick appearance."

A girl scurried off to tell Madame Robarde that her shop had been invaded by a diminutive Bedlamite.

"Really, Lady Claire, this is not necessary. I do not know how you talked me into this. Look at this place," Amanda said, with an encompassing, waving gesture that emphasized her growing dismay. "I have little doubt that even the most modest of garments will cost a sizable fortune."

"There is nothing modest about Natalie Robarde's garments," Lady Claire corrected, with an amused quirk of her eyebrow. "And her creations are well worth every farthing of the cost, though you must not tell her I say so, else she would surely raise the price."

"I must insist that we leave here," Amanda persisted with a sigh of exasperation, wondering how Lady Claire had managed to wheedle her into this untenable situation. "Surely Mrs. Peggoty could make me up some dresses. We could buy some cloth at the draper's."

"More bombazine, no doubt. Pah!" Lady Claire proclaimed dryly, fingering the stuff of Amanda's dress with disgust. "All these years you have offended what remains of my eyesight with those scarecrow garments of yours."

"They were within my means," Amanda said, her shoulders stiffening at the criticism. "And they were appropriate to my station."

"Do not get up on your high horse with me," the old woman said with a sniff, "for I know that it was pride more than necessity that kept you garbed in those foul weeds. You have refused my every offer of help lo these many years—"

"You have done so much already," Amanda protested. "I do not know what Marcus and I would have done without you, Lady Claire. It was you who—"

"Yes, yes, I am a veritable saint," Lady Claire said with a snort. "And you are a regular martyr; a lovely pair the two of us. T'was all very well to dress like a ragged nun when you had no funds, but now I shall allow no excuses. Sit up straight and stop looking like a rabbit in a poacher's net. Natalie Robarde is a modiste, not a butcher."

"You must be exhausted," Amanda objected, beginning to

rise from her seat. "You recall what Dr. Howell said about rest."

"And when have I ever listened to that fool's advice? I refuse to be treated as an invalid," Lady Claire grumbled, putting a restraining hand on the girl's arm. "Do not think to use my health as an excuse, Amanda; for you will not be allowed to leave Madame Robarde's without a decent wardrobe."

"But she is so expensive," Amanda complained. "Surely there is someone who could outfit me at a more reasonable price."

"You no longer have to count shillings and pence," Lady Claire's wrinkled face lit with a smile. "You have all the Hartleigh fortune in your pocket; might as well get a start on spending it."

"A case of too much, too late, I would say," Amanda said, the bitterness rising sour in her throat. "They cut my mother off without a penny piece. I want nothing to do with their dirty money."

"Stuff and nonsense!" Lady Claire exclaimed, her lips pursing in annoyance. "If it were me, I would wallow in their filthy lucre. I vow, if the high-and-mighty earls of Hartleigh can see you from their eternal torment in the depths of Hell, your pleasure will be the ultimate vengeance. Spend their money. Buy yourself a bit of ease, for you certainly deserve it."

"Do you think that it is proper?" Amanda began in concern. "A woman in my position . . ."

"There is nothing exceptionable in garbing yourself decently, I assure you. And although I many not act so on all occasions, *I* know what is proper."

"B . . . b . . . but," Amanda stuttered.

"I shall brook no 'buts' nor 'ifs,' 'ands' or 'maybes.' You shall buy yourself some acceptable clothes, Amanda Westford. Oh!" The elderly woman put a hand to her forehead.

"What is it, Lady Claire?" Amanda asked, taking the old woman's hand in concern.

"My vinaigrette," Lady Claire whispered.

Amanda fumbled with her friend's reticule, located the vial of sal volatile, pulled the stopper, and passed it beneath Lady

Claire's nose. The elderly lady's drooping eyes opened wide at the scent of the noxious fumes and she coughed vigorously.

"Perhaps we should return to your town house?" Amanda asked in growing guilt. "You are half–done-in after spending the entire morning with me in the solicitor's chambers."

"Poppycock! I have not enjoyed myself half so much in years," Lady Claire declared, her eyes bright both with the effects of spirits of ammonia and satisfaction. "I had a splendid time this morning, outfacing those crusty old windbags who were trying to cheat you of your legacy."

"They almost had my sympathy," Amanda said, looking anxiously at the pasty tint of her elderly friend's complexion. "Though you come barely to their shoulders, I vow you had those solicitors shivering in their stockings."

"As well they should have been! There is clearly no basis for contesting the will, although they would have had you think otherwise. It was abundantly apparent that you are the sole remaining heir of Hartleigh blood. The title must, of course, die, but the fortune is entirely yours."

"I cannot blame them for being somewhat skeptical of my identity," Amanda countered.

"Did you not see their faces when you produced your mother's marriage lines? When they realized that your parents' union was not a mere over-the-anvil match?" Lady Claire said with a dismissive wave of her hand. "Do not waste your pity on those fusty old legal gabblers. Gretna marriages are deuced hard to prove and they could have made it difficult for you, had your papa not done it up right and tight. At least that can be said for him."

"At least," Amanda agreed, having no illusions as to her father's motives for observing the legal formalities. A penniless drawing master, Henri Maisson had schemed to marry a fortune. To his everlasting disappointment, his earl's daughter had brought him only love. Unfortunately, that ephemeral emotion had quickly vanished with the realities of poverty. "But I still cannot draw on the money. I cannot even pay for the modiste."

Lady Claire waved a dismissive hand. "I shall frank you and then you may reimburse me, you tiresome gel, for I know that you will insist on it, just as you are determined to pay me for the Vicarage, even though I would gladly deed it to you."

"Indeed, I shall pay you, Lady Claire," Amanda said, reality slowly beginning to dawn. "In fact, it thrills me beyond measure to be able to pay my own way at last." The Midas hoard of the Hartleighs would soon be at her disposal; it was far beyond the realm of dreams. She gave herself a mental shake, telling herself that nothing that truly mattered had changed. "Although I still find it difficult to spend money so freely."

"Nothing difficult about it at all," Lady Claire declared vehemently. "You are the last of the Hartleighs, and a very wealthy woman."

"Calm yourself, Lady Claire," Amanda cautioned, worrying at her aged companion's agitated demeanor. "Remember your heart."

"If you are so concerned about my organs, I would suggest that you contradict me no further," Lady Claire snapped. "You shall be clothed as befits your new station, my gel."

Amanda had no more time to protest as a woman who was obviously Madame Robarde bustled in. "Ah, Lady Claire, a delight to see you, as always," she said in accented English, a genuine smile touching her lips. "Only for you would I leave ze customer waiting. Tell me how may I serve you today."

"No, Natalie, 'tis not I who requires your magic touch, but my young friend here, Mrs. Westford," Lady Claire said, slipping from her chair and drawing Amanda to her feet.

The modiste reached up and took the hat from Amanda's head, tossing it to the floor like a dirty rag as she looked the young woman up and down. "Your hair, Madame Westford. I would see eet loose."

Feeling much like a horse at Tattersall's, Amanda took the pins from her nondescript knot, letting the curls fall in a dark mane.

Madame Robarde nodded appraisingly. "Ze coleur of black opal. We dress her in blues, greens, silver for the eyes."

Lady Claire nodded agreement. "Do you think that her height will be a problem?" she asked. "She is unusually tall—although I must admit that everyone appears tall to me."

"Au contraire; it shall be made into ze asset. She is not what would be called a beauty," the modiste said frankly. "But she has ze air, zat which will make men look twice . . .

once I have gowned her, of course," she added. "Now if you would but excuse me, I must return to ze fitting room. My assistants shall bring ze fabrics and I shall return shortly."

"You must inform Madame Robarde that she is mistaken," Amanda said, when the modiste left the room. "I do not wish for anyone to 'look twice' at me, *especially* a man. I am a companion."

"You *were* a companion." Lady Claire corrected with quiet emphasis, seating herself once more. "Surely you do not mean to continue attending to a crotchety old woman's whims now that you have some wealth in your pocket?"

"Are you dismissing me then?" Amanda asked, her stomach twisting. Did Lady Claire mean to cast her loose because of her sudden change in fortune? It would only make sense that the elderly lady would wish to seek someone else to keep her company. *Leave Millford? Take Marcus from the only home that he had ever known?* "Can we not go on as before?"

The sudden look of panic in those gray pools tore at Lady Claire's heart. Amanda had endured so much. Lady Claire had no desire to poke at old wounds, yet the time had come to cease self-recriminations, to let go of the past and seize a new future. The tiny lady leaned over to give the girl's hand a reassuring pat as she began to probe obliquely. "It is just that now you can afford to go where you will, do whatever you wish. You no longer have to scrape for a living."

"It is all so strange." Amanda half laughed in bewilderment. "Like the fairy stories I used to dream of when I was a child. I would imagine that Mama's family had realized their terrible error and had decided to take Papa and myself back into their bosom. There was always food in my fantasies, for we were so often hungry. I only fear that I may wake up, as I used to." She ran a hand across the velvet armrest of her chair almost as if to reassure herself that it was all real. "But even if this dream is to go on forever, Lady Claire, you know that there is no place in the world that I would rather be than with you. I have found peace in Millford."

"Have you?" Lady Claire asked, deeply touched, her unspoken worry partially fading. Amanda did not intend to leave outright. In her seventy-five years, Lady Claire had learned that attachments formed by dependence often dissolved when need disappeared. Now that Amanda had a fortune at her disposal, she no longer required help. Not that she had allowed Lady Claire to assist her much anyway. All offers of comfort had been politely but firmly refused. It was as if the girl were placing a penance upon herself for past sins, denying herself pleasure out of some exaggerated sense of propriety. Nonetheless, the old woman was glad to learn that the newfound fortune would not cause her to lose Amanda's companionship. That would have been almost beyond bearing.

However, Lady Claire was far too honest and too concerned for the girl's good to let the matter rest. Amanda had lived like a hermit for nearly nine years. Reluctantly, the elderly lady pointed out the young woman's options, knowing full well that Amanda might yet choose to leave her. "You could create yourself a place in society now that you are an heiress," Lady Claire said.

"I would not subject Marcus to that," Amanda said, her mouth curving into a soft smile as she thought of her son. Although she had been in London for but a few days, she missed him and his steady stream of inquiries about everything and everyone he saw. It was the first time since his birth that they had been separated. Marcus would have loved London, yet she knew that she had been right to leave him in Cheshire, beyond the prying investigations of the solicitors. "I have no right."

"You have as much right as any of them, child," Lady Claire said, thumping her cane emphatically. "Your blood is every bit as good as theirs. You need not hang your head forever."

"There would be the inevitable questions," Amanda persisted. "I doubt that even the Hartleigh fortune could buy me the mantle of respectability, should the truth become known. In these things the female is always—" Amanda froze in midsentence, her gray eyes growing wide as the color disappeared from her face.

"Amanda, whatever is . . ." Lady Claire looked past her protégé to see Lady Whittlesea emerging from the fitting rooms.

Lady Whittlesea stared momentarily, as if confronting an apparition, her lips clamped together in a tight line before arching into a pasteboard smile. "Why, Claire! When did you come to town?" She advanced, pointedly ignoring Amanda's existence.

Lady Claire made no reply. A fractional rising of the chin made the eloquent statement—neither blindness nor deafness was preventing her from acknowledging the other woman. It was a merciless cut direct. Not even by a quiver did Lady Claire betray her satisfaction as Lady Whittlesea went stark white with rage.

A sharp intake of breath preceded a drawn-out "Well!" Only when Lady Whittlesea stalked from the salon with her maid trailing behind her did Lady Claire allow herself a slight smirk of victory.

"You did not have to do that, Lady Claire," Amanda said with quiet gratitude.

"Nonsense. That old hen deserved it," Lady Claire said, her voice trembling with suppressed anger. "It was her fault. Oh, why was I ever such a fool as to give you into her employ? I should have taken you abroad with me, but I thought that you would be far happier among those closer to your own age than saddled to an elderly spinster."

"Why do you persist in blaming yourself? I do not know what I would have done after Papa died, if not for you." Amanda took the old woman's hand, stroking it in a calming manner. "The offer to be the Whittleseas' governess was like an answer to a prayer. What respectable employment is available to a girl of seventeen?"

"Lady Whittlesea hired you out of parsimony, you know. She was the only one in that family who ever knew how to save a penny. Even then, her husband and son were all-oars-rowing down the River Tick. I still say she ought to have known what was going on in her own household," the old woman said, her voice quavering.

"That is all water over the dam," Amanda sighed, wondering how she could soothe Lady Claire's jangled nerves. The pulse beneath the wrinkled skin was visibly pounding like a post-horse's hooves. "And if there is burden of blame, then I must shoulder a large share. I cannot fault her for cutting me."

"Can you not?" Lady Claire sniffed. "Well *I* can. I vow, the biddy would have been clucking all over you had she known that you have inherited the Hartleigh treasure. Her son, Arthur, is desperate to snare an heiress, they say."

Amanda closed her eyes as the old pain flooded back. More than eight full years had passed, yet the very mention of Arthur's name caused the hurt to ache afresh.

Lady Claire watched the girl's reaction carefully but could discern nothing of Amanda's feelings. Did her young friend still harbor any affection for Lady Whittlesea's son? When the curtain of lashes opened once again beneath Amanda's troubled brow, the old woman saw a tempest in a gray sea. Gently, she explored the possibility of a renewed attachment. "You could easily have him, Amanda, if you wished."

Amanda laughed, but there was little humor in the sound. "You mean I could purchase him? Arthur would get his hands in my pocket, but I see no gain for myself. A Dutch bargain, it seems to me."

"You would gain a place in society, child. The Whittlesea name is old and honored," Lady Claire pointed out, satisfied that the girl cherished no kind sentiment for the Whittlesea idiot. Still she felt obligated to cite the obvious advantage. "If respectability is what you seek, you would have that as his wife. And Marcus would gain a father."

"Marcus has all the fathers he needs, Lady Claire, between Mr. Peggoty and you—" Her hand flew to her mouth as her elderly friend's lips twisted into a wry grin. "I meant—"

"I consider it a compliment, my dear. Prinny once remarked that I was one of the finest men he knew." Lady Claire chuckled but quickly grew serious once again. "All the friends and servants in the world cannot substitute for a father, dear. And what of you? Surely you deserve something more than the lonely existence you have led these years."

"I am not lonely. I have you—"

"I know, and the Peggotys; I have heard the catalogue. But much as we love you, gel, you know it is not the same as that one special man."

"You seem to have survived well enough without a man," Amanda pointed out. "Could you have experienced the world as you have if you had been tied to a husband? Would he have allowed you to travel to the far corners of the earth? Or use your funds to establish a school and orphanage at the Mills?"

"Perhaps he would have shared all these things with me," Lady Claire said wistfully, long-ago memories coming to the fore. "But do not set an elderly spinster up as your model, Amanda dear. For I must confess: before you and Marcus came along, I was a very lonely, disagreeable old woman."

"And now you are merely disagreeable," Amanda said, hoping to turn the subject.

Lady Claire would not be baited. "If you do not wish to ally yourself with Whittlesea, there are many other men who would be delighted to marry you."

"Marry my purse, is your meaning," Amanda said with a toss of her head. "I want your solemn promise, Lady Claire, that you will tell no one of my inheritance. I have no desire to be besieged by fortune hunters."

"But that is foolish, my dear," Lady Claire objected. "I shall not live forever. A husband could protect your interests."

"The money is mine now and it shall remain mine and mine alone," Amanda vowed, her expression adamant. "I will never again be forced to rely on the dubious integrity of a man." *Or my own,* she added silently.

"Do not judge all men by Whittlesea," Lady Claire said, but it was as if a shutter had closed over the girl's ears. Amanda's steady gaze was almost a palpable force. "Very well," Lady Claire relented with a sigh. "I shall tell no one that you are the Hartleigh heiress. But do not think that the secret will keep; the news is sure to be in all the papers eventually."

"Ah, but 'tis only Lord Hartleigh's solicitors who know that I am the late Earl's grandchild. I sincerely doubt anyone will connect the daughter of Charlotte Maisson to the retiring Mrs. Westford."

Further argument was forestalled by the arrival of Madame Robarde and her assistants. Never one to pursue a lost cause, Lady Claire turned her waning energies toward persuading Amanda to purchase a wardrobe befitting her newfound fortune.

It was well into the afternoon before the two women emerged from the modiste's establishment.

"My nightclothes were more than adequate," Amanda argued, coloring as she recalled the delightful silks and laces that she had been persuaded to purchase. "And I do not see why I could not keep my gown. It was still quite serviceable."

"My maid wears garments that have more panache," Lady Claire contended, as Madame Robarde's vendeuse handed packages to the waiting footman. "I cannot blame Natalie for refusing to allow you out in it. 'Tis luck indeed that she had several garments at hand which could be easily altered to fit."

"No one weel be seen leaving my shop in zees 'orreur," Amanda quoted, mimicking Madame Robarde's French accent.

"Even you must admit that it is a marked improvement," Lady Claire said, admiring Amanda's russet walking gown with its fashionable vandyked hem. "Shall we visit the confectioner's next? We did promise Marcus a treat for remaining behind in Cheshire. How I do miss that child, even his incessant questions. And he does love lemon drops, almost as much as my dear Sebastian." Lady Claire sighed and shook her head.

Amanda stifled a sigh and prayed that the reminiscence would not lead to yet another "Clever Sebastian" story. One would think that Sebastian Armitage was a boy himself, to hear Lady Claire speak of him, instead of a man of two-and-thirty. But Amanda had long since learned to keep silent where Sebastian was concerned, difficult though it might be. Anything derogatory that she might say about Lady Claire's miscreant godson was bound to agitate the elderly lady. It mattered not that Lady Claire was well aware of his notorious character, the gambling, the wenching, and the less than savory dealings that had made him infamous as "The Demon Rum." Nor did it signify that the reprobate had not contacted his godmother in years. It was plain that she still regarded him with more than common affection. More than likely, the elderly lady continued to think of him as the boy that she had known so long ago. Certainly, there was nothing that Amanda could discern about the man's present behavior that justified such regard.

"I think that we might bypass the confectioner's today," Amanda said, avoiding an argument by saying nothing. She looked at her companion in growing concern. She was clearly wilting. "I confess that I am fully expended. I do not know how you maintain such a hectic pace, Lady Claire."

"You shall not fool me with such folderol, for I know that you mean to spare my old bones. I must admit that I do feel a trifle fatigued," Lady Claire said, tucking Amanda's hand beneath her elbow. "Very well, after the confectioners, we shall return home."

"We can do without the sweets," Amanda suggested, disturbed by the fact that Lady Claire was leaning heavily on her arm for support. Although the small woman's weight was slight, the minute display of weakness was a measure of her weariness.

"We shall not!" Lady Claire proclaimed. "I want to see the boy's face when he gets those lemon drops that he craved."

"Marcus will be delighted with all the other things that you have purchased for him, I am sure," Amanda said. "The spinning top will send him into ecstasy. You are spoiling him, I vow, and me as well." She swept her fingers along the stuff of the gown in wonder. "There was no need for you to pay for this."

"Stuff and nonsense, child," Lady Claire said gruffly. "As if you would have taken any gifts from me before. You and your absurd notions of charity."

"Hardly absurd. You have done so much for Marcus and me over these years. You paid for the doctors—"

"Speaking of doctors, I have had news of the most amazing physician. They say he is a miracle worker, having dealt particularly with our poor lad's problem," Lady Claire said enthusiastically. "He uses the force of electricity, a marvel of healing."

"No," Amanda spoke as if carving her words in stone. "No more. Marcus had endured far too much already at the hands of those charlatans. The pain and the disappointment when all their efforts fail is far too much for a little boy to bear." *And for me,* she added silently. "It is barely worse than outright torture."

"Dr. Owen says that his appliance will—"

"As they have all said." Amanda shook her head. "Some of them well-meaning, but most cruel in their kindness. It was a waste of your money, but for a good cause. I am so glad that now I can pay you back at last."

"Do not poker up on me, gel," the elderly woman chided. "You know full well 'tis not the cost. I would fund all the physicians in England if they could but help the boy."

"Although I would hate to admit so, I am inclined to agree with Dr. Howell in this matter," Amanda said gently. "My son will just have to learn to live with his infirmity, to overcome it."

"Howell," Lady Claire said with a touch of scorn. "I suspect that his medical judgment depends most on the fee he believes that you may pay him."

"Nonetheless, I concur with his judgment in Marcus's case."

"Very well," Lady Claire said with a sigh of resignation. "I suppose that you must deal with it as you feel you ought."

The elderly woman's resigned expression filled Amanda with shame. "I am sorry," Amanda stated simply, her long fingers reaching down to gently clasp Lady Claire's fragile hand. "I know you mean well, and you have helped me vanquish so many dragons. You are a source of courage and strength to me."

"You have no reason to rely on me. You have more than your share of mettle," Lady Claire said, a catch in her voice. "And your heart is far more spacious than you are willing to acknowledge, for I have seen the breadth of its love. You have always been more than a mere companion to me, child. You know that."

As they walked to their waiting conveyance, Lady Claire said nothing more, yet her eyes spoke eloquently, acknowledging the ties of friendship that bound them. Amanda felt a warm, enveloping feeling as the difference in their ages faded in a concord of understanding. Perhaps it was the grief that Amanda had endured that bridged the chasm of the more than forty years that separated her from Lady Claire in age. But in the past, there had always been a barrier created by Amanda's uncomfortable consciousness that she was the recipient of largesse. Although the old woman had never demanded anything for her kindness, the knowledge of existing upon another's mercy had been constant cause for constraint. Now, that final boundary between them had been removed. They had always been friends; now, they were equals.

"Buy my lovely vyre-lets," a flower seller called. "Vyre-lets for yer lidy."

They were stepping into their carriage when Amanda heard the melodious cry. "Wait here," she said, pulling her purse from her reticule and running across the street. "I shall take the lot of them," Amanda told the astonished blossom-monger and then returned to the carriage with the basket of violets in hand.

"For you, Lady Claire," Amanda said, watching in delight. The elderly lady flushed with pleasure as she fingered the delicate petals in seeming disbelief. It was a long time since the young woman had felt the joy of giving.

Lady Claire buried her face in the buds to hide the glimmer of tears. Never, in all her seventy-five years, had anyone ever given her flowers. She closed her eyes, breathing in the sweet fragrance, as she blessed this sweet girl who had brought life to an old woman's twilight. Still, it was not quite the same, she thought, recalling the angry young man who had left her life forever. Lady Claire's chest tightened with a swell of emotion, but as she drew in her next breath, a spasm of pain sliced through her. The knife of agony cut at her breast.

"Lady Claire!" Amanda gasped as the ivory-headed cane dropped to the floor. She fumbled with the strings of her reticule, searching frantically for the vinaigrette with one hand as she attempted to support her friend with the other.

"Sebastian . . ." The name escaped Lady Claire's lips in a hiss of breath. She leaned toward Amanda, knocking the basket of violets from the seat. "Tell my . . . Sebastian that . . ."

Amanda leaned forward trying to hear her elderly friend's words for her rakehell godson, but there was only a sighing breath. Lady Claire's head lolled forward and the feathered turban tumbled to the carriage floor, to rest with a forlorn air amidst the flowers.

2

Sebastian rose from behind the vast mahogany desk and stretched like a cat, his bare toes curling into the Aubusson carpet as he eased the kinks in his arms and neck. Although several years had passed since he had sold his colors, the army-cultivated habit of early rising had been hard to break. It was barely midmorning and he had been up and awake for hours, yet the pile of papers that remained upon his desk was mountainous.

He was a fool to remain indoors on such a morning, he thought as he opened his windows wide to the Jamaican sun. A light zephyr ruffled his red-gold hair and teased at the open collar of his shirt, bringing with it the scent of blooming jasmine. O'Shea could easily take care of the correspondence, Sebastian knew, and that thought was somehow agitating. His enterprises had reached the point where they could almost run themselves, he realized with a growing restlessness.

He prowled through the library like a disturbed panther. It was time to move on, to hunt on new ground, he knew. Now that he had acquired the Burnside plantation, the final piece of his Jamaican scheme was in place. It had come almost too easily, fallen into his lap like an overripe plum. Perhaps that was the problem, nothing in his life had ever come without effort. Scratch, claw, and contrive had been the keys to survival and the invisible scars on his back had ground home a hard-learned lesson. Trust no one.

The light glittered invitingly upon the decanter that stood on the sideboard. Despite the hour, Sebastian poured himself a shot of rum. Critically, he held the crystal glass to the light, swirling the golden liquid as he examined the color and viscosity. He sipped, holding the liquor in his mouth, letting the taste bathe every part of his tongue before he swallowed. The elusive factors of smoothness and aftertaste were evaluated with a connoisseur's skill. Excellent on all counts; as different from the sailor's swill that Armitage Distilleries had once manufactured as a thoroughbred from a hackney horse.

There was a knock at the door.

"Enter," Sebastian said without turning from the window. "You are nearly an hour late, O'Shea."

The Irishman bustled to his accustomed seat, undisturbed by his employer's surly tones. " 'Twas the Burnside plantation that kept me, sir," he explained.

"Trouble?" Sebastian asked, whirling about without spilling a drop.

"Not o' the kind you're thinkin'," O'Shea said with a grin. "The slaves, sir, they thought I was yourself and even though I convinced them otherwise, they was all wantin' to touch me to thank me, as if I was some kind o' savior. They know well enough that you've freed the slaves on every other plantation you've come to own."

"Men work harder when there is something in it for themselves," Sebastian said gruffly. "Now give me the costs in pounds and pence."

"Never have I seen such misery as I have in those slave quarters," the Irishman said as he handed Armitage the column of figures. " 'Tis fitting, it is, that Lord Burnside threw this place away on the turn of a card."

"I would have gotten it eventually, one way or another," Sebastian commented coldly as he scanned the list. "It is the last bit of land between me and the cove. I had, in fact, been negotiating to purchase Burnside's property behind the scenes. However, since he was fool enough to put his patrimony on the baize, I simply took advantage of the opportunity."

"There's talk about you in Kingston," O'Shea said darkly.

"There is *always* talk in Kingston," Sebastian said, with a dismissive quirk of his brow. "There is precious little to gossip about in this benighted place. I provide something of a public service by my mere existence, it seems, between my high-flyers and my financial dealings."

"They say that your run of luck is unnatural," O'Shea continued despite his employer's cool stare. He knew full well that Armitage valued his honesty more than any other trait. "Two plantations you've won in as many years."

"Are there any who dare utter the word 'cheat,' O'Shea?"

The factor shook his head. "You know that they would not, not since you called Lord Halstead out when he accused you of cheating. Everyone knows that you could as soon have killed him as winged him if you had a mind to."

"Let them say what they please, then. I did not force Lord Burnside to frequent the gambling dens. If he had not lost his plantation to me, it would have gone to another," Sebastian declared with an air of finality. "It seems to be much as we expected."

"Aye," O'Shea said slowly. "We will offer the usual terms to the people there, I take it?"

Sebastian nodded. "A fair wage and a share if their cane crop exceeds our requirements. I fully hope to expand our rum production within the next year. We will build a new distillery in the cove; the harbor is deep enough."

O'Shea gave a whistle of admiration as he began to understand the scope of Armitage's plan. "So that is the way of it? Our shipping bypasses Kingston entirely. 'Twill give 'em all the apoplexy; you'll have no need of any of them."

"Exactly," Sebastian declared with satisfaction. No longer would he have to endure their contempt and curiosity, the silent snubs, the open derision of those who styled him a rakehell or those who hated his stand against slavery.

"*Your* raw materials, *your* labor, *your* ships to carry it," O'Shea said. "I vow there's many a man who would gladly sell his soul to trade places with the 'Demon Rum.' "

"Would you, O'Shea?" Sebastian asked baldly.

O'Shea looked at his employer, compared the lithe grace of Armitage's build to his own short stocky body. The Irishman contrasted his pudgy face and ruddy looks to Armitage's fine-chiseled features and olive-toned skin. Armitage was a striking man, modeled with the perfection of a piece of Greek statuary, but as O'Shea gazed into the depths of those quizzing blue eyes, he realized that they were as cold and bleak as bits of marble. He thought of his own loving Megan. Despite Armitage's flock of birds of paradise, it was a solitary life that the man lived and a lonely one. The glass prisms of the chandelier tinkled in a stray breeze. Silence was O'Shea's answer.

"I thought not," Sebastian said, his lip curling in mocking amusement.

The emptiness of that smile filled O'Shea with pity. He put his hand in his pouch to find a means of filling the uncomfortable silence. "I had nearly forgotten, Mr. Armitage, but I met the captain of the *Westwind* in Kingston this morning. He gave me several letters for you." O'Shea pulled out a vellum-wrapped bundle. "I'm thinkin' that this is the one that you were expecting from Bow Street."

Sebastian took the voluminous letter, breaking the seal with deliberate care. He was determined to betray himself to no one, not even O'Shea. Only when he had his emotions completely schooled did he scan the scrawled pages of the report.

Although Armitage's expression had not changed by so much as a hair, O'Shea could see that the news was not good. When his employer looked up at last, his eyes were barren.

"Not a trace," Sebastian confirmed the answer to the Irishman's unspoken question. "The Runners have not located her."

" 'Tis a cold trail they have to follow," O'Shea observed. "And it was barely five years ago that you began this quest of yours."

"No, O'Shea, this search began long before I met you, but it was only recently that I bethought myself to hire Bow Street. Yet they seem to have gotten little farther than I did," Sebastian said, his voice steady.

"What of the carter in Kent?" O'Shea questioned. "He says that he saw a red-haired girl enter the church that morning, holding a bundle."

"Who is to say just what was in her arms?" Sebastian asked, turning to the window. "It seems to me that Fielding's men are merely grasping at straws to justify their outrageous fees. As you say, the spoor is over thirty years old."

"Then why not let it go?" O'Shea asked. "She could be dead or . . ."

"Or worse?" Sebastian concluded, his voice bitter. "Do you think that I have not considered just what type of woman would abandon her child on a church altar? No, O'Shea, if Bow Street has lost the scent, I will find another, better pack of hounds. And another and yet another still until I hear the 'view halloo' that tells me the bitch has been run to ground."

"She may not even be alive, sir," O'Shea pointed out, shaken by the passion in Armitage's voice. If it was vengeance that he sought, the Irishman hoped that the woman was no longer among the living—for her sake, as much as Armitage's. The burning rage in those eyes would likely consume them both.

"Then I shall spit on her grave," Sebastian said, "but I will find her, O'Shea. My oath upon it. Now, what else has the good captain brought for me?"

It was as if the man had his emotions in a sack, O'Shea marveled, taking them out and putting them away as a child might a handful of marbles. Obediently, O'Shea took a look at the next letter in the packet. "A *very* pretty female handwriting," the Irishman said with a leer. "A billet-doux, I'm thinkin'. Must be one of your London doxies askin' when you'll be payin' a call?"

Sebastian's lip curled contemptuously. "Apparently," Sebastian said. "Although I find myself doubting that there is a one of them who can muster the intellectual effort required to put pen to paper. Undoubtedly she wants something, whoever she is."

O'Shea made a show of sniffing at the wrapper. "No scent, but that doesn't say much; it more than makes up for it in weight." He hefted the wad of paper in demonstration.

It was then that Sebastian noticed the seal, instantly recognizing the imprimatur in the wax. Lady Claire . . . how many years had it been? Why had his godmother written to him after he had made plain his wishes to sever the connection? She had lied to him, as his parents had, and the pain of that deception was with him still. For a moment, he was tempted to throw it away unread, loath to face the memories that this communication from the past was sure to rouse. Curiosity and painstakingly forged indifference warred within him. "Give it to me, O'Shea," he said.

From the first bald salutation, an unadorned "Sir," it was clear that Lady Claire was not the writer. The fine copperplate did not in the least resemble the elderly woman's spidery hand. He read on with growing trepidation.

". . . It pains me to inform you that Lady Claire is gravely ill. She had often spoken of you in the past . . ."

Sebastian read the contempt between the lines as the woman described Lady Claire's continued fondness for him, "despite the differences you may have had . . ." He wondered if the writer knew just what those differences were. His godmother's companion, as she described herself, attempted to cloak her feelings behind a veil of polite words, but the tone of concealed scorn was irritating, notwithstanding the fact he knew that he deserved it.

"Bad news?"

Sebastian stirred, realizing that he had been gazing fixedly at Amanda Westford's signature since finishing the last line. "My godmother . . ." he began rising to stare into the empty fireplace, the import of Mrs. Westford's words slowly penetrating. "She is dying." He handed O'Shea the letter.

"Your godmother, do you say?" the Irishman's brow wrinkled in puzzlement. "I had thought that you were without family since your uncle disowned you."

"Lady Claire stood by me," he recalled reluctantly. " 'Twas she who purchased my colors for me, but I paid her back, every last shilling with interest, though there were some days that I went without to do it."

"Gave with one hand and took with the other?" O'Shea said. "I know the type."

"No, it was not that way," Sebastian admitted grudgingly. It would have been far easier if she had been the least bit grasping, but she had demanded nothing from him in return. The image of the old woman had come to mind over the years, far more often than he cared to admit, but never without an accompanying sense of guilt. "When I sold out, I sent her a draft for £1,975 for the price of my commission and the money that she had sent me those early days. A few weeks later, I received a parcel containing nothing but the remnants of that draft, ripped to shreds."

O'Shea gave a long, low whistle of astonishment. "She must be a tough old besom and a rich one, too, I'd take it, to throw nearly two thousand pounds to the winds."

"She is," Sebastian said, wondering why he felt so suddenly bereft. There had been nothing between the two of them but childhood memories and, then, the weight of obligation. "Or, rather, she was ..."

"Don't be thinkin' that. The *Eastwind* is leaving today," O'Shea said, his hand fingering the stubble on his chin. "Seems to me you might catch the old bird before she makes her last flight and mend matters between you; get yourself an inheritance too, maybe."

"I would not go for the money," Sebastian said in annoyance.

"No such thing as too much money, you've told me that often enough," O'Shea observed. "But family—oh, that's far more precious."

"The *Eastwind,* eh?" Sebastian said, considering. His ventures ran smoothly without him; the managers whom he had put in charge did not require his constant direction. No one needed him.

Except one old woman ... a voice whispered.

"Send word to have my saddlebags packed and ready," Sebastian commanded, setting his empty glass on the desk. "I must be in Kingston by high tide."

Sebastian cursed the horse, the cheating innkeeper who had rented the sorry beast to him, and the antecedents of both. There had been no time to have his own cattle shipped and so Sebastian had been forced to make do with hired hacks. The horseflesh had been almost adequate in London and its environs, but once he had passed into Warwickshire he had found that even the pick of the available cobs had been barely fit for cat's meat. Certainly, the spavined nag that he currently rode was the sorriest of the lot thus far. Even though the sandstone towers of Chester Cathedral were barely an hour behind him, the creature was already panting like a spent runner at the finish line.

Reluctantly, he reined the horse in and dismounted on a grassy knoll overlooking the colorful fall landscape. As the animal grazed and rested, Sebastian gazed out over the distance, frowning as the sun began to dissipate the morning mist. The striking autumnal scene of reds, browns, and golds was little more than a taunting reminder of the long stretch that remained between him and the Mills.

Lady Claire was most likely bedeviling her Maker into rearranging Heaven to suit her, he thought guiltily. It had been a foolish impulse from the first. Even if she still lived, too many years of silence had passed. The bond of common memory that still remained would be far better forgotten and buried along with the rest of his past. If he had any sense at all, Sebastian thought, giving the bony nag a jaundiced look, he would turn around right now. Then again, this journey had little to do with sense. Somehow, his long-ago quarrel with his godmother had become a loose end in his life, raveling at the fabric of his peace. Perhaps the final knot could be tied at last, and he could leave the scrap of his existence behind him.

As Sebastian looked out over the glorious vista, he could see places that were teasingly familiar. His neckcloth suddenly seemed to grow tight around his throat. Home ... much as he tried to deny this sudden yearning, half-forgotten feelings touched him gently, inviting him to remember those days when he had roamed these very hills.

The right to call the Vicarage "home" had long ago been forfeited, yet he could still see it clearly in his mind's eye: the half-timbered Tudor parsonage tucked into the hillside, its patterned facade of dark and light whimsy a charming echo of the great manor house beyond. Memories rose unbidden of the child he had once been, but even those happy times were tinged with gall, their innocence forever spoiled like recollections of Eden after the apple had been tasted. Then, abruptly, the world had seemed to end, every door had been closed ... except Lady Claire's. Although it was she who had rejected his attempt to pay her, there was a debt still owed, despite the fact that his pride had long denied it.

Sebastian mounted once more, urgency overcoming all other emotions. Perhaps that obligation could finally be discharged and he would be free of this place forever. The horse, seeming to sense his need, responded with a mile-eating gallop.

The wrought-iron gates at the foot of the long drive were wide open. Although there were no black wreaths or other signs of mourning adorning them, Sebastian could still not be certain that he had come in time. He spurred the horse forward, promising the hack a banquet of oats and a palace of a stable as they rounded the bend.

The crook of the road hid the boy until Sebastian was nearly upon him. There was no time to slow. No opportunity to escape the bonds of paralysis, where the mind knows what is about to occur, but the body acts as if in a mire.

"Ware!" he cried to the small figure up ahead. There was seemingly adequate time for the child to move, yet as the distance closed between them Sebastian saw that the boy appeared frozen to the spot, his mouth open wide in a soundless scream as a stick he had been holding fell from his hands. The wide trunks of the trees lining the narrow drive were like the bars of a prison, preventing the rider from turning his horse aside. The terror-stricken young face was perilously close to the pounding hooves. Too late, Sebastian hauled at the reins, clutching the leather in white-knuckled horror as his horse's forelegs rose in protest. His arms felt as if they were being pulled from their sockets as he fought to control the shying animal.

Above the protesting neighs of his horse, Sebastian heard a terrified cry. A blue blur flew into the road. It was a woman, who tried to snatch the boy from his path. Failing that, she gathered the child to her using her body as a shield.

But Sebastian could not see if she succeeded against the flaying of those death-dealing blows. All his concentration was focused upon the battle between himself and his horse-flesh. Just when he thought he had mastered the animal, the beast reared in one final effort to rid himself of the burden that pulled at the bit so cruelly. For a brief, startled second, gray eyes met blue in mutual fear before Sebastian hurtled through the air in a flight that ended in darkness.

The taste of fear was sour on her tongue as Amanda waited for the slashing blow of iron-shod hooves. Her eyes were shut, her lips moving silently, as she tried to effect a rapid bargain with the Creator. Any pain, any penance would be endured if only Marcus was spared. Her world narrowed to that small stretch of gravel, the furious cries of horse and rider, the sound of hooves striking inches away, the small body that was heartbreakingly still beneath her as death rampaged around them.

Then there was a sudden quiet, the fading vibrations of hoofbeats. The horse was gone, yet she dared not lift her head. Amanda tasted the bitter salt of blood and knew that it was her own.

"Are you dead, Mama?"

The muffled question came from beneath her and she felt her eyes fill with tears. "No, Marcus," she said, trying unsuccessfully to force the quaver from her voice. "I am not dead." She rolled aside to reveal a dusty little boy. Amanda ran her hands over his body, brushing aside clinging dirt and bits of leaves.

"Why are you doing that, Mama?" Marcus punctuated the query with a sneeze.

"To assure myself that you have not taken any injury," she said, looking down at him in relief.

"I'm sorry," Marcus cried, a tear running down his dusty cheek. "I couldn't get out of the way. It all happened so fast."

"Hush, dear. It is not your fault. Who would expect anyone to come riding up this path like Jehu?" She brushed the tear away, her indignation growing. "Why, he did not even stop to see—" She halted in mid-sentence, her hand rising to her lips in a gesture of dismay.

Marcus's eyes widened as he followed the direction of his mother's gaze. "Look, Mama, look!" He pointed to the fallen rider at the foot of the towering beech. "Is he dead, do you think?"

Amanda rose stiffly to her feet. The few yards felt like an interminable distance as she forced herself to walk to the motionless body lying amidst the fallen leaves. Dizziness and fear nearly overcame her as she looked at that upturned face, trying to discern some sign of life. Inhaling deeply, she attempted to steady herself against a world that seemed suddenly gone atilt.

Amanda knelt beside him, disregarding the gravel that bit through the thin fabric of her gown, and placed her shaky fingers to the side of his throat. To her infinite relief, a pulse beat strong and steady. "Go quickly, Marcus, and get Mr. Peggoty. Tell him to bring the wagon." A trickle of blood ran from a cut at the stranger's lips. "Bandages, too. And be sure that Lady Claire does not hear of this, for if I know her, she would want to be in the thick of it and she is not yet as fully recovered as she would wish to believe."

"I'll go through the kitchen," the boy promised, picking up his crutch from among the leaves. "Will he die, Mama?"

"I hope not, Marcus. Now go, as fast as you can." Amanda watched her son's limping progress until he was out of sight. It was nearly a mile up the winding roadway to the Mills, but she dared not leave the stranger with only a little boy to tend him. It was bad enough that Marcus had already begun to blame himself for the accident. If this man died . . .

She shook her head, trying to banish the thought. With gentle fingers, she touched the stranger's body, examining him much as she had Marcus.

There seemed to be no bones broken. Blood matted his auburn hair. Carefully, she pushed it aside, biting her lip in worry as she probed for the source of the spreading crimson stain. A surface wound above his eye was bleeding prodigiously and a lump nearly the size of a hen's egg was rising above his ear.

She undid the folds of linen from his neck, cursing all the while. The elaborate elegance of the knot and the clumsiness of her fingers brought Amanda perilously close to tears. At last, she was able to pull the linen free. Using the length of fabric to staunch the flow of blood, she pressed steadily, trying to stem the scarlet tide. Other than that, there was nothing she could do but wait and hope. His face was ashen and she felt for his vein once more, watching the steady rise and fall of his chest as if she could keep him breathing by the sheer force of her will.

"Help is on the way," she whispered as if to reassure him, but it was she who needed comfort as the minutes stretched interminably. She wondered at the thin stuff of his jacket, wholly inadequate for a late-autumn afternoon. Hastily, she removed her own cloak, thinking to cover him with it, but a brisk gust whipped icily through the flimsy fabric of her gown. "So much for fashion," she said with a snort of disgust, wishing heartily for her old, warm, serviceable wools as she bent to wrap the cloak about him. Unfortunately, there seemed no way they could both be warm, unless . . .

Surely, it is not good for him to lie thus, with nothing between his body and the cold hard ground, she told herself. *You are only trying to give him some ease, nothing more.* Yet, the prospect of so intimate a contact, even with an unconscious man, caused her to quake at her own temerity. However, the rising wind soon whipped away the proper in favor of the practical.

Amanda scrambled into a sitting position, bracing her back against the nearby tree trunk. Then, hesitantly, she slid her hand under his back, tugging him closer, shifting his head into her lap. It was awkward, but she managed to spread her cloak, partially covering them both while she scanned the road, listening anxiously for the sounds that would mean help was on the way.

"Please do not die," she whispered. She lifted the clotted linen hesitantly from the head wound, ready to cover it once again with a clean corner of the makeshift bandage. But there was no need. The bleeding had stopped. With a sigh of relief, she stroked the stranger's hair gently away from the site of the injury. So intent was she upon him that the distant rumble startled her. Thunder . . . she shivered as a wisp of memory touched her like a chill autumn wind. She watched the ominously clouding sky with growing dismay.

Sight, there was none. Only sound. An ache tattooed in his head like a drumbeat. Bombs were bursting all around him. The death calls of wounded horses emerged with the cries of shattered men in a cacophony of death. Sebastian waited for final oblivion, prayed that the smoke would never clear so that he would at least be spared the sight this time. . . . *This time . . . different . . . The ground yielding beneath his head . . . soft hands skimmed his body . . . he tensed . . . battlefield looters? . . . No, these fingers were gentle, tracing the line of his lips like a trade wind kissing the shore . . . A woman's touch. . . .*

"Please wake up," Amanda whispered, gently wiping the blood at his mouth with the stained linen stock. She had once heard that the longer someone suffering from a head wound remained unconscious, the less likely they were ever to regain their senses. Although she knew it had been but a few minutes, time seemed to stretch interminably. She thought of Marcus, trudging slowly up the long, winding drive to the Mills with the ill weather closing in and cursed herself for a fool. It was she who should have gone for help, but it was too late for second thoughts. She could not leave the stranger alone now. She searched her mind for prayers, but the only words she could recall were those of the Psalm singer. *Yea, though I walk through the valley of the shadow of death, I will fear no evil: for thou art with me.*

"Stay with me," Amanda begged softly, searching his face for any signs of consciousness. "Stay."

A woman's voice . . . penetrated the smoke. The acrid scent of sulfur changed to a fragrance of flowers. Roses . . . roses and female flesh bending in an intoxicating aroma . . . the cold ground had become a lap. . . . She cradled him with her softness, calling from afar. Although his mind reeled with pain, he hoped that the dream would go on. . . . He could put no name to that quiet voice, attach no face to those gentle hands. . . . He had no one. . . . The ache in his head was joined with a deeper anguish, one that wrenched at his very soul. He reached for those fingers and grasped them, trying to hold back the loneliness of death. "Too late . . . ?" the question slipped from his lips.

Even though she knew that this was a man she held, his gesture was one of a child, seeking comfort. "No, there is time yet," she whispered, her rigid posture relaxing. It was obviously the answer he sought. He sighed and shifted his head, nestling against her thigh. A positive sign to be sure, she thought. And what had been the cause of his heedless hurry?

Who is he? Amanda wondered. His clothes showed the sure hand of a master tailor. Despite the coating of road dirt, his Wellington boots had the look of new leather, and his pantaloons, too, were in the fashionable Wellington style, revealing long, well-muscled legs. Yet, the sorry-looking animal, which was nonchalantly cropping grass by the roadside, was entirely at odds with his master's appearance.

The horse, she decided, was an anomaly, the signs of wealth and breeding were unmistakable, from the aristocratic arch of the rider's cheekbones, to the finely veined surface of a wrist that most likely had lifted nothing heavier than a brandy snifter. Just the type of man she had come to despise, she told herself, lifting his limp hand from the ground to tuck it beneath the cloak. A blood red ruby gem, set in a band of heavy gold, glittered on one of his long, shapely fingers, their dark tan contrasting with light skin of his palm. Already, reddish welts had appeared; the marks of the reins, she realized.

Regardless of her feelings, she told herself as she brushed back a wave of his hair from the darkening bruise on his forehead, she owed this man a debt. He had struggled for her son's life, yet she could do nothing for him, nothing except shield him as best she could.

Pain ebbed into pleasure as the womanly fingers wandered from his hair to his forehead, stroking, soothing. He would have been well content to remain so beneath the ministrations of that comforting touch, but he felt something wet and warm fall on his cheek.

"Sir, can you hear me?" Her voice rose, pleading as much for her own sake as for his. A sudden ache filled her, a longing that she dared not name, not even to herself. Fanning his cheeks, his long lashes were like sable brushes, darker than his hair and so full that a woman might envy them, but there was nothing feminine about him, for all that he seemed so vulnerable. His face might have been conjured from a Michelangelo painting with its high, sculpted planes and noble lines.

Amanda had thought herself long past the power of a handsome face, if only by virtue of the hard-learned lesson that such appeal was the first step on the road to Hell. Having been to perdition once, she had no intention of visiting there again. All the more reason that this feeling of attraction was uncommonly foolish. Tears of frustration began to sting at her eyes.

Moisture slid to his lips and he tasted salt. Tears? She was crying for *him,* and he felt strangely moved. Some women in his past might have cried for themselves, but to his knowledge, no woman had ever cried for his sake. Sebastian reluctantly opened his eyes and the world came into hazy focus.

Amanda almost gasped as the stranger's lids flickered apart. The brief glimpse of blue that she had seen before had not prepared her for the peculiar hue of his eyes. The shades of sea, sky, and gemstone blended together in an azure gaze that gradually fixed upon her. Her heart skipped several beats.

"The boy . . . ?" He tried to raise his head and get his bearings, but yielded to the tender but firm pressure of her fingers. She leaned over him with eyes as gray and unfathomable as a stormy sea.

"Remain still," Amanda admonished him, disturbed to find

that her untoward fascination was not the least bit abated by the stranger's consciousness. "He has gone to fetch help."

"He is damned lucky," Sebastian said, wincing as his lips tightened into a scowl. "Why did . . . not get out of the way? Witless young idiot . . . could have been killed . . . I damned near was."

Amanda's hackles rose, the sympathy and tenderness that she had felt dissipating at his harsh tones and the offensive characterization of her son. People often coupled Marcus's twisted leg with a simple mind, so his attitude was not unexpected. However, she felt oddly disappointed. "My son is not lacking in sense. In fact, if anyone's lucidity is in question, it is yours, sir."

"Indeed?" The single word held a wealth of scorn. Sebastian noticed that anger had turned the woman's eyes the shade of molten silver. "And how have you . . . determined that?"

"Only a fool would ride ventre-a-terre up a private drive," Amanda said, looking down at him. Although she regarded him from a topsy-turvy vantage point, she could see his eyes narrow in annoyance. She fueled her anger, finding it a far more comfortable emotion than the strange sensations that she had felt just moments before. " 'Tis obvious that you had absolutely no regard for anyone who might be in your way. Only a complete addlepated, inconsiderate, boorish, jackass—"

"Spare me . . . the list of my virtues," Sebastian said in rising annoyance. He felt as if he had gone ten rounds with Mendoza and now the shrew seemed intent on showing him the sharp side of her tongue. And although it was galling to admit, she was somewhat right. He *was* partially responsible for the accident. Still, so was the boy. "There was more than . . . ample time for your son to move aside," he reminded her, "and you can be sure that both of you would likely be ground into . . . the drive gravel if not for my horsemanship."

"Such modesty! 'Tis a poor horseman, indeed, who cannot remain on his animal's back. And a cruel one who would drive a wretched creature like that to more than a sedate trot," Amanda declared with a snort, pointing at the grazing horse, whose reins had snagged in the branches. "Pitiful thing. It is shaking so badly that it can barely stand."

"I confess myself surprised that you chose to tend me instead of my horse," he said with cool contempt.

"We all make errors in judgment," Amanda retorted tartly, knowing that she had scored a palpable hit. He was reddening beneath his tan. "The animal seemed to be doing well enough by itself once it got *you* off its back." All at once, she felt him shifting. "What are you doing?"

"Getting up," Sebastian said, spitting out the words as he tried to take stock of his injuries. "Your lap, Madame, has suddenly become a decidedly uncomfortable place. My ears have begun to ring." He pushed her cloak aside.

"Are you sure you ought to be on your feet?" Amanda said, her brow furrowing in worry. She was being more than a little unfair, she knew. What was it about this man that caused her to react in such an outré fashion?

"Of course," Sebastian said, clenching his teeth as he lifted his head slowly and eased onto his side. Using the nearby tree trunk for support, he managed to raise himself on hands and knees. "Then you can take care of my horse." His head spun sickeningly and he closed his eyes for a moment. Every bone in his body was crying foul. But he *would* get up. There was no time to bandy insults; he had to reach the Mills.

"I did not mean . . ." Amanda murmured guiltily. She rose in haste to stand by his prostrate figure. The weight and pressure of his head had numbed her legs, sending prickles of pain up her thighs, nearly causing her to stumble. Stooping, she touched him lightly upon the shoulder "Let me help you," she offered, extending her hand.

"I do not require your assistance, Madame," Sebastian said, turning his head awkwardly and craning his neck to eye her from the damnably uncomfortable kneeling position. "I cannot pretend to aspire to the importance of an equine."

The top-lofty hauteur of his rebuff from a position of hands and knees would have been humorous, had it not been accompanied by his wince of pain. "May I counsel that you attempt to sit first," Amanda suggested.

Although it galled him to admit it, the woman was right. His limbs turned to liquid as he attempted to ease himself from his knees to a sitting posture. His heart was banging in his chest with a hammering beat, and his head was pounding with sickening regularity. Just when he felt on the verge of

collapsing to the ground, he felt her hands from above grasping the stuff of his jacket, bracing him. The woman's wiry
strength was surprising, for he would have sworn from her
delicate face that she was as frail as a feather. She helped him
achieve a sitting position, leaning his back against the tree
trunk.

A groan issued from his throat. The effort had nearly un-
done him. There had been worse falls in his lifetime. *Just a
moment's rest is all you need,* he assured himself. *The world
will soon come back into focus.* Once the woman's gamine
face ceased to swim before him, he would be on his way, he
promised himself. Slowly, her wavering ripe red lips pursed
to a provoking line; curls that had obviously come loose from
their mooring pins were no longer blurred but cascaded in a
riotous fall that was the color of starlit darkness. She would
have been beautiful were she not fixing him with a gimlet
stare.

"You are as white and quivering as a blancmange, sir,"
Amanda said. "Perhaps you should lie down once more. Help
is on the way."

"Are you volunteering to play at pillow again?" Sebastian
asked, enjoying the blush that crept up her long neck to suf-
fuse her face. Outraging the sensibilities of so-called proper
females had become one of his most pleasurable pastimes and
excellent way of deflating any pretensions they might have.
"You do have a most comfortable thigh, Madame. But another time perhaps; I have urgent business."

"Of all the disagreeable, conceited apes!" Amanda's fists
balled by her side.

"You flatter me," Sebastian said, taking a deep breath. His
chest felt as if someone had taken a mallet to it, but it would
seem that nothing was broken. "However much I might enjoy
a roadside dalliance, I must be on my way."

Amanda watched, speechless, as once more he began to
rise. He was shaky as a newborn foal, yet this time she made
no move to help him. A mouthful of gravel was as much as
he deserved, she decided as his hand inched up the tree trunk.
She picked up her discarded cloak and made a show of
dusting it off. The ungrateful wretch.

Within a few moments, he was upright and looking down
at her with a look of amusement and superiority, seeming al-

most to know that she had hoped for him to fall. There was a thunderous boom, as if to punctuate his triumph.

"Farewell, Madame; much as I enjoy tarrying here with you, I fear we are in for a storm." Sebastian said, realizing that she was a Long Meg, nearly as tall as he. He took a step forward, putting full weight on his left foot for the first time. It was an error. The pain struck in a bolt, searing through his body. As his ankle collapsed, he felt himself going down. The woman lunged toward him, trying to support him, but she was too late. The two of them went down in a tangle of limbs. He landed on top of her, nose to nose, eye to eye.

Like air from a bellows, Amanda's breath was pushed from her by the force of his weight. The stranger's cerulean eyes widened impossibly and for a moment he just stared at her with a startled expression. Once more, thunder echoed, the air heavy with that peculiar atmosphere of anticipation and foreboding that comes before a storm. The surroundings were still; even the birds had fled the sky as time itself seemed to unwind slowly. In those few heartbeats, Amanda felt as if she saw something in those blue depths, something as wild and powerful as the wind that began to blow through the trees. She was carried away to another storm, another time, the last time that they had been together. *The nursery window had been opened wide, whipping the curtains into a frenzied billow, shutters banging on the brick. As he had come closer, the whiskey on his breath proclaimed that he had been drinking and there had been a look in his eyes . . . She had just told him what she had begun to suspect and all her happiness had evaporated before his fury. . . .*

Past merged with present as Amanda abruptly became conscious of the stranger's maleness and, despite the injuries, his strength. She was alone and helpless beneath his body. Her breath came in frantic, uneven gasps as her vision began to blur through a veil of tears. It could not be happening, not again. She had to get away. "Get off of me . . . you blundering oaf," she panted in desperate bravado, battering at him with clenched fingers.

She was afraid. Even through the pangs of torture that ran up his leg as she squirmed beneath him, he could feel her fear. The facade of her flippant words was ridiculously easy to penetrate, for those silver eyes were mirrors into her soul. She continued to struggle, writhing, lashing like a willow against the tempest, her hair loose about her like a dark thunderhead. Her small fists pounded against his sides and were it not for his bruises, they would have had no effect at all. Yet he could not help but grudgingly admire her for the effort, however futile. She was an unusual woman, one who would put herself in front of an on-coming horse to shield her son, who would risk enraging a man in a position to do her considerable harm. Then, to his surprise, she gave a final shove with the flat of her palms, causing him to slide off of her. His leg shot arrows of agony through him as it jarred against the ground.

Amanda turned over and scrabbled away, putting a cautious distance between herself and the stranger before attempting to rise. He groaned, turning his head on the excruciatingly hard gravel and fixing her with a basilisk stare. "If I were intent ... on rapine, Madame," he said, his tones made terse by white-hot pain, "be assured that I ... would choose a more comfortable place to do the deed."

The heat rose to her cheeks. Embarrassed by her foolish panic, and unaccountably annoyed that he had recognized it, she realized that she had likely compounded his injury. The blood had all but drained from his face, giving him a ghastly aspect and his jaw was clenched tight, as if only the power of his will kept him from crying out in torment.

Trying to dismiss her unwelcome memories, Amanda fought to control her trembling. She forced herself to approach him once again and kneel beside him. "Your leg?" she asked, reaching out to touch his boot tentatively.

"Do not do that!" He inhaled sharply as the leather pressed against the tender flesh.

"It might be broken," Amanda protested. "I just thought . . ."

"Do not think," Sebastian exhorted, pulling his foot away. Excruciating pain instantly caused him to regret the motion. "Women are not much good at the process anyway."

Before Amanda could frame a retort, flashes of lightning, punctuated by deep rumbles of thunder, rippled across the distant hills. There was a rush of wind that sent a shower of leaves tumbling down upon her. Stomach churning, she looked frantically up the road. Surely, they would come soon, before the storm. She prayed that Marcus would make it to the Mills before the worst broke.

The kneeling woman had stiffened; her eyes reflected the leaden sky in a look that bordered on outright terror. Just his luck, to be dependent on a female who melted in the rain. Sebastian craned his neck painfully, trying to ascertain his location. The Vicarage. If he recalled correctly, the short footpath that led to the cottage was but a few feet away.

"We must find shelter," he said, but she continued to stare at the darkening sky like a statue fixed into place.

"Help me up!" he ordered, raising his voice above the storm.

The vociferous demand in his tone rivaled the roll of thunderclaps that burst nearby. Amanda shook herself, trying to control her unreasoning fear. "I . . . I do not know if I can," she said in dismay. "And help is on the way."

"I would not wager on their arriving before the storm breaks," Sebastian said with a touch of acid in his tones. "The rain will turn the incline of this road into a veritable bath of mud and I, for one, have no desire to wallow in the midst of it. If you will assist me to stand?"

Recovering herself, Amanda cast him a dubious look. "You recall the results of your last effort, I presume."

"There seems little choice," Sebastian said, putting out his hand toward her. A crack from above served to stress his point. Reluctantly, Amanda reached for those outstretched fingers, trying to suppress a swell of panic as his large palm snared hers with a firm grip. Trembling, she bent, allowing him to drape his arm over her shoulder. With great care, they rose in tandem, attempting to keep as much of his weight as possible off of his injured leg. As he stood upright at last, his face grew ashen, and for a moment she feared that they would come to grief again. Indeed, they nearly did take a spill when she took the first step up the road, for he seemed determined to go in the other direction.

"There is a shorter way to the Vicarage," he said from between clenched teeth. "Through the woods."

How did he know of the path? Amanda wondered. *She and Marcus had always preferred to use the road because of its smoother surface. And how had he come to be familiar with the Vicarage?* But this was not the time for questions.

Slowly, Amanda helped him make his way up the narrow track. She could feel him flinch every time his injury made contact with the uneven ground, but he did not utter a word of complaint. "Only a little bit more," she said in encouragement, when she felt him flagging.

He kept his eyes on the ground. The mud seemed to suck at his boots, threatening to pull them from his feet, and roots appeared suddenly to trip him. But, throughout it all, she would not let him stumble. Half carrying, half dragging him at times when he misstepped, she stood hip to hip with him, like a pillar against the wind, sustaining and guiding.

By the time they reached the door of the Vicarage, Amanda was sodden, her waterlogged clothes making every step seem like a league-spanning journey. His handhold around her shoulder had become bruising but, even so, she realized that he was attempting to spare her from the full burden of his bulk.

She sighed in relief as they went in out of the weather; however, that sense of solace was doomed to be short-lived. The past few days had been unseasonably warm, so there had been little need for heat. Aside from their lack of beds, the rooms on the first floor were subject to drafts. A look at the stranger's face was less than encouraging; his pallor was alarming and his teeth were beginning to chatter with cold. Amanda racked her brains, but there seemed no way to avoid taking him up the stairs.

"Just a bit more," Amanda coaxed, trying to conceal her apprehension as she looked up the narrow flight. Never had it seemed so steep. The stranger nodded. Taking a deep breath, he gripped the stair rail with both hands. He was going to attempt to haul himself up. "No, surely you do not think that you can do this alone," Amanda chided, drawing his arm around her shoulder once more. "Do not be afraid to lean on me," she said, her expression a study in grim determination. "I am far more enduring than I look."

"Yes," Sebastian said, surprised by the strength of will and purpose that he saw in that delicate face. "I am beginning to believe you are." Despite the weary sag in her posture and the worry in her eyes, she shifted closer to support him. Her hand slipped behind him and round his waist, in a firm and reassuring embrace, as he began the climb. For all her softness he could sense a spirit that was forged of steel, a warmth and courage that seemed to flow from her. She demanded no less than his all, forcing him to tap resources within himself that he did not know he possessed. His world narrowed to a mountain of fourteen stairs and a velvet voice alternately coaxing and bullying him up toward the summit.

The woman panted as she pushed open a door. "Into . . . bed . . . with you now," she said, easing Sebastian onto the mattress. "We are going to have to get you out of those wet clothes."

"I am . . . flattered by your eagerness," he began to quip, fighting the assault of pain.

"Sir, presently you are most definitely not a sight to rouse my passions," the woman said, fixing him with a contemptuous stare. She pulled a quilt from the chest at the foot of the bed and draped it about his shoulders. "It seems for the present that you are to be a guest in my home. I will thank you to keep a civil tongue."

"Your . . . home?" Sebastian asked, a jolt of recognition penetrating the haze of pain. "The Vicarage . . . Are you the vicar's spouse then?"

"Scarcely," the woman said, the corners of her lips rising wryly. "Although one need not be a clergyman's wife to be offended by your overwarm badinage. You speak like a gazetted rake."

"I am . . . a gazetted rake," Sebastian murmured in feeble irony.

"Are you, indeed?" the woman asked with a throaty chuckle. "Then you must have been entirely lost, the only thing that lies at the end of this road is the home of Lady Claire, an elderly spinster. It was she who built the new rectory in the village, nearer to the church."

A jagged memory of his purpose momentarily eclipsed the pangs that tormented him. From the woman's words it was not quite clear if his godmother was still among the living. "You . . . must . . . tell me . . ." he stammered softly.

"This may hurt," the woman warned, bending to kneel at his feet, her dark hair tumbling about her shoulders. She began to tug experimentally at his boot. Her touch was gentle, but the stab of agony severed the last fragile bonds that held him to consciousness. A thought that was part comfort, part dread slipped through his mind. He had come home.

3

Amanda barely had time to lift her arms as he pitched forward. There was little bracing her as she caught him full on and the press of his weight pushed her back, nearly bringing them both down to the floor. With his head pillowed against her chest, she grasped the bedpost. She attempted to struggle up from her knees, desperately trying to keep him from falling and further injuring himself. The bristle of his unshaven cheek scratched against her neck and she could feel the rapid rhythm of his breathing, sending a shiver down to her toes. It took several deep breaths of her own to stop the panic, the sense of helplessness. She could not let him fall.

Broaching her last reserves of strength, she maneuvered the deadweight onto the bed, almost falling upon him as she levered him up. Although she held the front of his shirt in an attempt to ease him back slowly, the wet fabric slipped from her sore hands, causing her to cry out in pain as he fell back onto the mattress. By the time she had shifted his legs and spread the blanket over him, she was panting with effort.

Blankets would not be enough, she realized as the chill began to permeate her very bones. Shivering, she knelt by the small hearth. Although the logs had already been laid, it was difficult to get a fire burning. Her hands shook as she struck fruitlessly at the flint, trying to get a spark, then nursing the nascent flames with kindling. The cold of the flagstone floor crept up her spine with icy fingers; nonetheless, she tended the fire until the wood caught fully. Although the room gradually grew warmer, Amanda knew that she could not leave the stranger to risk an inflammation of the lungs. His wet clothes would have to be removed somehow.

Clasping her arms around herself, she stood by the bed wondering what to do. If the drumming sound of rain on the

roof was any indication, there would be no one coming soon
to assist her. It was entirely improper, she knew, to be alone
with a man in this manner, much less to unclothe him, but
even the god of propriety had to bow to the necessity of the
situation.

You have undressed Marcus thousands of times, she admonished herself. *It is not as if you have never before seen
a bare male.* Yet, as she put her arm around his neck in an
attempt to lift him, his rain-soaked hair brushed like liquid
fire against the back of her hand. The shiver that crept down
her spine had absolutely nothing to do with the cold.

Amanda tugged at the sleeve of his riding jacket, but between the close-fitting tailoring and the rain-taut fabric it was
like trying to remove a second skin. The minutes passed as
she continued her vain effort, cursing tailors who cut their
clothes so skimpily and men who filled their garments to the
inch. He started to quiver violently, his lips coloring with an
alarmingly bluish tinge, forcing Amanda to make a rapid decision.

Hastily, she covered him once again, and ran to her room.
Out onto her bed went the contents of her workbasket, scat-
tering in a tangle of yarns and silks. She grabbed the shaft of
gleaming metal at the center of the jumble and rushed back
to the stranger.

The beat of rain on the roof intensified into a steady din
and the roll of thunder became a constant cannonade, but for
the first time in years, she was not acutely aware of a storm's
fury. Since that long-ago night, she had always feared the
echoes. She could hear his voice in the reverberations, feel
his anger. "Stupid bitch," the thunder seemed to growl, "stupid bitch."

But now the man upon the bed had become the fulcrum of
all her fears, the rapid, shallow sound of his breathing making
her mindful of her own inadequacy. She could not give way
to her cowardly inclinations. Her efforts might very well determine whether the stranger lived or died. She was determined not to fail him.

Trying to keep her hand steady, Amanda carefully began to
cut his clothes away, snipping at sleeves and seams, adding
bit by bit to the pile of wet rags by the bedside. His shoulders
were square and muscular, his jacket almost devoid of pad-

ding. It seemed a shame to destroy such fine workmanship, yet there was little choice, she reflected as she sheared down the neck of his shirt. The dank linen came away with a ripping sound to reveal the healed seam of a scar running from his shoulder, through the dark damp swirls of hair on his chest, to the midriff. She traced it gently with her finger, realizing that this man was no stranger to pain.

Despite all modesty, she found her eyes drawn to the flat plane of his stomach, so different from the childish lines of her son. There was no use trying to fool herself into believing him no different than a boy, for there was nothing the least boyish about this man. The lean musculature had its own peculiar beauty, a symmetry and strength that held her momentarily enthralled. This was a man who could unnerve her with his vulgarity, yet risk himself to hold a frightened horse in rein, who could force himself to walk injured through the pouring rain, yet try to spare her from carrying his full weight. It was this confusing mixture of virility and valor, of power and compassion, that stood at the heart of what she recognized as a most dangerous fascination. How strange to have conceived and borne a child and yet feel so very ignorant.

He moaned softly and she drew away her fingers as if they had been burned. Why was she moping about like some besotted schoolgirl when every second of delay put him at greater risk? Quickly, she concealed the distracting torso with the blanket, but her resolution flagged when she turned her attention to the bottom half of his person. His wet breeches left little to fancy, the clinging cloth limning every ropy sinew, from waist to calf. With fumbling fingers, she tried to loosen his pantaloons at the waist, but the waterlogged fastenings resisted all effort.

Scissors poised, she closed her eyes and attempted to swallow the huge lump that was suddenly constricting her throat. But before she could open them again, she felt iron fingers tightening about her wrist.

"Madame," the stranger said hoarsely, his eyes unnaturally bright. "I realize that I may have offended your sensibilities; however, that scarcely justifies turning me into a damned soprano."

Amanda all but choked as the import of his accusation

sank in. "Nonsense," she said briskly, trying to calm the agitation in those blue depths. "If I were attempting to unman you, sir, be assured that I would choose a sharper instrument." She snapped the blades open and ran the thumb of her free hand across the edge in demonstration. "These are quite dull, I am afraid. They have made sorry work of your clothing."

"My clothing?" he asked distracted, his voice rising. "You have hacked apart my garments? I have nothing more than what was once on my back and the clothing in my saddlebag."

"I am sorry," Amanda apologized with patently false sweetness, her lips tightening into a thin line. "I can see now that you would have preferred to be a well-dressed corpse."

The shaking of her hand penetrated Sebastian's befuddlement. Save for the rapid beat of her pulse, the woman's wrist was like a block of ice. Dimly, he realized that she was still attired in her own wet, muddy clothing. She had not even stopped to make herself comfortable after the grueling trek up the stairs, it seemed. And her hands—the lines of her palm were crisscrossed with raw scrapes. She was likely in considerable pain. Wounded, freezing, utterly fagged, yet she had tended to him, before herself. He could see himself mirrored in those silver eyes and for the first time in years, he felt shame.

"It is I who should be sorry, Madame," Sebastian said gruffly, letting go of her hand. "I have been vexatious and more than uncommonly rude."

"You have," she agreed, stifling a sneeze. "Now if you can assist me, we will soon have you snug. The pantaloons."

"The boots must come first," Sebastian said, moving his foot experimentally. But rather than the shock of pain that he had expected there was a growing numbness that filled him with dread. "You are going to have to cut the right one off, I fear, and quickly. Perhaps your husband's razor, if it is sharp."

"Decided to trust me, have you?" the woman asked, the suspicion of a smile hiding in the corners of her mouth. "Unfortunately, my son has not yet reached the bearded condition, and his father is no longer with us, so there are no razors to be found here. We do have some rather sharp knives. Will they do?"

"They will have to," Sebastian said, closing his eyes against the throbbing of his head. He tried to wiggle his toes; to his relief, the digits responded but he could feel the intense pressure of his skin swelling against the leather. It was not a good sign. He heard her footsteps retreating hurriedly down the stair, felt himself floating, suspended in a sea of pain.

"Sir?"

The one questioning word held a wealth of anxiety. He could feel the warm touch of her breath on his cheek as she bent close. He inhaled the faint odor of the rose scent that she wore, trying to determine why the smell was familiar, but the reason eluded him. He opened his eyes to find his would-be surgeon looking at him, her quicksilver eyes filled with apprehension. She held a gleaming knife out for his inspection.

"It is our butchering knife and a most wicked blade, as you can see," Amanda said, laying the honed blade carefully on the night table. "Many's the time I have inadvertently put a little bit of myself into the stew."

"How very reassuring," Sebastian mumbled to himself, watching with sick fascination as the firelight played on the metal. Ironic if he had narrowly avoided amputation in the field hospitals of Spain only to be hacked into a peg leg by a clumsy female with a kitchen knife. "I am sure that it will serve," he said aloud. "Best go at it now, while I can still guide you if you cut too deep."

"Are you sure that you wish me to attempt this?" Amanda asked, silently hoping that he would demur. What if she hurt him, caused him to be crippled? She would never forgive herself.

"It is necessary," he said quietly, trying to convince himself as much as her. The prognosis for success was less than promising. She was pale with apprehension, but he remembered the steady strength that had gotten him here. She was capable of far more than she believed. "Promise me that if I lapse into unconsciousness, you must go on. Your oath."

"Very well." Amanda nodded, trying to swallow her fears. She lit a branch of candles by the bedside, but the light still seemed insufficient to play the surgeon by.

"Perhaps I should wait for help to come?" she said, hopefully, listening for the sound of footsteps on the stair.

"Waiting will only make matters worse, I believe. You will have to do the honors," he murmured, reaching out to grasp her fingers. He attempted a smile.

"But 'honor hath no skill in surgery,' " she answered with a tremulous grin, trying to make a joke of it, but it was all she could do not to snatch her hand away from his hold. He was only trying to encourage her, she told herself.

"Falstaff. . . ." Sebastian searched his memory for the source of the quote. "Well, though I may owe God a death, 'tis not due yet, so let us hope that honor *can* 'set to a leg.' " An unusual woman to be sure. Seemingly so frail, yet strong enough to half carry him. Bold enough to undress him, to cite the Bard's bawdiest creation; yet he could feel her shrinking from his touch. But although his curiosity was piqued, he would not seek the answers now. "Remember, go on, no matter what."

Amanda nodded, and reluctantly picked up the knife. Breathing deep, she put it to the leather, stopping at once as he stiffened.

"Wait," he said raggedly, putting a restraining hand on her wrist. "Look in the pocket of my jacket."

Amanda set the knife down and searched through the tattered pile on the floor for the remnants of his pockets. The first she found was empty, but the second contained a battered but sound silver flask. She unscrewed the cap. "Whiskey?" she asked recoiling in repugnance. "But I thought you wished to remain aware."

"Not mere whiskey, Madame, but rum." He sighed, his eyes lighting with relief. "The best Jamaican rum. Unfortunately it will take far more than this trickle to put me three sheets to the wind. However, this might serve to help take the edge off of what may prove to be rather rough surgery." He tried to lift himself up on his elbow, but even that minute movement nearly proved to be his undoing. His complexion blanched and Amanda hastened to help.

The stranger looked up at her sardonically, as if daring her to touch him once more. Resolutely, she slipped her palm beneath his head trying to raise him up, but it was soon apparent that she could not both support him adequately and help him drink in this manner. She slipped round behind him, bracing him from the back. The warmth of his bare skin penetrated the damp thin stuff of her dress, as she crooked her arm round him. Trying to ignore the sudden heat that seemed to sear her to the core, she attempted to hold him steady. Fingers splayed against the rough reddish stubble on his cheek, she held the flask to his lips with her other hand.

Her palm was clammy, and she was wound tight as a spring. Sebastian could feel the tension in her, the pell-mell pummeling of her heart as he leaned against her softness for support. There was more to her reaction than the fear of what she had to do, of that he was certain, but the throb from his head was overcoming all coherent thought. Greedily, he gulped the fiery liquid down, choking as the rum seared his throat, but finishing it to the last drop. She let him down slowly, leaving him feeling strangely deprived as she withdrew the comfort of her embrace. Once more she looked at him, uncertain, her eyes wide with trepidation.

"Go on," he urged, wondering if he was being a fool by allowing her to put the knife to him. But the nature of the sensation in his leg was beginning to change, his toes becoming cold and unresponsive, a circumstance far more worrisome than her inexperience. "Cut. You can do it. You must."

Amanda began to saw against the wet boot, knowing that even the slightest motions were causing him exquisite agony. Yet, he did not cry out. Luckily, the leather was relatively new and supple, but it still required prodigious effort to cut. Slowly, she stripped away the layer of tanned hide, exposing his foot inch by torturous inch. Although the room was still chilly, she found herself perspiring with nervousness as the knife penetrated dangerously close to his swollen flesh.

"Good girl," he murmured, his voice strained. He held himself steady, hard-pressed not to pull away as he felt the cold steel through the stuff of his stockings, but, though she was sheet white with fear, her hand was gentle and sure. "Go on."

She could not bear to pause and look at him, for she knew that face was sure to be contorted with pain. Her wrist ached, the cuts on her palm stung from the effort of controlling the blade's course but she dared not stop, knowing that she might not have the strength or the courage to go on. At last, she reached the base of the heel. Gently, she stripped away the stocking, revealing an angry black-and-blue, bloated mass. Amanda stood and straightened, the knife slipping from her stiffened fingers and clattering to the floor.

"Done," she said with a weary sigh. Finally, she risked a look at her patient. A trace of blood welled at his bitten lower lip and handfuls of blanket were bunched between bloodless, clenched knuckles.

"And well-done, Madame," he whispered faintly, his eyes glistening with withheld tears. "Well-done. We could have used hands like yours in the field hospitals."

That explained the scar. He was a soldier, Amanda thought with a brief frisson of concern. *But there had been many men who had taken part, many places where soldiers had fought and died. It did not signify.* She flushed at the look of frank admiration in his eyes and turned her attention to his other boot, succeeding at last in tugging off the remaining Wellington.

Sebastian almost reveled in the pain as circulation began to return, finding even excruciating agony preferable to the sensation of numbness.

"C . . . can you remove your pantaloons unassisted, sir?" the woman asked hesitantly.

A decidedly ribald reply rose to mind, but the look on her face stopped him. She was blushing once more, her countenance a mixture of discomfort and . . . could it be— innocence? How peculiar in a widow. Intrigued, he plumbed those gray depths further and once again identified that expression lurking in the corner of her eyes . . . outright dread. He had seen many things in women's eyes, passion, calculation, distrust, anger, disappointment, and speculation, but never obvious fear. "I will make an attempt, Madame," he said, adding with conscious provocation, "however, you are missing a definite opportunity." As he had hoped, she went red to the roots of her hair and the terror in her eyes vanished.

"Indeed, sir, you will give me leave to doubt that you have anything unique for viewing," she replied indignantly, deliberately turning her back.

The saucy reply was all the more piquant for its defiance of his expectations. He knew that the mouse had teeth, and could quote Shakespeare, but he had been unaware till now that she had any claim to wit. To his dismay, Sebastian found that laughter and the rib cage were intimately connected. As he lost his tenuous hold on consciousness once again, his last thoughts were ones of regret. His pants would be sacrificed to her shears after all.

"Ahoy, Mrs. Westford!"

"Up here, Mr. Peggoty," Amanda roused, putting her scissors aside in relief, as the heavyset servant puffed up the stairs.

"Would ha been sooner, I would," Peggoty said, mopping his brow with an already-wet handkerchief. "But Father Noah's own weather out there, it is. Had to leave the wagon in the middle o' the road, I did, so mired it was. Slipped the horse from harness and slapped him on home."

"And Marcus?" Amanda asked anxiously. "Is he with you?"

"Nay, ma'am," Peggoty shook his hoary head. "He's a plucky one, he is, your boy. Made it to the door just before the buckets started pourin'. Wanted to come with me, he did, though he's plumb wore out. The devil's own time it took to convince him to stay put at the Mills, so consarned he was for you. Came lookin' just where the lad tole me to, I did, but you was gone. Found the feller's horse though, and brought him up with me. Figgered he had come to hisself and I'd be findin' you here at the Vicarage and right I was. Now where's the man what come to grief?"

Amanda pointed toward the bed. "He took a blow to the skull and he has some bruises, but it is the right leg that seems to be the worst of it. I do not know if it is broken. Have you sent for Dr. Howell?"

"Aye, sent one o' the footmen, I did. Ain't gonna slog through this though, Howell. He don't like to get wet, that 'un, as is; and the road's turned into a river. Always does in the wet," Peggoty said, his expression doleful as he lumbered toward the bedside. "Ain't seen such a blow since I rounded the Horn. Lucky thing you got off'n the drive afore it came pourin' down."

"This man knew that the road would become impassable," Amanda said, brushing a stray lock of hair from the stranger's forehead. "Is that not most peculiar? He was familiar with the Vicarage too."

"Ain't seen him before, as I recall." Peggoty shrugged his broad shoulders before pulling aside the covers and hastily replacing them. The old sailor glanced at Amanda in consternation, taking in the scraps of cloth and leather heaped on the floor with a cluck of surprise. "'Tain't the thing for you to be strippin' him down like that, Mrs. Westford."

"I know," Amanda said, shaking her head at her own temerity. "But I had to, you see. I could not very well let him freeze to death."

"That's so, I reckon," Peggoty said, his weathered face breaking into a smile. "And lucky it is, I'd say, that you didn't wait on ceremony, knowin' how you feel about the proper. Lady Claire would be proud o' you, she would. Just what was needed, you did."

"Did you manage to get out without Lady Claire's knowledge?" Amanda asked, feeling a bit more at ease. Peggoty did not condemn her, so perhaps others would be equally understanding. She could not afford to risk her reputation.

"Aye, she knows nothing," Peggoty said, as he lifted the blanket once more. "Else 'tis here Lady Claire'd be, fog or flood, knowin' her, bless her heart. Missus Peggoty has the boy hid in the kitchen, she does, and mebbe we can have him home come morn with milady none the wiser."

The stranger's sweat-sheened torso glistened in the firelight and Amanda quickly looked away as Peggoty began his examination. "Well let us pray that she does not find out," Amanda said, keeping her eyes fixed on the fire. "For I would hate for anything to destroy the marvelous progress that she has made in these past few weeks."

"Aye," Peggoty agreed. "Thought we was goin' to lose her, I did. But when she started onto cursin' the doctor what wouldn't let her leave Lunnon, she was on the mend, I knew. And more of it due to you than the leeches, I'd say, stayin' by her night n' day the way you did. Fact is," he said, carefully covering the stranger once more, "ain't much that a surgeon could ha' done for this gent what you ain't did already. Seen men with legs twice this bad and dancin' the hornpipe come mornin'. Don't seem broke to me. I'll just wrap it up and we'll see if the sawbones don't say the same when he comes."

A flash of lightning illuminated the room, followed by a ripple of thunder. "If he comes," Amanda said, suddenly feeling the cold. " 'Tis as you say; I doubt that Dr. Howell will stir from his house on an evening like this. Besides, it is coming on to nightfall. It would be suicidal to attempt the drive after dark." She shivered violently and sneezed.

"Bless me if you ain't half-froze, and shakin' like the tops'l in a nor'wester," Peggoty said in concern. "Go on with you and change out o' those wet things. Else you'll be the one that the doctor'll be comin' to see, I'm bound."

"And what about you, Peggoty?" Amanda asked. "You are far wetter than I."

"This is but a mizzle, I'd say, compared to some o' the storms I've weathered after I took the King's shillin'," Peggoty said heartily. "Now go on with you and don't worry your head about me. Bein' an old salt and knowin' what the sky promised, I bethought to bring meself a change o'togs, I did. I'll take care o' him."

"Are you certain that you do not need help?" Amanda asked.

"You done seen more'n what's fit for a lady's eyes, seems to me. I'll be fine by meself."

Amanda nodded and hurried to her room, trying to keep her teeth from chattering until she was out of Peggoty's sight. The row of buttons down her back seemed endless to her benumbed fingers as she stood before the looking glass. *It is ruined,* she thought in dismay, surveying the mud-spattered, torn skirt. Her heart sank for a brief moment as she recalled the cost of the deceptively simple gown. Yet, even as she agonized, a curious thought dawned. Madame Robarde would gladly make her another. In fact, Amanda could easily afford a dozen.

She pushed aside the well-worn woolen that she had been about to choose in favor of a new blue merino, savoring the soft fabric as she pulled it on. Not nearly as practical, she thought critically, examining her appearance in the pier glass. But there was a novel delight in not being sensible. She found herself wondering what the stranger might think of the rather fashionable woman who peered back from the mirror.

With a rueful shake of her head she turned away, going back to her wardrobe for the wool. If this was the effect of fine feathers, then she had best shed them for more drab plumage. Preening like a popinjay for a man whose name she did not even know, absurd!

"Mrs. Westford," Peggoty's voice came from beyond the door. "He's getting a mite restless, I'm thinking. Mayhap there's a fever coming on."

Amanda quickly hung the older gown away. It was unconscionably foolish to be worrying about what she wore. Especially when the man who had saved her life and her son's might not live to see it.

All through that long night, she and Peggoty fought for him, trying to quench the fires of a rising fever.

"Mama?" he whispered in a longing voice that wrenched at Amanda's heart. "Please don't go away this time, Mama."

She smoothed his brow and held his hand, making promises to the child that this man had once been. "I am here," she said softly. There was a terrible loneliness in that cry, a little boy's fear in that handhold. Too many nights she had sat beside this very bed, listening to Marcus's nightmares, the secret torments that plagued the mind set free in the throes of suffering.

Her patient moved restlessly and she dipped a cloth into the basin, touching the cool compress to his forehead, but he writhed away from her, his face contorted as if he witnessed some unspeakable horror.

"No!" he screamed, sitting bolt upright, the sheets slipping from his body. " 'Tis a bloody lie. A lie. *You* are a bastard, liar," came the anguished cry.

She tried to soothe him, ease him back down into the pillows, but he pushed her aside, the force of the blow sending her reeling to the floor. Peggoty rushed to her aid.

"Is it all right you are, Mrs. Westford?" he asked, helping her to her feet.

The stranger was quaking, rivulets of perspiration running down his neck. He raised his hand in a beckoning motion.

"Rally men! To me! To me!" Sebastian shouted . . . *smoke from the ammunition made his throat raw . . . can't see . . . a feeling like a vise around his stomach . . . Damn Picton for ordering this charge into hell . . . falling . . . they were all falling . . . Lady Claire . . . why was she here in the battle-field? "Beware!" He ran toward her, trying to get her out of the way . . .* "Too late," he moaned, shaking his head, tears pouring down his cheeks. "Too late."

"There laddy," Peggoty said taking him by the hand. "Calm yourself." But the man struggled against him, trying to get out of the bed.

"Have to get there," he cried. "Too late! Debt must be paid."

"Let go, Peggoty. He will do himself injury," Amanda said, wondering what terrible memory was causing him to cry thus. He had not seemed like a man prone to weeping. "Let me try."

"Seems to me, 'tis him doin' you harm that you ought to be afeard of," Peggoty said, but he reluctantly released his hold.

The stranger's gaze was entirely disconcerting. "It is not too late," Amanda kept her tone even, approaching him with caution. It was difficult to discern if he heard her.

"Are you sure?" he asked, his voice plaintive with a depth of sorrow. His hand snaked out to grip her wrist tightly, pulling her to sit nearly beside him.

Peggoty lunged forward, but Amanda waved him away. "No, there is still time," she promised him, trying to be as convincing as she could. "But you are injured. You must rest."

He nodded slowly, his eyes clearing for a moment. "Who? . . ."

"Amanda," she said. "My name is Amanda."

"One who is loved," his fevered mind translated aloud, as his free hand rose to trace the ridge of her cheekbones.

Feather-light, the long fingers slipped to touch the line of her lips. Closer he drew her, his hand tangling in her hair. She knew she ought to pull away, but she was losing herself in his need, the longing reflected in those glittering sapphire depths.

"Do not leave me," he whispered hoarsely. "Promise me."

She knew that it was someone else he saw, that it was an-other woman whose vow he sought, but she could not deny him. "I will stay," Amanda agreed, as one ensorcelled, allow-ing herself to be pulled closer yet.

She closed her eyes, forgetting Peggoty's presence, aware of only this man beside her whose overwhelming loneliness seemed to match her own. She waited, wanting, but confused by this strange need that was both craving and compassion. Desire and dread mixed as she felt the warmth of his breath.

His dry lips brushed her forehead with a kiss, a child's token, a gesture of tenderness, but hardly the kind of communion that she had anticipated. Amanda swallowed her disappointment, wondering at her own audacity. Was she so lost to sensibility, so desperate that she longed for the kiss of a stranger? And an insensible one at that. "Rest now," she told him, suddenly glad that those glazed eyes could not discern the breadth of her embarrassment. "Sleep." She reenforced the command with a gentle push on his shoulder.

Obediently, he lay back and closed his eyes, his fingers still twined tightly with hers.

Peggoty let out a relieved sound. "A close business that was," the old sailor declared. " 'Twas hard to tell whether he was out to strangle you or have a smack at you, I'd say, so out of his head he is."

"His breathing appears to be easier now," Amanda said, watching the slow up-and-down movement of his chest. Her own heart was beating a frantic tattoo.

"Aye, seems t'be restin' more calm," Peggoty said, misunderstanding Amanda's agitated look. "And 'tis rest you're needing, Mrs. Westford. Fair to frazzled, you must be. I'll mind him."

She felt totally spent, but the desperate clutch of those fingers held her fast. "No, Peggoty," she demurred. "You go next door to my room; it ought to be warmer by now."

"Is it sure you are, Mrs. Westford? Seems to me you're needing your bunk more," he said, shaking his head doubtfully.

"I made a promise and I intend to keep it," Amanda said, assuring him with a smile. "You know full well that I have spent many a night like this."

"Aye, that you have, ma'am," Peggoty said, his hoary head nodding in acknowledgment. "But there's no tellin' what a man might do in the throes of a fever. Why I recall once in New Guinea, a mate o' mine—"

"None of your yarns, Peggoty," Amanda said, sensing a

long story in the offing, "else we shall both be up half the night. If there is any difficulty, I will call you. Now get yourself some sleep."

The old seafarer nodded his head, knowing that he could not dissuade her. She had that selfsame stubborn look that Lady Claire got when she had the wind in her sails. "Aye, aye. I'll be givin' you a 'spell-o' in an hour or two then," Peggoty told her, as the door squeaked closed behind him. "Sailor's lingo for a *rest*, that is. Next watch is mine."

"Aye, aye," Amanda agreed, settling herself back into her chair. The cushions were old, but they conformed exactly to her contours, molded by nights of long vigils. The fancy-worked covers on the arms could not fully conceal the worn upholstery frayed by worried hands. However, this time, it was not Marcus's face lying pale against the pillows, but a man whose name she did not know and whose outwardly lascivious character seemed less than savory.

Yet as she listened to the sounds of his delirious dreams, she came to know some of those things that individuals confine to the deepest recesses of the soul, seldom revealed even to their closest companions. In the rallying cries and retreats of battle, the frenzy that comes in the heat of a fight, the disasters of defeat and death, she felt his welling grief, the unspoken bond between men who face destruction together. There were no victories, no joys in his fevered mutterings, only inexorable loss and terror. Even mumbled fragments of thought conveyed a crushing sense of solitude that resonated deeply within Amanda herself. And through it all ran the poignant thread of "too late . . . too late." Almost as soon as her reassurances calmed him, he would begin to fret again.

Amanda did not know the hour when the din of rain on the roof finally stopped. Fatigued as she was, she could not snatch any rest. The uneasiness began in the silence, a niggling worry that grew like a shadow in the night as she wondered at the stranger's identity. In the moonlight, his hair seemed like the glowing embers at the heart of the coal. If she lived to Lady Claire's age, she would never forget the look on his face as he struggled to master his horse, the instant when their eyes had met and she had known that they stood at the brink of death. *These feelings,* she told herself, *are a result of obligation.* He had saved her life and her son's; it was only natural to feel responsibility.

Which one was he? Amanda wondered, trying to distract herself from these curious emotions. *The ribald skirt chaser who seemed to delight in defying convention?* The bandage that Peggoty had put round his crown made him seem boyish and oddly vulnerable. *Or was he the battle-hardened soldier who had shed tears when he saw his men dying?* She leaned forward, adjusting the rough bit of linen that had tilted rakishly above his eye. *Was he the child begging his mother to stay?* Her hand strayed to his cheek. She checked herself, pulling back abruptly, recognizing those intangible emotions at last. Longing. Had nearly nine years changed nothing then? Was she still the same half-brained girl that she had been at seventeen? A fool for a handsome face and a winning smile?

Memories of passion and pain mingled as the door to her yesterdays opened. She had believed in him, walks in the moonlight when all were abed, hushed laughter and breathless kisses. Ruthlessly, she closed that portal, clinging only to the pain to armor herself against further hurt. *Remember,* she adjured herself. *Remember the price you paid.* She got up and looked out into the darkness, her mind racing with forbidden thoughts. The few pleasant memories that she had of Marcus's father were tainted by bitterness. There was no sensible reason for this strange surge of desire, yet it was strong, almost compelling, but it was surely wrong to feel so. Certainly no proper female ought to have this fearsome need to be held, to be touched . . .

When she seated herself by the bedside once more, Amanda methodically recalled ever licentious word, every suggestive remark that the stranger had uttered. A wicked man, far too handsome by half, he was dangerous indeed, and she would do well to rein in her base instincts. The recounting of his perfidies, however, had a distinctly curious effect. Like so many lost sheep, the charges she mustered against him leapt the fence of her imagination and sent her into the boundaries of sleep.

4

The candle on the bedside table flickered as night winds penetrated the shutter, casting dancing shadows into the small looking glass. Like a struggling half-drowned swimmer, Sebastian broke the surface of consciousness, blinking his eyes in the twilight between waking and slumber as oddly familiar shapes took form. The slope of the whitewashed ceiling was as well-known to him as the battered Chippendale desk in the corner by the door. The Stubbs print that his father had purchased hung in the shadows, but Sebastian knew it by heart, the proud piece of horseflesh pawing the earth, almost diminishing its owner, who stood at the reins. He heard a peculiar scratching sound and identified it immediately as the limb of the old oak, rubbing against the windowpane as if in greeting. He looked for his toy soldiers, but they were not upon their customary shelf; instead he saw the dimmed curved outline of a sword hilt and felt confusion. Perhaps his leaden troops were in their secret hiding place or scattered on the floor, in the midst of a battle . . .

A sense of wonder filled him. By some unknown magic, he had come home. Familiarity wrapped itself around him like a warm blanket with a child's sense of security. Surrounded by the accoutrements of boyhood, he closed his eyes, half listening for the sound of his mother's laughter drifting up the stairs, the booming bass of his father's voice as he practiced the week's sermon. This was *his* room, his sanctuary, the place where he had dreamed his childish fancies, planned to be a soldier for the glory of England and the Armitage name . . . foolish boy that he had been. *Lies, all lies.* Only tin soldiers could fight and not bleed and die; only children could believe in a future where glory came without a painful price.

He turned his head abruptly, as if looking away from those

youthful memories could ease the sudden ache deep within. His breath caught sharply as the movement caused the screw round his skull to tighten its grip. The throb in his ankle was but a minor distraction by comparison. The pain of reality called him back to the here and now; the sensations of the past faded like the paper on the wall. *It was warm, so very warm . . . Why was the fire burning so brightly?* He was all in a sweat. When his headache eased, Sebastian opened his eyes again, only to wonder if he was dreaming still.

The boy, the road, the woman . . . a jumble of images tumbled through his brain. But was this the female that he had met upon the roadside, the Amazon who had hauled him up the stairs and wielded a butcher knife against his boot? Cheek leaning against the chair's wing, lids shuttering her eyes, lips parted in sleep, the moonlight from the window made her into a fairy being, capable of flying away into the night on pixie wings. This ethereal woman seemed to be clothed in a veil of luminous silver, streaks of light glowing in the velvet darkness of her hair as if it were adorned with stars.

Meticulously, he recorded each detail, the way the mercury light caressed her cheek like a lover, her lashes thick and lustrous upon her cheek, the creamy rise and fall of the lace at her throat. Her hand lay close to his, relaxed in repose, a ray of moon nestled in her upturned palm as if the very beams were creatures of the night that she could tame.

Slowly, almost of their own volition, his fingers crept into hers. He found himself half expecting to find her skin as cool as the moonlight she wore like a gown. But the warmth of her hand marred the perfection of the illusion. She was a woman of flesh and blood and Sebastian felt an unreasoning surge of disappointment at her actuality. Then her long fingers curled around his, clasping his palm in an innocent gesture. A long time indeed since any woman had proffered her hand with such trust. It was oddly pleasing, albeit done unaware, the feel of that gentle hand in the quiet night, demanding nothing from him. Stealthily, carefully, he brought her fingers to his lips and drifted back into sleep.

There was music. The distant sounds filtered into the nursery. There was a ball below; Amanda knew somehow. Cur-

*tains blew in the spring breeze swaying in time to the tempo.
The children were gone. She was alone in the deserted nursery, flying across the schoolroom floor in a solitary waltz.
The door burst open and the stranger, resplendent in full evening dress, stepped from the shadows. Suddenly the room was
filled with branches of candles, the tapers shedding gentle
light. With a wave of his hand, her somber bombazine transformed to silk; satin slippers replaced worn leather. Like Me-
dusa's hair, Amanda's dark tresses acquired a life of their
own, piling high upon her head to nestle within a sapphire ti-
ara. And then he held out his hand beckoning . . . his face
grim . . . She shrank away. "Do not be afraid," he whispered,
"dance with me. . . ." Slowly, compelled by the demand of
those azure eyes, she stepped into the circle of his arms and
began to move to the music. As they swayed, clouds began to
gather upon the ceiling. The rhythm became thunder, harsh
and demanding. Yet they whirled on unheeding until the rain
began to pour. They whirled through the sheets of water as
the candles extinguished one by one till they danced in total
darkness, holding each other in a circle of warmth amidst the
storm. "Do not be afraid. . . ." he whispered and she felt the
touch of his lips. Then lightning flashed, but it was not the
stranger's face she saw. Arthur . . . he was laughing mock-
ingly. "Can your son waltz?" he asked.*

The metallic rap of the door knocker below startled
Amanda from her dreams. Bewildered and feeling curiously
bereft, she blinked at the flood of sunlight, stirring in her
chair, attempting to recollect just how she had come to be sitting in Marcus's room. As she started to stretch away the
knots in her neck and back, she felt the resistance of a warm
hand clasping her own, certainly not the hand of a boy. The
stranger! His countenance appeared more in the realm of normal than it had been the night before, the unhealthy feverish
flush had abated. His breathing seemed deeper, less labored.

Her hand flew to her hair with the sound of footsteps on
the stair. She must look as raggle-taggle as a tinker, hardly in
any condition to face the gossiping physician. Therefore, it
somewhat relieved her to hear the yell on the stair.

"Mama! Mama!" Marcus called, pounding up the treads
with an uneven gait. The door opened with a loud groan from

the hinge and the boy limped into her skirts. "What happened? Did you get wet? Is he dead?"

But Amanda's relief was short-lived, as she heard another familiar voice echoing in the hall.

"Andrew Peggoty, you wave-shaken fool!" Lady Claire bellowed, her words punctuated by the dull thud of her cane. "How dare you order my staff to deceive me!" Her plumes bobbed in outrage as she leaned on the lintel to catch her breath.

"For your own good it was, milady," Peggoty stammered, staggering into the room.

"My own good!" Lady Claire said. "And what of Amanda's good? If I had not arrived here before the doctor, we would like as not have a scandal on our hands. You know that Howell has precious little liking for Amanda since she refused to allow him to bleed me. I shudder to think of the broth that he might stew over her spending a night alone with a stranger with only a servant to lend her countenance," she muttered, turning to scold Amanda. "I vow, I do not know how you could be so foolish."

"It was I who requested that the servants keep this from you," Amanda said in Peggoty's defense. "Because I feared exactly the consequences that are occurring now. You ought to be resting, Lady Claire. Dr. Howell expressly forbade strenuous activity and, in that, I would tend to agree with the man."

"Pah!" Lady Claire said with a dismissive wave of her hand. "His sole distinction is that he is the only physician between Millford and Chester. It pays to have his advice only so one might do the exact opposite. Now, let me have a look at this stranger. I have set more than a few broken bones in my time."

Reluctantly, Amanda stepped aside and the elderly woman hobbled toward the bed. Abruptly, she stopped, standing stock-still. Her face parched the color of ash.

"S . . . S . . . Sebastian," Lady Claire stammered, her voice low, "S . . . S . . . Sebastian."

Amanda could barely hear the whispered name. She rushed to her friend's side as Lady Claire began to sway.

"Quickly, Peggoty! We need to get her to a bed," Amanda

demanded, rushing to help, but the older woman shook her head.

"No ... the chair ... take me to the chair," she commanded.

"Peggoty, is she sick again?" Marcus asked anxiously.

Sebastian awoke to a veritable Babel of voices. His head had begun to pound and he was about to tell them all to shut their faces, but one quavering utterance stood out among the cacophonus chorus.

"Sebastian," she called soft as a sigh.

He opened his eyes to find Lady Claire peering into his face. The parchment of her skin was more wrinkled than he recalled. Somehow, time seemed to have shrunken her in upon herself, distilled her to an essence. Those wise eyes were rheumy, touched with tears, but still piercingly blue. Her thinning gray hair was adorned with a ridiculous turban of the kind that she had always favored.

In an ironic twist all his suppositions had been reversed. Instead of attending her sickbed, she was attending his. During the journey from Jamaica, he had wondered what he would say to her after all these years, but that was when he had expected her to be dead or dying. Now, all of those fine speeches of reconciliation deserted him. It was far harder than he had expected to put those bitter memories aside, to swallow the pride that had driven him for all those lonely years.

"Get away from me, all of you," Lady Claire exclaimed, waving her hand as if shooing away a swarm of flies before turning her attention to the man in the bed beside her. Her fingers sought and found his to clasp them tightly.

She was trembling. And the unspoken fear in her countenance moved him to compassion. He set himself aside in an effort to reassure her. "You need not worry ... Lady Claire," Sebastian said, his aching head temporarily forgotten. "If you recall, I spent a great part of my childhood being pitched off of horses."

"Sebastian," Lady Claire repeated, overwhelmed by the moment.

Any doubts that Amanda might have had as to the stranger's identity were suddenly laid to rest when her friend bent to kiss him gently on the cheek. *Sebastian?* The name reared up and hissed at her. *How many Sebastians would be riding neck or nothing up a private drive in a remote corner of Cheshire?* Amanda's stomach suddenly knotted.

"You young idiot," the elderly lady said, her voice husky with emotion, eyes glistening. "I have been longing to see you this age, but not laid out for the churchyard, boy."

"You on the other hand, look quite well . . . for a woman with one foot in the grave," Sebastian said, surveying her lined face warily. Impossible to act as if nothing had changed, to slip into old patterns. He was no longer a boy to be alternately scolded and coddled. "When I inquired after you at your town house in London, I was told that you had demanded to be brought home to Cheshire, even though you were on your deathbed," he said coolly.

"Deathbed?" Lady Claire snorted. "I have cheated the Reaper more times than I care to admit. Who has told you such folderol, godson? And how came you to London in the first place?"

Amanda began to gnaw at her lower lip. He certainly did not look like a rake. From Lady Claire's disapproving descriptions of her godson's riotous life, Amanda had expected a much more world-worn visage, some outward signs of dissipation, a paunch at the very least, but Sebastian Armitage, if this was he, had none of these external characteristics, other than a tendency toward rude speech. Still, with the stranger's identity thus confirmed, there was naught that she could do but admit culpability.

"I am afraid that I am responsible for Mr. Armitage's presence," Amanda confessed. "The doctors were not at all hopeful in those first days, Lady Claire, and you had mentioned Sebastian's—I mean, Mr. Armitage's—name in your final moments of consciousness. So I wrote to him in Jamaica." Her eyes met those of the man in the bed briefly, but she quickly looked away.

"You?" Sebastian asked, the fog in his head clearing somewhat. Certainly she looked like no companion he had ever encountered. With her hair tangled wildly and her complexion glowing rosily with obvious mortification, she seemed little more than a schoolroom miss. Only the presence of the towheaded boy was proof positive that her years were well beyond her looks. She was a mother. A widow, he reminded himself, and a most straitlaced one no doubt, he thought, recalling the obvious disapproval of her letter. "You are *that* Mrs. Westford?"

"Yes," Amanda admitted, a sinking feeling in her stomach. "I am, but I wrote you a second letter immediately when it was apparent that Lady Claire was on the mend."

"No doubt it ... awaits me in Jamaica," Sebastian said ruefully. "I came as soon as I received the first message."

"Did you truly?" Lady Claire asked, wiping the corner of her eye.

"She ... described your condition in the direst terms," Sebastian said, giving Amanda a glowering look. "Yet I find you in the ... rudest of health."

"Are you disappointed, then," Lady Claire said, stiffening slightly, "to come all the way to Cheshire and find me alive and quite well? Shall I take to my bed once more? Is that what is required for my godson to finally pay me a visit? I had never expected to see you again this side of Heaven, boy."

"If Heaven is your expectation, Lady Claire ... then it is fortunate indeed that I came before you took your final journey," Sebastian said, trying to keep his tone deliberately light. "For I believe it was you who first told me ... that I was bound on a course straight for Hell."

"Yes," Lady Claire said with a touch of sadness, "I did indeed and you have not minded my advice yet."

The ill-hidden distress on the old woman's face was a reminder of why Sebastian had never wanted to come back. Now he would have to face them all, everyone who had known him as a boy. The Reverend's son ... the disappointment ... the fraud ... and now ... rakehell ... Cit, and other appellations that he had no wish to dredge up. He closed his eyes, wishing heartily that he had stayed in Jamaica, where no one could touch him, could rouse those old feelings once again. The vise began to tighten around his head.

"We must get the doctor here at once," Lady Claire demanded, seeing her godson's brow furrowing in pain. "He must be seen to immediately."

"Don't look like much beyond a lump on the pate to me, milady," Peggoty said. "Ankle got twisted, but a few days off it and he should be fine enough."

"I asked you for the physician, not an opinion," Lady Claire said with a glare.

"Aye, aye, milady," Peggoty said, hurrying to obey. "It's settin' sail at once I am." The hinge groaned as he pulled the door open.

"And tell Howell that *I* will pay his fees, if that is what is keeping him," Lady Claire called.

"I can well afford to compensate the doctor," Sebastian protested, his voice strained. "I am no longer needful of your charity."

"Aye, boy, I know you can," Lady Claire said, pain in her words. "You saw fit to pay me every penny you ever had from me, with *interest,* as if I was a damned cent per cent-er." She slipped out of her chair, shrugging aside Amanda's hand. "Thinking you near ready to be put to bed with a shovel I merely wished to assure that Aesculapius's henchman would do his best for you. Amanda, when Dr. Howell arrives you may introduce him to my godson, Sebastian Armitage, a fellow that Midas himself would envy. Tell the scoundrel to charge him whatever he chooses, for *Mr. Armitage* can pay the shot." She took up her cane and stalked out of the room.

Amanda stood momentarily rooted as the old woman slammed the door behind her.

The jarring sound made him wince and, momentarily, Sebastian regretted the rum that had accompanied the impromptu surgery the night before. "Please, go after her," Sebastian whispered, closing his eyes against the throb

Amanda looked at him uncertainly. "Are you sure?"

"I will look after Mr. Armitage, Mama," Marcus offered.

Amanda nodded and ran out of the room, leaving the door open behind her.

Sebastian shivered. "There is a draft from the hall, lad," Sebastian said. "Would you close the door? And lift it slightly as you shut it, it will not make noise that way."

"Truly?" the boy asked.

Sebastian did not note the peculiarity immediately, but as the child walked across the room, there was a break in the usual pattern of steps. The bedridden man's eyes flew open and he immediately saw the reason. A crutch. Had the child been injured in the accident after all? But as the boy walked back toward the bedside, Sebastian could see that the young one handled the stick with the familiarity of a well-used appendage. The boy was lame.

"You are right, sir. It does not make noise at all," Marcus said, his eyes glowing with admiration. "Mama has oiled it any number of times, but it would still squeal."

With sickening clarity, Sebastian recalled his comments upon the roadside to Mrs. Westford. No wonder the woman had taken a belligerent stand. Her son could never have gotten out of the way in time. "What is your name, lad?" Sebastian asked roughly.

"Marcus, sir," he answered, approaching the bed hesitantly, his crutch tapping in an irregular rhythm. "Marcus Westford."

"Ah, the man of the household. I am pleased to meet you," Sebastian said, extending his hand in the fashion of one man to another.

"And I, to make your acquaintance," Marcus said in his most grown-up manner, grinning with delight. "How did you know about the door, sir?"

"This was once my room," Sebastian said. How foolish to feel sad, but the ache was undeniably there. "For sixteen years."

The boy was visibly impressed. "That's very long. Longer than it has been mine for sure. We have only lived at the Vicarage, since just after I was borned. Almost eight years is a fair amount too, ain't it?"

"Empires have risen and fallen in less," Sebastian said, smiling as he remembered a child's concept of time, the moments lasting forever and years the province of ancient history.

"Napoleon's did, didn't it?" Marcus asked as he set his crutch aside and settled himself in the chair near the bed. "Mama said he called himself an emperor and that is why my papa had to fight him."

"Your father was a soldier?" Sebastian asked.

"Yes, he was," the boy said solemnly. "He died at a place called Toulouse. That's in France, you know."

"I know," Sebastian said softly, closing eyes that had suddenly begun to sting. That fatal April day was one that he would never forget, pushing his men forward against the French forces, the sounds of steel clashing, the sulfurous smoke and the ground slippery with blood. "Who was your father with, lad?"

"The Third Division, sir," Marcus said proudly. "Mama says that the Third charged the Frenchies and there never were any braver men than they was. Lieutenant Edward Westford was his name. Did you know him?"

Nor had there been any more uselessly slaughtered, Sebastian added silently, shaking his head, *damn Picton's hide.* It was Picton who was largely responsible for the debacle. Wellington had ordered a feint against Napoleon's general, Soult. Instead General Picton had chosen to disobey and forge ahead with disastrous results. The Third, including most of Sebastian's own command, had been decimated, their lives thrown away because of one man's glory hunger.

It had been a narrowly won battle. Eight thousand men had died uselessly at Toulouse. Barely an hour after Wellington had entered the town, the news of Napoleon's abdication had arrived. Sebastian had written the requisite letters to wives and mothers of the fallen, forwarded their belongings and then, despite Wellington's wishes, resigned his commission. Jamaica had been as far away as he could get from the continent and his memories.

"That's my papa's sword up there," Marcus said, pointing to a dress scabbard mounted upon the wall. "Ain't it grand?" But Mr. Armitage made no answer. He was awake and staring, but not seeing.

"Sir? Are you well?" Marcus asked, with concern. "I really ought not to be chattering like this. Mama says I always ask too many questions."

The boy's anxious voice pulled him from the past. "Other than a sore head and a less than sound ankle, I reckon that I am in good order," Sebastian said. All in all, it was true. He had been injured far worse in the past. He took an experimental breath, running his hand over his chest. His ribs were not cracked, it seemed. And his ankle was painful, but he would lay a monkey it was not broken. Only the blow to the skull was somewhat bothersome, for he knew that such injuries were sometimes worse than they appeared. But he was not about to worry the child on that score.

Marcus relaxed visibly. "Mama would skin me alive if she knew that I was keeping you from resting. It is my fault that you were hurt, I suppose—my stupid leg—so I would not blame you if you do not want me to stay. Should I leave?"

For a moment, Sebastian wished him gone. His head was bothering him, and the memories that the child had stirred were more uncomfortable still. Yet Sebastian recognized the look of longing on the lad's face, the fear of being dismissed along with the knowledge of its inevitability. In all likelihood, young Marcus had seen a great deal of rejection in his short life. But it was the guilt in the boy's voice that was the deciding factor.

"You need not fault yourself for the accident," Sebastian told him. "As your mother pointed out, simple caution on my part could have prevented it." The boy's shoulders straightened as if a physical weight had been removed. "And, in actuality, I would likely expire of boredom if you were not here to talk with."

"Truly?" Marcus asked, scarcely daring to believe his luck.

The boy's face lit like a Vauxhall display and, for a moment, Sebastian could see the likeness to his mother. Although Mrs. Westford had never smiled upon him in quite that way, nor was she ever likely to do so. "Yes," Sebastian said. "Being in bed is deadly dull."

"Ain't it just," Marcus agreed with sympathy. "I used to spend a lot of time in bed. I know how many cracks there are in the ceiling."

"There used to be forty-three," Sebastian recalled.

"Sixty-seven now," Marcus corrected.

"And I see the spiders still spin webs in the east corner," Sebastian said.

"Please don't tell Mama."

"Of course I shall not," Sebastian agreed solemnly. "Ladies do not realize the inherent value of spiders and such."

"Exactly!" Marcus concurred, surprised at such superior understanding in an adult. "Mama might do something foolish like clean them away. And then where would that leave me, I ask you? One can only read for so long and Mama is a poor partner for cards. She loses all the time."

"Does she?" Sebastian asked in growing amusement.

"She does." Marcus nodded, dropping his voice to a confidential whisper. "But sometimes I think she does it on purpose to let me win."

"Never say so," Sebastian said in feigned disbelief. "How entirely like a female to think that a man cannot bear to lose an occasional game."

"Is it because she's a female, you think?" Marcus asked, somewhat puzzled. "Lady Claire always plays to win and sometimes she cheats, even when we play spillikins."

Sebastian was hard-pressed not to smile. "She used to cheat when I was a boy too. However, one ought not to say such things about a lady."

"Even if they are true?"

"Even if they are true. No gentleman ever would take any action that would impugn a lady's reputation."

Marcus sighed. "It is often hard to know what a gentleman ought to do."

"Yes, sometimes it is," Sebastian agreed, an ache in the pit of his stomach, as he thought of Lady Claire's pained look. "It is very hard, even when you are grown."

Amanda found Lady Claire in the parlor. Luckily, Peggoty had already thought to light a fire and the elderly woman stood beside the radiating warmth, staring into the flames.

"Why do you not sit down?" Amanda asked, putting a hand on Lady Claire's arm and gently steering her to the settle by the hearth.

"I have made a muddle of it, haven't I?" Lady Claire asked, shaking her head as Amanda tucked a blanket about her. "For sixteen years I have been longing to see him and in a mere two minutes I have spoiled it all."

"He is tired, Lady Claire, and feverish," Amanda said, her guilt growing by the second. "He is bound to be querulous under the circumstances."

"All the more reason not to worry old wounds," the old woman said. "But fool that I am, I could not keep my tongue between my teeth. Why did I have to bring up the sore subject of that draft he sent me."

"Surely it is admirable that he wished to pay back his debts," Amanda said, bending down to add fuel to the fire.

"He *knew* that I wanted no payment," Lady Claire said. "I would have given him far more than a commission if he had let me. Bad enough that he threw that gift back into my lap, but to add interest upon the money was like a slap upon the face. Treated me like a common dun, Amanda, I who supported him when he had nothing."

"Perhaps that is why he felt he ought to repay you," Amanda ventured, recalling the overwhelming burden of Lady Claire's generosity. "It is very difficult to have nothing . . . to be as nothing, to forever feel that sense of obligation. Many is the time since I inherited that I wished to compensate you for what you have done for Marcus and myself over these years past."

"And *I* have told you that I was mortally insulted every time you advanced that ludicrous notion," Lady Claire said with a dismissive gesture. "What I gave to you, at first, I did for your grandmama's sake; she was once one of my dearest friends. And later, I must admit, my support stemmed from selfishness; you and Marcus have become very dear to me. Surely you know that what I did, I did out of love?"

"Yes," Amanda said, smiling at the old woman's indignant look. "I know that *now*. The question is, does your godson know it yet."

"Of course he does." Lady Claire shook her head scornfully. "I vow it is nothing more than foolish pride that caused him to behave so."

"The only thing that the destitute may have in abundance," Amanda reflected, stirring the fire as she recalled how shock and rebellion had quickly turned to shame and resignation. "It is difficult for females to comprehend sometimes, how important that sense of dignity is to a man. We are a bit more practical I suspect. For a man pride is all, yet when I believed myself to be in love, I had no self-regard, no honor, no shame."

"Then it was not love, my dear," Lady Claire said softly. "Love does not demand that you sacrifice yourself entirely, only that you be willing to do so if need be. It exalts you, brings out the best that you have to offer, and offers you the best in return."

Amanda looked up at her, startled.

"You wonder what an ugly, aged spinster could possibly know about love." Lady Claire asked, her lip curling in a sad half smile. "More than you think my dear, more than you would ever imagine, despite my wrinkled phiz. You forfeited everything—"

"Do not attempt to make me into a saint," Amanda said, pulling up a nearby chair. "You know full well that I am not blameless when it comes to Marcus's father."

"You were more sinned against than sinner," Lady Claire retorted. "Yet you would sooner forgive anyone else than yourself. You were barely old enough to have your hair out of plaits and—"

"—should have known better," Amanda concluded bitterly, gathering the folds of her skirt in her hands as she avoided those sympathetic eyes. "After all, I had my parents' own marvelous example to guide me. But I believed myself to be in love. I wanted him . . . so very desperately." She shook her head as she recalled how she had lived for his smile, hungered for his kiss. "No, Lady Claire, the fault lies within me." Her face reddened as she recalled the visions that had visited her that previous night. Surely they were indicative of her wanton nature, to dream of embracing a nameless man, kissing him, having his arms around her. "Sometimes, I still feel . . . a longing within me for something more . . ." her voice trailed off into a shamed whisper. "Why can I not be content?"

"Oh my dear," Lady Claire said, clasping her hand. " 'Tis no crime to be lonely. If it were, I would have been in gaol for most of my life. But you have brought Sebastian back to me."

She looked at her elderly friend, wondering how she could explain this strange desire. As she and Lady Claire had followed the rake's progress of Sebastian Armitage, Amanda had come to believe the man was synonymous with everything she disdained. Nonetheless, although all logic and sensibility would dictate otherwise, it was his face that was now haunting Amanda's dreams. If only she had not impetuously written that letter. In truth, she had never thought that a man of his ilk would bother himself to come. Yet he had run all the way from Jamaica for the sake of an old woman who was not even of his blood, and had been injured in an effort to save others from harm. A most uncommon rogue. "And by bringing your godson here, I am responsible for yet another disaster."

"No," Lady Claire said, bringing Amanda's fingers to her dry lips and bestowing a kiss. "I bless you for that, my dear.

I am glad that he came before I make my crossing into eternity. Unmended quarrels and unfinished business are ill burdens to carry into the next world. There is much to settle and I am grateful for the opportunity to do so."

"But his injury," Amanda said. "That, too, is my responsibility. He was thrown from his mount in an effort to avoid doing Marcus and me injury."

"Never you fear; he comes from a line of hard skulls and thick ones," Lady Claire joked with effort. "He will take no harm."

She was whistling in the dark, Amanda knew. In all the time that she had known her, Lady Claire had been virtually imperturbable, the veritable rock in all emergencies. When Marcus had fallen and broken his arm, it was Lady Claire who had held the boy and soothed him while the bone was set. Through the search for a remedy to Marcus's disfigurement, the crises, the hopes, and the failures, Lady Claire had been there, solid and dependable. Yet now every sound made her start. Despite her show of bravado, the old woman's eyes were constantly flitting to the door, her glance filled with frantic distress. Amanda realized that any assurance that she might attempt was found to have the opposite effect. She could only pray that the doctor would arrive swiftly and render an optimistic prognosis.

"No less than three weeks abed," Dr. Howell pronounced.

"That is absurd," Sebastian protested. "For a knock on the head and a twisted ankle?"

"I vow, you are just like your godmother," the physician sniffed. "You seek my advice only to ignore it. I ought to bleed you, to relieve your feverish condition, but you refuse me. Laudanum would be the most efficacious of physics, yet you will have none of that either. You do not seem to recognize the severity of your condition. Many a thrown patient I have seen, hale and hearty one day and in the earth the next."

Lady Claire gave a cry of dismay. "We must send to Harley Street at once," she said, gripping Amanda's hand with the force of panic. "Immediately get him the best treatment that money can purchase. I know the King's medical man personally."

The elderly lady was shaking like a leaf in the wind, her

face wiped of all trace of color. The veins at her neck seemed as if they were threatening to pop. "Dr. Howell, the fever is almost gone," Amanda said, throwing the physician a warning look, "and Mr. Armitage himself claims to feel much improved. Surely he *is not seriously ill, is he?*"

Howell perceived that he had gone too far. "There there, Lady Claire," he said soothingly. "I did not mean to distress you. I have certainty that your godson will recover fully, *if he does as I say*. He must not, however, under any circumstances, be moved," he said, looking at Amanda maliciously."

"You mean that I cannot take him back to the Mills?" Lady Claire said in consternation.

Amanda bit her lip in dismay. She had hoped that Armitage would be gone before nightfall. The longer that he stayed under the roof, the greater the hazard of scandal. Her first instincts had been entirely correct. He was dangerous. Everyone in Millford knew of 'The Demon Rum.' As a native son, Armitage's career had been followed with avid interest. His army heroism and his rapid rise to wealth had assumed the force of local legend. Even the less savory aspects of his character were elbow-in-the-rib tavern talk among the Millford men and clucking 'fancy, the vicar's son,' disapproval among the women.

Sebastian watched the exchange with interest. He had seen physicians of Howell's ilk before, grasping toadies who knew more about the Exchange than nostrums. He half suspected that the doctor's orders were governed more by a desire to milk a well-to-do patient than actual need. However, the obvious antipathy between the practitioner and his godmother's companion piqued his curiosity. It might even have been somewhat amusing had Lady Claire not spent half the time avoiding his eyes, talking about him, but never to him. But it was up to her to end the foolish farce; he would be damned if he would apologize first.

"Then I suppose there is no help for it," Lady Claire said, recovering her composure. "If my godson stays, then I must as well, to lend Amanda countenance. His reputation must be protected," she added with a sniff.

"You cut me to the quick," Sebastian said.

Lady Claire pointedly ignored him, taking Amanda by the arm and leading her toward the door. "I am determined not to be an encumbrance to you. Let us see, I shall need at least one—no, two footmen. I do not mind a bit of rough living. There is no room for them here of course, but they may come by day. The Peggotys can stay. Let me see, we shall need cutlery, feather tickings, some wines from my cellar . . ."

The catalogue of absolute necessities continued as the two of them left the room.

"Rough living indeed," Sebastian commented.

The physician gave a humorless laugh. "Not as rough as it used to be here, Mr. Armitage. Mrs. Westford has acquired airs well above her station in these past months. Ever since she returned from London with Lady Claire, one would think her quite the grande dame. Her manner of dress is far too modish for a mere companion and, of late, she has been quite free with the ready in the village. Why, just last week, the butcher said that she ordered a sirloin of beef and I have heard that she is purchasing beeswax candles these days," he added with a knowing nod.

"All manner of luxuries, eh?" Sebastian inquired, marveling that the physician had not consulted about Mrs. Westford's hedonistic habits with the baker and greengrocer as well.

"Indeed so," Howell agreed. "One of my patients mentioned that she had made an inquiry regarding the acquisition of a horse and carriage."

"Did she?" Sebastian asked, taken somewhat aback. Of all of Howell's banal catalogue, this was certainly the most troubling bauble. The purchase of a horse and equipage was, in the usual run, well beyond the means of a mere companion, not to mention the tax and the heavy expense of stabling and care. "And you say that this has all occurred since my godmother's illness?"

"Yes," Howell said, with a look that spoke significantly. "Mrs. Westford has taken up the reins since then, ordering everyone about as if *she* were the mistress of the Mills. She and her son were in residence there for the duration of Lady Claire's illness and since then, there have been all manner of deliveries coming through the village. New furnishings and the like for the Vicarage. In fact 'tis only two weeks ago that she returned to the Vicarage and she has been making inquiries regarding the hire of servants *for herself.*"

"She does not live at the Mills?" Sebastian asked. "Surely a companion ought to domicile herself with her employer?"

"No, she never has," the physician said with disapproval as he put his unused lancet back in its case. "Lady Claire has never treated her quite as an employee, and that, no doubt, has been nurturing her top-lofty ways. Why, Mrs. Westford has even used her influence to turn your godmother against me, countermanding my orders at every turn. That woman would not allow me to bleed Lady Claire although it was clearly required."

"Yet she did recover," Sebastian felt obliged to point out.

" 'Tis a matter of luck that Lady Claire is still with us, if you ask me," Howell said, gathering up his things. "I shall be by to visit you tomorrow, and see how you are getting along."

And therein lies the crux of the matter, Sebastian thought. Jealousy was obviously the cause of the doctor's denouncement of Mrs. Westford. Yet, if his accusations were true, they might bear examination. Lady Claire was a kindhearted soul and many was the time within Sebastian's childhood recollection that her generosity had been abused. If Mrs. Westford was out to bilk his godmother . . . It was a possibility he was strangely reluctant to entertain.

5

Arthur, Lord Whittlesea, looked disdainfully at the cold mound of eggs on the sideboard. "Really, Mama," he protested, replacing the cover with a moue of distaste and staring at his reflection in its dull surface, "you just must speak to the servants. The silver is so tarnished I can barely see myself. As for this!" He speared a kipper and held it up in disparagement. "One can scarcely break one's fast on such slop. I vow, I have never seen such purse-pinching, not one above a half dozen dishes and none of them with more appeal than a pile of horse droppings."

"Count yourself fortunate, Arthur," Lady Whittlesea said with a sniff, raising her lorgnette momentarily from her perusal of the morning paper. "If the Sommers heiress does not come up to scratch, you may be sampling the fare in Fleet and you need not worry about the state of the silver, for it shall be seized and sold. I have managed to put off most of the duns thus far, but you can be sure that they will soon be swarming like flies to the carrion if an engagement is not announced soon."

"You need not fear, Mama. She wants to be a 'milady' far too much," Arthur said, continuing his survey of the breakfast array. "If I attempt to rush my fences, the nag may very well refuse to take the leap."

"You really *must* do something," Lady Whittlesea said, rustling the paper angrily. "Why can you not just set the date? You say that Mr. Sommers was more than well pleased with the match."

"He is more than pleased!" Arthur snorted, helping himself to some kippers. "The Cit is in alt, knowing that he is about to purchase the Whittlesea name for his daughter. But he is being difficult about the settlement. 'Tis not nearly enough. I should be paid her weight in gold to wed that fat cow."

"Arthur," Lady Whittlesea warned. "Remember the last time. Do not be too greedy."

"She believes that I intend to take her riding on Rotten Row, for pity's sake," Arthur said with a laugh. "A bovine on horseback. I refuse to make myself the laughingstock of White's. Bad enough to be leg shackling myself to a mushroom, but I see no need to flaunt my mésalliance. I fully expect that 'Madame Moo' is going to pasture herself in the country after we are wed."

"You had best beware, else there will be no need to worry about your friends' sensibilities," Lady Whittlesea fumed. "Nor, in all likelihood, the terrible humiliation of wedding yourself to one of London's biggest heiresses—"

"Certainly the biggest!" Arthur guffawed. " 'Twill be like kissing a balloon."

"I do not give a fig as to what you choose to kiss, so long as you do it soon," Lady Whittlesea said.

"I vow, it is so demeaning. To sell our name like so many ells of cloth. The Whittleseas go all the way back to the Conqueror," Arthur protested.

"So I have told the vintner, the butcher, and the cook," Lady Whittlesea said acerbically, "but it fails to impress them. Madame Robarde even had the audacity to tell me that she no longer wished to accept my custom until my bills are paid."

"I am certain that La Sommers will jump at my suit," Arthur said, adjusting the intricate folds of his cravat with an expert hand. "There may be others who think to use their titles to tow them out of the River Tick, but not a one of them has countenance and style above a toad's. I will call on her father this afternoon. He will see reason, I suspect. Even a Cit's daughter has eyes, y'know."

Lady Whittlesea looked at her son, silently conceding the point. Although Arthur was well past his fortieth year, his blond good looks were enough to turn the heads of most females. However, his perpetually empty pockets and propensity for the company of high-flyers won him no plaudits among the mamas of eligibles. Even the most horse-faced of heiresses were kept from his company. The Cit's daughter was their best hope. "You are a dear boy, Arthur," she said with a pleased smile, her eyes returning to the daily tittle-tattle about the doings of society. All at once, a name caught her eye. "I cannot credit it . . ." she whispered, dropping back into her chair. "It is beyond belief, I vow . . ."

"Is it Lady Hertford again?" Arthur said, stuffing a fork full of kippers into his mouth.

Lady Whittlesea shook her head dumbly.

"What is it, Mama?" Arthur asked. "You look absolutely ghastly."

"Ever the gallant," Lady Whittlesea murmured, holding out the offending page. "Do you recall Lord Hartleigh's grand-daughter?"

"Did I meet her at Almack's?" Arthur wondered, putting a finger to his lip in deep consideration, "or was it at Lord Ratherby's rout?"

"Neither!" Lady Whittlesea snapped. "Her grandfather disinherited her mother."

"Then why in the world does it signify?" Arthur asked, puzzled. "The chit is of no interest to me. It is money we need."

"The old earl's son was not in the petticoat line, if you recall, and there was no direct heir. The papers have been filled with speculation."

Arthur waved a dismissive hand. "You know full well I have no interest in those rags."

"It would seem that the last of the Hartleighs is a female, the granddaughter," Lady Whittlesea said faintly. "Everything goes to her . . . every last farthing."

Arthur brightened. "Is she pretty?" he asked.

"In a common sort of way." Lady Whittlesea's voice dripped with venom. "At least, *you* once thought so. She previously made her living as a governess."

The gears in Arthur's head began to whir and click until the growing disbelief in his eyes signified that his thought processes had come to a conclusion. "You cannot mean . . ."

"Amanda Maisson," Lady Whittlesea hissed in fury. "She is an heiress now."

Arthur ran his hand through his carefully arranged hair. "I had always thought you too harsh on the girl," he accused.

"Me? *You* were cheering me on, if you would but recall!"

she cried. "It was you who . . ." Her lips thinned with fury, but relaxed slowly into a crafty line. "Perhaps we have *both* wronged her," she said in treacle tones. "Maybe we ought to make amends somehow."

"Whatever do you mean, Mama?" Arthur asked, scratching his head. "You do speak in riddles sometimes."

Lady Whittlesea gave her son a contemptuous look. "I believe the young woman is presently unwed. When I saw her last, in fact, she was wearing widow's weeds."

"You have seen her?" Arthur asked. "Do not say that she has chosen to show her face in polite society."

"She was in the company of that dreadful Lady Claire in Madame Robarde's salon," Lady Whittlesea recalled. "If you remember, 'twas Lady Claire who recommended the chit for employment as our governess eight—or was it nine?—years ago. She did mention that the girl was Hartleigh's grandchild then, but it was apparent that her family would not acknowledge the connection. Lady Claire was ever one for taking wounded birds under her wing."

"Even soiled doves?" Arthur snickered.

"Arthur! I will not have you talking so of my future daughter-by-marriage," Lady Whittlesea declared.

"What? But I thought that the Sommers chit was . . ." Arthur shook his head.

"Leave the thinking to me," she said, patting her son on his hand. "It should be an easy matter to find the Hartleigh heiress's direction. And when we do, you shall go to her and proffer your humblest apologies. The Hartleigh treasure trove makes the Sommers fortune appear the merest pittance."

"Of course," Arthur said, his smile mirroring his mother's. "Amanda was mad about me. I shall offer her my hand in redress, and I have little doubt that she will accept."

"Oh, she shall wed you," Lady Whittlesea said with a harsh laugh, "and gladly. The outcome is clear."

"To my sweet bride-to-be," Arthur said, raising his cup of coffee in salute.

Sebastian squinted, trying to see if the line in the corner of the room was indeed a crack or merely a trick of the dying light. Yes, it was a crack . . . sixty-nine, he counted triumphantly. The boy had obviously missed some. Most of the day had been slept away. The ache in Sebastian's head had abated and the pain in his ankle had been reduced to a dull throb. Although he was feeling far better, it was now a question whether he would die of ennui or hunger. Lady Claire's salty servant had refused outright to fulfill Sebastian's request for a book. "Surgeon said you ain't to be doin' nobbut like that," were the sailor's precise words. And Sebastian's query about food had been met with a sympathetic stare that boded no good.

There was a soft scratch at the door, almost too hesitant to be a knock.

"Come in," Sebastian called.

"Peggoty said you were awake, but I wasn't sure," Marcus said, his gray eyes impossibly wide as he peered shyly into the room. "Mama told me that I was not to bother you."

"No bother at all," Sebastian said gruffly. "I was just wishing for some company to while away the time till dinner."

"Mrs. Peggoty is making it now," Marcus said, his nose wrinkling with a mixture of distaste and compassion. "She cooks for Lady Claire at the Mills."

"So, my godmother is taking up residence," Sebastian said in amusement.

Marcus nodded. "She is moving in all sorts of things. Mama says that Lady Claire has brought everything but the hip bath. I hope she stays forever."

"Do you?" Sebastian asked curiously.

"Lady Claire is the funnest lady I know," Marcus asserted. "She never tells one to go to bed before dark, or not to take another helping of trifle because it'll make one sick."

"She must have changed since I knew her," Sebastian said with a nostalgic smile. "For she was forever mouthing Franklin's homilies about being 'early to bed and early to rise,' and telling me not to make a pig of myself."

"Do you like working at the newspaper?" Marcus asked, changing the subject with childlike abruptness.

"Newspaper?" Sebastian raised his brow in puzzlement.

"Yes, Mrs. Peggoty said that you are a gazetted rake. Which gazette is it you work for?" the boy asked innocently. "And what do rakes have to do with journals?"

Sebastian nearly choked. Only the boy's concerned expression kept him from losing himself utterly. Nonetheless, it was a few minutes before Sebastian could speak.

"Are you well, sir?" Marcus asked. "Should I call Mama? Perhaps I had best leave."

"I am f . . . f . . . fine, lad," Sebastian sputtered out, at last. "P . . . please stay." He looked about for some means of entertaining his guest. What would a boy enjoy? His eyes scanned the room as he tried to think back. "Tin soldiers!" he said in triumph. "Just the ticket."

"But I have none," Marcus said.

"But I do," Sebastian said, his excitement growing. "Go to the farthest corner of the eaves, move the stool aside and tell me what you see."

Marcus obeyed his commands, crouching with difficulty as he peered into the darkened corner. "Why, the board is loose," he said, dropping his crutch with a clatter.

"Move the board," Sebastian instructed, drawing himself up against the pillows in anticipation. "Inside the space there should be a box. Feel about for it."

Marcus groped in the darkness, putting his hands on a smooth wooden surface and sliding it out of hiding. "What is it, Mr. Armitage?" he asked, using his crutch to help him scramble to his feet, holding the large casket under his arm with difficulty. " 'Tis very heavy."

"You must call me Sebastian now," Sebastian said solemnly as the boy proffered the begrimed box, "since my treasure hold is known to you, it only seems fitting."

"Treasure?" the child breathed.

"Yes," Sebastian said wiping the smudge from Marcus's cheek. "You must promise me never to reveal its location to another living soul."

"I swear," Marcus agreed, lifting his head in an oath-taking gesture. "Upon my father's sword."

"Very well." Sebastian smoothed the dust lovingly from the rough oak, his fingers finding the crudely carved initials "S.A." It had not been touched since he last hid it away. The latch was rusty, but it gave way to pressure, flipping open to reveal all the worldly goods of a fourteen-year-old boy, for Sebastian reckoned it had been at least eighteen years since he last laid eyes on it.

"Oooh," Marcus exclaimed in appreciation as Sebastian

poured the multicolored contents of a leather pouch onto his hands, "I have never seen marbles quite like that."

"Lady Claire brought them for me, from Egypt, I think," Sebastian said, picking up a huge ancient key.

"What does it open?" Marcus asked in awe.

"I never knew," Sebastian admitted, "but it seemed useful to keep it just the same."

Marcus nodded at the wisdom of this. "And what is that?" He pointed at a glint of gold in the corner.

"I had forgotten I had this," Sebastian said softly, picking up the ormolu frame and gazing at the miniature portrait. So, his uncle had not gotten everything after all.

"Who are they?" Marcus asked as he carefully replaced the marbles in their sack.

Sebastian hesitated briefly, his emotions in a jumble. The sight of those beloved faces drew him back beyond the years of bitterness and pain. "The people who raised me," he whispered.

"Your mother and father?"

Sebastian nodded, letting the distinction pass.

"I wish that I had a portrait of my papa," Marcus said with a sigh. "Mama says that I look much like him, but it is not the same as an actual picture."

"No," Sebastian said softly as he replaced the miniature in the box. "One wants to know, to see for oneself." He reached to the very bottom of the box, lifting out a large canvas sack. "This is what I am seeking," he said, opening up the thongs and spilling the jumble out onto the sheets.

"The soldiers," Marcus said, his eyes wide with delight. "But they are so oddly dressed."

"Saracens and crusaders," Sebastian said, picking up an example of each. "Lady Claire bought them for me on one of her journeys. But they can be whoever you wish with a bit of imagination, Romans and Gauls, settlers and Indian warriors."

"Or Frenchies and English soldiers," Marcus ventured.

"If that is your preference," Sebastian agreed. "Now if you will move the table this way, we could set them up."

"You mean you would *play* with me?" Marcus asked in patent astonishment.

"Unless you would prefer to wage war against yourself," Sebastian said.

Within a few moments they had drawn up the leaves of the low bedside table and set up a makeshift battlefield.

"Form square!" Marcus ordered, setting up his pikemen in the traditional formation.

"Shall we make these catapults stand for cannon?" Sebastian asked, his stomach growling fitfully.

"Sounds like you already got some artillery to me," Marcus giggled.

Sebastian grinned in answer. "Several batteries it seems. I hope Mrs. Peggoty hurries herself."

"She likes Mama's new Rumford stove," Marcus said, setting up his catapults. "Says it's ever so much better than the one at the Mills. Says it's like magic it is."

Very expensive magic, Sebastian thought to himself. "Get ready for the first charge, Westford," he declared, but he was not speaking strictly to the boy.

Amanda paused at the door, listening to the sound of Marcus's merriment. It was a long time since she had heard the boy laugh and she savored the sound. These past few months had been all whispers and silence, filled with the unspoken fear that they would lose Lady Claire. There had been precious few smiles and even less occasion for guffaws such as those that currently emanated from the room. A deep base joined Marcus's treble in a delightful combination. Mr. Armitage? Curious, she set the tray that she was carrying on the hall table and peered into the room.

The scene that spread before her was beyond belief. Marcus was kneeling by the bedside.

"P'choom, P'choom," Marcus cried, his hand swooping across the table. "We've got 'em on the run, men."

Leaning back against the headboard, the sheets pulled to his armpits, Mr. Armitage watched the action with every appearance of dismay. Amanda recognized the battered tricorn perched at a crazy angle upon the man's head. It was a hat that she had purchased from the ragman for Marcus to play with. The effect of the shabby chapeau was particularly peculiar since Lady Claire's godson wore no shirt, the dying rays of the setting sun turned the hair upon his chest into threads of copper.

"*Zoot alors!*" Sebastian cried leaning over the table. "I, Napoleon, send my curses upon you as well as my cannonades." He gave a low, whining whistle punctuated by an explosive "Pachoomm!"

"And I, General Westford, vow to bring you to your knees!" Marcus threatened, moving his mounted soldiers forward. "Damn your eyes! Sound the charge!"

"Taratata! Taratata!" Sebastian raised his hands to his mouth to give the mock trumpet a reverberating effect, but he lowered his fingers sheepishly as he caught sight of Mrs. Westford watching, her hands on her hips in an attitude of bemused disbelief. With a look of boyish chagrin, he pulled the hat from his head.

"Mama! Mama!" Marcus said excitedly. "We are near the chateau of Hougemont."

"Houghemont?" Amanda asked, trying to place the familiar name. Lady Claire had followed her godson's army career avidly and had hoarded every mention of every engagement and skirmish in which his regiment had participated. However, the folio of clippings had ended with the battle of Toulouse. Mr. Armitage had sold his commission soon after. It was quite unlikely that he had ever encountered Edward Westford. Nonetheless, she felt uneasy.

"It was near Waterloo," Sebastian explained. "As I told your son, I preferred to stage a battle in which I did not directly participate."

Amanda nodded in understanding. "I would imagine the memories might be overwhelming, even in mock play."

Sebastian looked at her, surprised by her insight. Her face was unlined and young, but there was a darkness in those gray eyes, a sad wisdom, the knowledge that comes only from experience, from suffering.

" 'Tis time for Mr. Armitage's supper, Marcus," she said.

"But we were having such fun!" Marcus protested with a pout. "I have nearly won the war."

"*Au contraire!*" Sebastian said, affecting a French accent. "Napoleon ees not so easily vanquished, monsieur. But an army does run on its stomach and my corps is on the verge of rebellion."

"But I doubt he'll want supper once he sees it," Marcus speculated. "Sebastian, are you fond of—"

"Mar ... cus ..." Amanda warned, her eyes narrowing. "We do not address adults by their Christian names, nor do we say words of four letters that begin with 'd.' Now, put the soldiers away."

Mothers, Sebastian thought, *some things never did change.* The attenuated way in which she had said the boy's name was a universal reproof and the look that accompanied it held an implicit threat. Marcus seemed to recognize his hazard instantly, pulling himself hastily to his feet and gathering up the soldiers. "I gave him leave to call me 'Sebastian,' Mrs. Westford," Sebastian said in the child's defense. "After all we are comrades-in-arms. We shall continue the battle tomorrow, boy. Try to remember your positions."

"Truly, sir?"

"Truly, lad," Sebastian promised.

"*If* Mr. Armitage is up to it," Amanda added, somewhat bewildered. Although her experience with rakehells was a limited one, this reprobate had a decidedly odd kick to his gallop. Clearly, her son had been enjoying himself; he lingered as he put the figures away, dawdling deliberately. And Lady Claire's godson seemed honestly to regret the end of the game. Yet she could not help but disapprove of Sebastian Armitage even as a temporary playmate for her child. Despite the boyish appeal in his smile, Mr. Armitage was all that she must scorn, a womanizer with more money than morals, a man of sensuality without sensibility.

"Tomorrow morning, Sebastian?" Marcus asked, drawing the canvas bag closed.

"Afternoon," Amanda said firmly. "Else he will be at your door at cock's crow, Mr. Armitage."

"That's not true, Mama," Marcus protested.

Amanda raised a questioning eyebrow.

"Well, I would have waited at least until after breakfast," the child allowed sheepishly.

Sebastian could not help but grin at the exchange. It was like hearing an echo of himself.

It was little wonder that the man broke hearts, Amanda thought, as their eyes met in understanding. It was the measure of his charm that the mere sharing of a humorous moment could be an intimate invitation. The smile transformed his face making him seem accessible, vulnerable, almost attainable. And she felt a dangerous longing to see his smile again, but this time directed entirely at her. *Fool . . . idiot . . . imbecile;* she thought of a half dozen other synonyms for stupidity, but none of them seemed severe enough. *Are you so lacking in wit as to be half-seduced by a smile?*

"I shall get your tray, Mr. Armitage," she said. "Put the soldiers away, Marcus. Lady Claire wishes to hear how you are progressing on the pianoforte."

"She is angry," Marcus said in an undertone, as he picked up his crutch. "You can tell by the way her eyes are squoonching."

"Squoonching?" Sebastian asked.

"Like this," Marcus demonstrated, his lids narrowing in imitation of his mother. " 'Tis best to say you're sorry and be done with it."

"But why would she be annoyed?" Sebastian asked, his puzzlement genuine. "I have done nothing wrong."

"Sometimes she gets that way," he said with a half shrug. "Remember, when you make your excuse, you've got to *look* like you mean it, else it won't jump the fence. Mama can see an excuse that ain't got heart in it."

"Tough to bamboozle, eh," Sebastian said.

"Very," Marcus said with a sigh.

"Marcus!" Amanda called from the hall.

Marcus conferred a warning look upon him. "Voice is squeaky, too," he observed with a connoisseur's air. "Might as well cry surrender."

"Marcus!" Amanda entered the room, putting the tray down by the bedside with a clatter. "You are keeping Lady Claire waiting."

"I'm sorry, Mama," Marcus said, hanging his head in contrition. "That is terribly rude of me."

Amanda's expression softened. "Yes, it is, but if you hurry, I am sure that she will forgive you."

Behind her back, Marcus paused at the door, giving Sebastian a slow, encouraging wink.

The scamp, Sebastian thought, turning his attention back to Marcus's mother. Her movements were stiff and controlled, as if she had her anger on a leash, but barely contained. The young sage had indeed assessed the situation correctly. Apologize, Marcus had recommended, but for what? Surely, he had nothing to regret as far as Mrs. Westford was concerned. Indeed, if any apologies were due, they were owed him for the wild-goose chase that had laid him low. But somehow, he doubted such regrets would be forthcoming from Mrs. Westford. It was only when he heard the distinctive sound of the boy's crutch on the stair that he knew. There was, indeed, an apology owed.

Nonetheless, Sebastian found himself somewhat reluctant to say the words that he knew were required. In matter of fact, it was difficult to bring to mind the last time that he had needed to proffer his regrets to anyone. Wealth diminished the need to appease with words and he had almost forgotten how to go about it. The click of utensils against the crockery was almost menacing, and the look in those "squoonched" eyes was fit to cut.

"I owe you an apology, Mrs. Westford," Sebastian began, deciding to take the most direct approach.

She looked up from the tray, startled.

"I must apologize for my harsh words when we first met," he said, hastening to keep her off-balance. "I did not realize that your son was lame. He could never have gotten out of the road in time."

Amanda searched his face for signs of shammed sympathy, but found no falsehood in his steady gaze. The azure depths contained real remorse. She had made every effort to protect her son from the brutal realities of the world. And even so, however much she had tried, she had been unable to shield him entirely. "There are many who look upon his deformity with fear and superstition, or worse, with treacle pity, as if his wits were as twisted as his limb," she explained. "I feared that was what you meant when you woke on the roadside."

"It occurred to me that my words might have been so misconstrued," Sebastian said. "He is a fine boy, Mrs. Westford, and not the least bit bitter about his circumstances that I can discern."

"Marcus is by no means a saint," Amanda said with a smile.

"Nor am I," Sebastian said.

"That, Mr. Armitage, is a definite understatement," Amanda said, busying herself with the tray.

From the way she banged the crockery about, it was clear that she was still somewhat annoyed, although he could not for the life of him discern why. It would appear the time had come to take yet another leaf from young Marcus's book. "I am lamentably crude and I regret my rough behavior," Sebastian apologized. "However, I suspect that any remorse that I might tender will not change your ill opinion of me."

"And how do you know that I think badly of you, sir?" Amanda asked, unfolding a linen napkin and handing it to him. Where would he tuck it in? she wondered preposterously as she recalled his state of dishabille. Once again, she shuffled the silver about industriously, hoping that she would not make a fool of herself by blushing once more.

"It was quite apparent in the tenor of your letter," Sebastian said, wishing that she would look at him. If he was forced to spend three weeks under her roof, it would make his stay more pleasant if the two of them got along, he reasoned. Moreover, if there was something havey-cavey about Mrs. Westford, it would be far easier to detect if she were not forever on her guard.

"And I had thought myself quite the clever diplomat," Amanda said, her lips pursed wryly. "Tiptoeing nimbly all around the truth."

"And just what do you perceive as the truth, Mrs. Westford?" he asked.

"Do you honestly wish to hear, sir?" Amanda asked, trying to keep hold of her temper. The very affability of his tone was beginning to annoy her. "You are a known rakehell, a man whose poor reputation and questionable dealings are known even in this remote corner of Cheshire."

"I believe the term that your son used was 'gazetted rake,' " he chuckled. "I do not deny it."

Amanda was momentarily taken aback. As she had feared, Marcus *was* being corrupted by Mr. Armitage's presence. Where had an eight-year-old boy learned of gazetted rakes? "No, you seem to take considerable pride in your infamy," she said, banging the spoon down on the tray. "Even though your ill repute is the cause of substantial pain for Lady Claire and certainly not the stuff of which little boys should be speaking."

"Do you think that I would deliberately hurt my god-mother, or your son, for that matter?" Sebastian inquired tersely, wondering just how much Lady Claire had told her.

"*Deliberately,* sir, is a most important reservation," Amanda tried to calm herself as she explained. "Most of the injury I have seen in my life has not been the product of intent. The harm that comes through thoughtlessness or lack of consideration is just as damaging as any deliberate evil."

"And you, I take it, believe me to be heedless?" Sebastian asked. Her eyes were gray as the back of a looking glass, reflecting her concern, doubt, and confusion even as they examined him. He felt as if she were searching the deepest recesses of his soul and, somehow, finding him wanting.

"What else can I think?" Amanda said, her eyes like twin flints, striking sparks with every word. Perhaps the time had come for plain speaking. "I have heard much about you, Mr. Armitage, and little of it is good. Perhaps you believed that your godmother would never learn of the life you lead in distant Jamaica. Unfortunately, that is not the case. She has wept over you; the rumors fed to her by letters from so-called well-meaning friends have caused her no end of grief. The doings of the infamous Sebastian Armitage are the subject of great interest in this humdrum corner of England."

"Is it my fault that the world is filled with busybodies who have nothing better to do than talk of me?" Sebastian asked in rising annoyance.

"You make my point, sir," Amanda said. "I doubt that you embarked on your course contriving to cause Lady Claire pain, yet you have. She worries about you. For reasons that I cannot fathom, she loves you."

"For a *paid companion,* Mrs. Westford, you are rather opinionated," Sebastian declared. How dare she read him a scold. No wonder a woman of her looks was still a widow years after Toulouse if she was so entirely composed of prisms and prunes. "Lady Claire was always fond of me, that is true, and she was there to help me when I was in need—but love? I would say that you exaggerate the depth of her sentiments. Even if what you say has some truth, my affairs are certainly no business of yours."

Amanda stiffened at his tone of condescension. For a brief moment, she felt like putting him in his place. Obviously he expected her to grovel, but she was not his inferior and it gave her no little satisfaction to know that she no longer had anything to fear from those who might try to intimidate her. "As a *paid companion,* Mr. Armitage, the welfare of my patron ought to be my paramount duty. As your godmama is my *friend,* the impact of your behavior is a matter of deep concern to me." Let him think of her whatever he wished. It did not signify in the least; what was of importance now was Lady Claire's health.

"You are treading dangerous ground, my girl," Sebastian warned. "It has been more than sixteen years since anyone has dared to tell me to my face how I ought to behave."

"Then it is well past time that someone else did, someone who will not be disregarded," Amanda retorted, relishing the amazement on his face.

"And what makes you think that I will listen to *you?*" he asked, drawing himself up in the bed.

The blankets fell to his hips. Although bandages covered the livid bruises and scrapes, Amanda felt the heat flooding her face as she suddenly recalled her dreams of the previous night. *They had danced once again, his lawn shirt flowing in the moonlight as they whirled. He had whispered in her ear, telling her that she need not be afraid of what was to come* . . . Quickly, she gathered up her wits. "You will listen to me, sir, because I believe that you do have some fondness for your godmother, else you would not be here."

He nodded, as if conceding her a point, but from the crook of his lip, it was obvious that her discomfited reaction to his half-naked state amused him. Amanda focused on his eyes; certain it was far safer to engage that icy gaze than to look elsewhere. "You were but a boy when you left here. Lady Claire still thinks of you as such, and so has managed to dismiss your capers as a youth's wild oats. But I do not know if she can pass them so lightly, now that she has seen with her own eyes that you are a man grown."

"As you do?" Sebastian could not resist interjecting.

"You must be quite cold, lying bare like that," Amanda said, affecting a nonchalant air. "Peggoty will fetch you one of his nightshirts from the Mills. Unfortunately we could find none among your things."

"I do not habitually wear a nightshirt, Mrs. Westford," Sebastian said, watching closely to see her reaction. Sure enough, the blush spread downward, flooding her with color from cheek to neck.

"Do you think you shock me?" she asked, her voice rising despite her efforts to keep it on an even keel. "I vow you put me in mind of Marcus when he tries a gutter word or two just to see the effect. But childish tricks will not put me off. You have asked for my view and I shall give it. Do you know that Lady Claire talked of little else but you these past few weeks she has been abed? She has collected scrapbooks of your army exploits, even kept the little notes of thanks that you sent for gifts that she gave you when you were a boy. Is it any wonder that your antics have nearly broken her heart?"

"Does Lady Claire also know that you have so waspish a tongue, Madame?" Sebastian asked, feeling a spark of shame. It seemed that the world was far smaller than he had thought. He had believed that his godmother would lose interest in his activities once the connection was severed. Apparently, her affection had been far stronger than he anticipated.

"You may tell Lady Claire whatever you choose," Amanda said in open defiance. "This is *my* house and I will say the truth as I see it."

"*Your* house, Madame?" Sebastian asked, seizing upon the opportunity to steer the conversation away from himself. "To my knowledge, Lady Claire has always owned the Vicarage."

"You have been away a long time, Mr. Armitage," Amanda said. "Do not think to use my position to intimidate me into silence. Whatever you may say, Lady Claire will know that I have her interests at heart. I have nothing to fear where you are concerned."

"You are very sure of yourself," Sebastian said.

"I suppose so, for *a paid companion,*" Amanda threw his own words back in his teeth. "But if you truly care for your godmama, Mr. Armitage, you will behave yourself during your sojourn here, recover as quickly as you may, and take yourself back to your Jamaican debauchery."

"You seem very anxious to be rid of me," Sebastian said, "and I find myself wondering why?"

"I should think it would be obvious. 'Tis your irresistible charm," Amanda said, her tone sarcastic, but her heart knowing that she spoke far more honestly than she wished to admit. She wondered whether her fears were for Lady Claire or for herself.

To her surprise, he lay back against the pillows and laughed. It was a delightfully deep and resonant sound, sending a delicious shiver down to her toes.

"Oh, that hurts," he said, clutching his hands round his bruised ribs.

"The truth usually does, Mr. Armitage," Amanda said, regaining her composure and returning to her theme. "Sometimes the greatest havoc is caused by carelessness. That is my worry. Your godmother is not a well woman and my son has suffered far too many disappointments for one so young. I will try to keep them from grief if I can."

"I did not come here to cause harm," Sebastian said, serious once more. It was clear that Lady Claire had kept his secret. Nonetheless, if Mrs. Westford was speaking the truth, the old woman was far fonder of him than he had realized.

"Just the same, harm has already been done," Amanda pointed out, sadly, knowing that by bringing him here, she had caused it all. "Lady Claire is so greatly distressed by the quarrel between the two of you that I fear her recovery may falter. Yet she has determined that she will stay here at the Vicarage to be my chaperone until you are fit to leave. And poor Marcus feels that he is at fault for it all."

"And so I have been the cause of your world turning upside down?" There were dark circles of weariness beneath her eyes. The unmistakable signs of fatigue were there in the tired sag of her shoulders, the wilt of that graceful neck. She was like a spent thoroughbred, on the verge of collapse, yet hell-bent on the finish mark. "I am sorry, Mrs. Westford." To his own astonishment, he actually meant it. "I shall apologize both to Lady Claire and to your son. I have already done what I could to disabuse the boy of the notion that he is to blame for what has happened. I told him that he was not at fault nearly as much as I was."

"Thank you, Mr. Armitage," Amanda said, amazed at his admission. "Marcus has far more in his dish than he can deal with. One more portion of guilt on his plate would be difficult to bear."

She smiled at him, not with the engaging fireworks grin of her son, but with a slow, steady almost tremulous expression that reminded Sebastian of an unexpectedly beautiful dawn, the first light followed by a breathtaking brightness. It was a smile that almost demanded a reply in kind.

The corners of his mouth lifted reluctantly, as if it was a rare, nearly forgotten motion. Yet, from that tenuous beginning, the grin inched along until it arched its way from ear to ear, the corners of his eyes crinkling in a beguiling way. His smile was an offering of peace and something more . . . something that she dared not dwell upon. She turned away, fussing deliberately with a tray. "Your gruel is getting cold, Mr. Armitage."

"Gruel?" Sebastian said, his nose wrinkling at the word. "Surely you jest, Mrs. Westford."

"Dr. Howell left strict instructions. You are to have nothing but light fare for the next few days."

"Hoping to send me into a decline, I would wager," Sebastian mumbled.

"Mrs. Peggoty made you a delightful oatmeal gruel."

" 'Delightful gruel' is an oxymoron," Sebastian declared, his mouth setting in a stubborn line. "There is an inherent contradiction between 'delight' and 'gruel' and when *oatmeal* is placed in between the two words, the paradox becomes utterly insoluble."

Amanda dipped a spoon into the bowl. "Then you shall taste an oxymoron. I assure you, Mrs. Peggoty is an excellent cook."

"Have *you* tasted it, Mrs. Westford?" he asked, his eyebrows raising to convey how unlikely he thought *that* possibility.

"Well . . ." Amanda prevaricated, "not exactly."

"Aha!" Sebastian accused, his arms crossing over his chest. "I knew it! Well, why deny yourself the pleasure, if oatmeal gruel is such a culinary delight?"

"I have never had the occasion to require it," Amanda said, a trifle primly. "I am rarely ill."

"Do you know why gruel is served only to the sick, Mrs.

Westford?" Sebastian asked with a mocking smile. "Because they have not the strength to resist it."

"And you do," Amanda observed, putting down the spoon with a sigh. "Well, I suppose then we shall have to starve you into submission, for I must confess that I do not have the strength to shove it down your throat."

"I shall make you a proposal, Mrs. Westford," he said, a devilish gleam lighting his eyes. "For every spoonful that you consume, I shall eat one."

"How very infantile," Amanda said, replacing the cover on the bowl. "I would not stand for such nonsense from Marcus."

"Are you afraid to try it?" Sebastian asked, his head cocking to one side. "That *culinary delight?*"

"Very well," Amanda said, with counterfeit sweetness. "One for me, then, and one for the baby."

"You first," Sebastian stipulated.

Amanda lifted the cover once more and dipped a spoon into the cooling, almost glutinous mixture, after lifting the utensil in mock salute, she popped it into her mouth.

"Swallow it," he commanded in amusement as he watched her trying to control her facial expression.

"Ambrosia," she said at last, gulping down the mass with difficulty. It seemed somehow to lump in her throat. She dipped the spoon in the bowl once more. "Your turn to sample the nectar of the gods."

"No wonder Olympus is no more, if this was their sustenance," Sebastian commented. "It cannot possibly be as good as you make it look, your appearance of utter enjoyment, as if—"

"The more you delay, the colder it gets," Amanda commented drily, her tongue busily trying to root the last bits from her mouth. "Unless you are reneging on your promise." She held out the spoon in challenge.

"It is fuller than yours was," Sebastian said, his lips verging on a pout.

"A spoonful for a spoonful," Amanda reminded him with a daring look.

Sebastian closed his mouth around the metal and swallowed quickly. "Wholly met my expectations," he choked.

"Another for me," Amanda said, gulping down the gruel hastily.

"Revenge, that is it," Sebastian muttered darkly. "You are out to retaliate for my previous rudeness. You will stop at nothing, 'tis obvious to me now."

"Yours," Amanda said, laughing aloud now. "Come on, open wide."

Her eyes were like quicksilver, sparkling with amusement. It was almost worth the taste of the gruel. He touched her wrist lightly, helping her guide the spoon into his mouth. Her hands were long-fingered and delicate, yet callused as if they had seen hard work. "There," he said, grimacing. "Shall we end the farce now?"

"As they say," Amanda began to speak but found it difficult to keep her voice steady. His fingers had circled around her wrist once again, and she found herself praying that he could not feel the increasing rapid rhythm of her pulse. *This is no different from feeding Marcus,* she told herself as he steered the spoon to his mouth once again. But she could not help but be conscious of his nearness as she leaned closer to him. She felt the puff of his breath upon her fingers as he swallowed. Even had her eyes been shut to the sight of the hard, flat planes of that well-muscled chest, the smell of soap mixed with his musky smell informed her senses that it was not Marcus here beside her. Peggoty had helped Sebastian bathe; his hair was neatly combed. It framed his face in luxuriant waves, absurdly tempting her to touch it. "Waste not . . . want not." She barely managed to choke out the words before polishing off another mouthful. The unpleasant taste was almost welcome, helping her to refocus her confounded senses.

"I would rather want, thank you," Sebastian said, marveling as she swallowed without so much as a moue of distaste. "How can you eat that swill?"

"Actually, this is quite palatable, compared to some other things that I have eaten in my lifetime," Amanda said. She could not afford to let him know just how much he affected her or else he would become totally intractable. Man grown though he might be, he had a little boy's instinct for mischief. However, she thought as she inclined closer, the fiction of detachment was difficult to maintain. "Now you."

There was no defining just what was in the air here. Discord had yielded to humor and rapport, but now as her head bowed nearer, Sebastian felt a peculiar craving to feel if her hair was truly as soft as it seemed, a desire to determine just how those full lips would taste. *Is there anything that could melt the ice in those enigmatic gray eyes?* he wondered. Obediently, Sebastian opened his mouth, allowing her to slip the spoon inside. "You have gotten some of that slop on you," he observed, bringing the delicately veined wrist to his lips.

His tongue flicked out, wiping the bead of meal away. Amanda shivered at the moist touch, nearly dropping the spoon from suddenly numb fingers. She looked away in confusion. "You ought not to do that," she sputtered, drawing back as if he had bitten her.

"I vow that bit almost had flavor," Sebastian said teasingly, as he released her hand, "even though this rivals some of the muck we foraged during my Peninsula days. What could you have eaten that is worse than cold oatmeal gruel?" Instantly, he regretted the question. Quicksilver turned to a shadowy gray and the softness slipped from her face.

"When one is hungry, Mr. Armitage, one sometimes must sacrifice taste for survival. Necessity is a spice that makes almost anything palatable," she said, her words clipped. "My turn."

He watched her take the spoon, her face full of pain as she swallowed and turned it back to him. The rest of the meal was a dismal affair, but he took his turn until the spoon scraped the bare bottom of the bowl.

"You had one more than I," he protested, attempting to recapture the accord they had achieved.

"Next time, you shall be first, Mr. Armitage," she said, a ghost of her former smile touching her lips. "I shall give Mrs. Peggoty your compliments. Surely she will give you an extra large helping. And I think that Mr. Peggoty shall have the honor of feeding you. You may try your tricks on him if you will, lick him on the wrists if you dare, but I must give you fair warning. Mrs. Peggoty is thinking of making you calf's foot jelly. Perhaps you might prefer *that* to gruel?"

"You are a wicked woman, Mrs. Westford."

"Yes, so I have been told," she replied stiffly, picking up

the tray and juggling it one-handed as she closed the door behind her.

Sebastian slipped down in the bed feeling suddenly cold. He drew the covers close around him as he wondered about Mrs. Westford. He could have sworn it was not the flirtation that had set her off so much as his innocent question. A woman of contradictions, he thought, starting into the glowing firelight. Dr. Howell's words came to mind unbidden. The dress that she wore made the most of her well-formed figure, its lines of simple elegance showing her graceful curves to advantage. He had purchased enough female wardrobes to know that the gown was the work of a superior and undoubtedly expensive modiste. Lady Claire, it seemed, attired her companion in the first stare of fashion. Yet, those haunted eyes had contained an abiding sorrow. Mrs. Westford had obviously known poverty and hunger. An enigma, he thought as he tried to swallow down the last mealy taste of grain. What better amusement for an invalid than a puzzle to solve?

6

"How is he?" Lady Claire asked, waiting for Amanda at the bottom of the stairs.

"Contrary and disagreeable to the point of being intolerable," Amanda said, wearily putting the tray down on the hall table. "It would seem that he is on the road to recovery. He ate his gruel."

"That noxious stuff!" Lady Claire exclaimed. "I cannot credit it. Why, when you attempted to serve *me* those granary sweepings, I threw them into the fire. However did you manage to get him to swallow it?"

"Cajolery," Amanda said, touching her wrist, lightly. It was still moist. "And the threat of calf's-foot jelly."

Lady Claire gave a delicate shudder. "Calf's-foot jelly; a low blow, but a necessary one, I suppose. A bit of opposition is just what that boy needs, I suspect. He has become used to getting his way. And you did not back down," her elderly friend said with a nod of commendation. "You are changing, gel; nothing like a bit of gold to give you confidence."

"Yes, I suppose that I have undergone something of a transformation," Amanda said, her smile rueful. "Heaven knows the old Amanda would not have put a flea in your godson's ear."

"Just what did you tell him?" Lady Claire asked uneasily.

"Exactly what I thought," Amanda said. "That his behavior was the outside of enough and that he has caused you a great deal of grief."

"Never say so." Lady Claire shook her head in dismay. "All that will do is anger him. He has ever had a contrary disposition, I fear, although I do no know how he came by it."

"I thought that you had just said that opposition is what he requires?" Amanda asked, puzzled. Lady Claire was not normally a here-and-thereian. This vacillation was wholly unlike her. "I think that he wishes to reconcile with you, Lady Claire," Amanda added, putting a comforting hand on the elderly lady's shoulder.

"Do you think so?" Lady Claire asked, doubt reflected in her eyes.

"What other reason could he have for coming all this way?" Amanda asked, guiding her friend from the drafty hall to the warmth of the parlor. She settled Lady Claire in a chair and then automatically began picking up the spillikins from the table, putting the wooden rods in their box.

"I do not know," Lady Claire said, her fingers knotting worriedly. "Why would he come back here, when he was loath to return all these years?"

Amanda looked at her in surprise. "Why would he not wish to come back?" she asked, a spillikin stick poised in her hand.

"Memories, I suspect," Lady Claire said, avoiding Amanda's questioning gaze. "All at once, his life was ripped asunder, the two people that he loved most were dead and he thought himself alone."

"But he had grown up in Millford?" Amanda asked, unable to understand. "He had you to help him. Why would he deliberately uproot himself from everyone who might care for him? His father was most beloved. There are still many people here who speak of the 'blessed vicar' with reverence."

"Nathan Armitage was one of the kindest men I have ever met, a most unworldly individual," Lady Claire recalled, wishing that she could tell Amanda the whole of it. Of all people, Amanda would understand; but the elderly lady owed Sebastian her silence. "He and his wife were my dearest friends. It was a devastating blow that accident . . . and their death nearly destroyed Sebastian." The wizened woman stared into the flames, lost in memories. "But he made it through . . . became a hero in the Peninsular campaign . . . thought that might be the period to him then—there are none so brave as those who feel that they have nothing to lose. Then he sold his commission and hied himself off to Jamaica, where he has been these past few years."

Some of these facts were already known to Amanda. Lady

Claire had often spoken of her godson's valor and agonized as well over the chaff the rumor mill blew her way. Although he had visited both England and the Continent since leaving the Army, he had made no effort to contact his godmother. It had been close to sixteen years since the elderly lady had last seen him. Yet the pain in those faded blue eyes had not seemed to diminish with time, nor had the abiding affection resonating in that tremulous voice waned. If anything, the wound that the rift between godmother and godson had caused seemed to grow deeper, more hurtful.

"I suspect that in a way, I am as much a part of that painful past as this very house," Lady Claire acknowledged, her voice close to breaking. "Sebastian abided me for a time since he had no choice but to accept my assistance. But he ended that connection with me as soon as the chance came."

"But you have not yet answered my questions. Why would he turn his back on all he once held dear?" Amanda asked, putting the last piece in the box. "My parents and I were never in one dwelling long enough to call it 'home.' We were constantly one step ahead of the landlord. If I had a single pleasant recollection of my childhood, I would hold it to my bosom and cherish it. Unfortunately, there is nothing good for me to remember."

"Sometimes, my dear, it is simpler to seal the past away, good and bad, and begin anew," Lady Claire said. "I suspect that Sebastian thought it so."

"But the past cannot simply be put away like a game of spillikins," Amanda said, closing the lid with a snap. There was something that her old friend was concealing, but curious though Amanda might be about Sebastian Armitage, she would not directly press Lady Claire. "Our history is always with us, lurking there like a ghost, materializing to howl and clank the chains when we least expect it."

"Yes," Lady Claire said softly, "no matter how much we would wish it otherwise, our past haunts us."

"Perhaps your godson has finally come to that realization," Amanda said. "Perhaps he is ready to turn around and face his specters foursquare."

Lady Claire shuddered inwardly. "He might do best to let sleeping ghosts lie, I would say," she ventured. " 'Twould be more than enough for me if he reconciles himself to the present, as you have."

"Think you so?" Amanda asked, putting the game on the mantel above the hearth. She had no wish to return it to its proper place upstairs in Marcus's room and risk another confrontation with Sebastian. "I am not reconciled so much as resigned, Lady Claire. I do what I believe is best for my son. Yet I live in mortal fear that someday, somehow, the web that I have spun to secure Marcus will be sundered."

"Nonsense," Lady Claire said staunchly. "You have no reason to worry. Certainly the past cannot find you at this edge of the world. Money is a most powerful shield, child, it can buy you protection, silence—"

"But is it proof against the truth?" Amanda asked, kneeling beside her friend. "I know that we thought this the proper path at the time, but now I find myself wondering."

"There is no going back, my dear," Lady Claire said, her blue eyes darkening almost to slate, as Amanda gave voice and substance to the nebulous fears that had plagued her. "In five, threescore, and ten years, I have learned that much."

"Well?" Arthur Whittlesea asked, as his mother came in the parlor door. "What have you found out?"

"It was extremely difficult," Lady Whittlesea said, untying the strings of her bonnet. "Lady Claire's town house is all shut up and the remaining servants were extremely insolent. They absolutely refused to give me her direction, for all that I waved a handful of silver under their noses. Leave a note, they said, and *they* would forward it."

"Perhaps she is abroad," Arthur said with a moan. "And taken Amanda with her. It may be months before we catch up with them. We do not have much time. The duns will soon realize that I am no longer courting the Cit's daughter."

"You will not need Miss Sommers." Lady Whittlesea smiled like a cat in the dairy. "I have found that Amanda is *not* over the sea," she said. "Do you recall that I had encountered Lady Claire at the modiste's? Well, although La Robarde was less than forthcoming, it was a simple matter to bribe one of her girls. It seems that your Amanda has had her gowns sent to somewhere in Cheshire."

"Somewhere in Cheshire?" Arthur asked, his face falling.

"That is all that you could garner? So we now know in which haystack the needle resides. Might as well be somewhere in China for all the good that does us."

"Lady Claire's ancestral home is just north of Chester. And I have it on good authority that Amanda is presently there. Lady Harrismere's estate is not far from the Mills and *she* says that the old witch is at her last prayers. The doctor expected Lady Claire to fall with the leaves," she declared, her voice smug. " 'Tis a relief to know that we need not deal with the old battle-ax."

"What battle-ax could stand up against you, Mama dear?" Arthur said fondly. "You are far sharper at the edges."

Lady Whittlesea looked at him askance, trying to decide if she had been complimented. "Well, Arthur, do not just stand there. Order your bags packed and we shall set off at once."

"My valet left this morning," he said sullenly.

"Do not sulk, Arthur. You are a Whittlesea," his mother reminded him. "We have always dealt with adversity. Why, when Cromwell came into power, do you recall the Cavalier Whittlesea's actions?"

"He cut his hair and saved his neck," Arthur spouted the lesson learned from the cradle. "Cozied up to Cromwell and made a fortune."

"And who would forget, when your namesake, Arthur, Lord Whittlesea, was offered a fortune to betray the Crown to the Jacobites at Culloden?"

"He took the Scots' gold and then turned them over to the 'Butcher Cumberland,' " Arthur said, inspired. "You are entirely correct, Mama. I shall pack my own bags."

"Good boy," Lady Whittlesea said approvingly. "I shall summon my abigail and we will be off to Chester."

"Your abigail left with my valet," Arthur said. "Said that she was tired of waiting for her wages."

"Why the ungrateful wretch," Lady Whittlesea exploded. "After all these years she has been with me."

"Adversity, Mama," Arthur said with a sly smile. "You are, after all, a Whittlesea."

"Yes," Lady Whittlesea agreed. "But only by marriage."

"Where is this to go, Mrs. Westford?" the footman asked, setting the striped silk settee down in the entryway.

"In the parlor, I suppose," Amanda said with a sigh.

"Not too close to the fire, mind you, the cinders are dreadful," Lady Claire chimed in as she entered the hall, a plate of pastries in hand. "Really, Amanda, you must get yourself a new fire screen, or better yet, you may have one of mine."

" 'Tis not necessary, Lady Claire, truly. You have moved half of the Mills here, I am sure, from the feather beds to the copper hip bath. It seems an utter waste of effort when all these furnishings will just be going back in short order," she protested as she watched the footman trudge out for another load.

"That is as may be," Lady Claire declared, with a smug look on her face. "Nonetheless, I have no wish to exist like a nomad while I await Sebastian's recovery and I intend to assure my godson of every comfort. You may keep the furnishings as my gift for the inconvenience he has caused you."

"No, I shall not," Amanda said, with a smile. "I would not dare, considering the new things that I have ordered to be sent from Ackermann's."

"Where d'you want this, Lady Claire?" the footman asked, groaning beneath the weight of a heavy chest.

"Take care!" Lady Claire warned. "That is my china. Set that in the kitchen for Mrs. Peggoty to unpack."

"China? I had thought that you did not mind a bit of rough living," Amanda asked, unable to keep her sarcasm contained.

"Even in the wilds of Araby, I had the basic necessities of civilization with me," she said with a sniff. "I always traveled with my own linen of course, china and cutlery, for one never knew when someone would drop by for tea. Have I ever told you about the sheik who asked me to marry him?"

"No, Lady Claire," Amanda said, knowing that the story would be forthcoming whether she said yea or nay.

"He was a handsome devil, although I daresay that the only thing he thought attractive about me was my red hair. The Arabs think a ginger head is lucky and he offered my majordomo a herd of camels and two flocks of goats for my hand. However, on the shelf though I was, I had no wish to be his fortieth wife. We had to steal away in the dead of night. It was an anxious time, I vow."

"I would suppose so," Amanda said, hiding a smile. "Tell

me, Lady Claire, how is it that you were allowed such latitude? You managed to travel the world over as a lone woman, yet no one condemned you for it."

"Age, child," Lady Claire said, "and the fact that I had the features of an ape leader. I was well past fifty when I began my journeys. As so elderly and ugly a spinster, I was held to be above reproach. No one believed that I would have the opportunity to stray from the path of propriety, so I was given far greater freedom than most. My curse became my blessing. Why are you suddenly curious about these questions now, Amanda? I vow you are becoming almost as quizzical as Marcus."

Amanda stopped to consider. "I suppose I have always been curious," she said with an embarrassed look.

"But you never before felt that you had a right to ask," Lady Claire concluded. "The air of assurance is most becoming. You have lost the look of perpetual apology, as if you needs must make excuse for the very air you breathe."

"I suspect you may be right," Amanda said, ruefully recalling her conversation with Mr. Armitage. Would the poverty-stricken Amanda Westford have dared to read him the Riot Act? She sincerely doubted it.

"Mrs. Peggoty has made the most lovely pastries," Lady Claire said, setting the tray down on the hall table. "Shall I have her put the kettle on and we may take a dish of bohea?"

"No more gruel, by Heaven!" Armitage's voice roared down the stairwell. "I vow the water in the chamber pot is probably superior to this swill. I will not eat it, I say."

"It would seem that your godson is gaining strength this morning," Amanda remarked, her eyes sparkling in amusement. "I swear, he sounds just as you did when you were on the mend."

"Do you think so?" Lady Claire asked, a pleased smile lighting her face.

The crash of crockery came from above. "To the very dot above the 'i'," Amanda said. "I suppose that I should go up. He has eaten so very little and Dr. Howell was quite specific. . . ."

There was a shriek from the kitchen.

"My china!" Lady Claire cried as she heard the sound of shattering porcelain.

"I shall see to the china," Amanda said, turning toward the kitchen.

"Insult my woman's cooking would you?" Nautical oaths echoed down the stair.

"And I shall see to Sebastian," Lady Claire said, with a sigh.

"Are you sure?" Amanda asked, her look questioning. "You have been doing far too much since yesterday morning. Why, you have traveled back and forth between here and the Mills a half dozen times at the least."

"It is shameful, at my age, to be so dreadfully cowardly," Lady Claire said, putting her hand on the banister. "I have simply been avoiding what I know I ought to do. I am certain that I shall pass another sleepless night unless I confront my godson. But I have not the foggiest notion what to say."

"Do you want me to come with you?"

"No, my dear," Lady Claire said with a sigh. "This is betwixt Sebastian and myself. Only the two of us can resolve it, I fear."

There was another crash from the kitchen. Amanda gave her friend an encouraging nod as she hurried off to rescue the porcelain.

Lady Claire paused and looked at the dish of pastries. She set her cane aside and slipped two of the largest into her pocket before taking up her stick once more to begin the slow climb. What could heal the breach of distrust? she wondered. What words could she find to bridge the years?

"If this were a ship, lad, I'd have you keelhauled, I would," the old sailor threatened, "you damned near burnt me with the flyin' slop, you did."

"I warned you not to try to jam that spoon down my gullet!" Sebastian said, his jaw thrust out like a pugnacious child's. "And you may tell Mrs. Westford that if she wished me to eat it, she can jolly well come up and feed it to me herself."

"She will not!" Lady Claire said, stepping into the room. "Amanda is worn to a frazzle, young man. Between the two of us, the poor gel is being danced off of her feet. Now go down, Peggoty, and fetch another bowl."

"See, now you've done it," Peggoty hissed as he scrambled to obey the order, "gotten us both in a stew, you have."

"I vow, you act like a little boy as well as look like one," Lady Claire said, eyeing Sebastian in amusement. "You are virtually swimming in that nightshirt."

Sebastian pulled up the voluminous sleeve in irritation. " 'Tis one of Peggoty's. I do not *own* any nightshirts, but Mrs. Westford insisted that I make loan of Jack Tar's sail-cloth."

Lady Claire nodded. " 'Tis no wonder you came to grief in Jamaica, if folks go running about without nightclothes on. That may do in warmer climes, but not here in England."

"Ah yes, England. The land of utter morality, where everyone is wrapped in the hypocrisy of nightclothes, keeping their indiscretions under wraps," Sebastian said, his eyes narrowing. He was becoming extremely wearied of being treated like a naughty child. Yet he found himself holding back his anger. There was a look in the old woman's eyes that was almost a plea.

"I did not come here to pick a fight with you, boy," Lady Claire said, with a sigh.

"Then why are you here?" Sebastian asked bluntly. "If you mean to coax me into eating that pig slop, you might as well save your breath."

"You ate it for Amanda," Lady Claire reminded him.

Somehow, the idea of a spoon for spoon bargain with his godmother had little appeal. He folded his arms across his chest stubbornly. "I won't."

"Do you recall when you had the measles?" Lady Claire asked. "You were about nine, if I am correct."

"Vaguely," Sebastian said, the cajoling tone in her voice making him distinctly uneasy. She was up to something.

"The doctor forbade your mother to go near you. She had never had the illness," Lady Claire continued.

"Yes," Sebastian said, the circumstances returning to mind. "She was with child again and they thought that this time she might be able to carry the baby to birth."

"I—happened to be in residence," Lady Claire said, her thoughts distant. "Since I had suffered through the spots already, it was I who came to nurse you through it. Do you recall what I did with the gruel that they sent you?"

"You poured it out the window," Sebastian said with a reluctant smile, "and snuck up delicacies from the Mills, pastries and jellies and all my favorites."

"And your dear mama thought me quite the wonder for coaxing you into eating that loathsome mess," Lady Claire reminded him with a smirk of satisfaction. "Celia was happy, because she thought you well nourished and you were pleased because you were fed to the gills. So . . ." She fished a pastry from her pocket and waved it under his nose. "Warm from the oven, boy. And there is another for you, if you make a show of eating the gruel. Amanda is quite worried and I would not put another problem in her sack for the world."

"She is worried about me?" Sebastian asked in surprise. "Why?"

"The gel feels indebted to you," she said, handing him the bun. "Feels 'tis her fault that you came to grief in the first place since it was she who brought you here. And it is thanks to you that both she and Marcus escaped unharmed. Seeing you well again is the first step in making amends."

"Or getting rid of me," Sebastian said, biting into the flaky sweetness.

"Whatever do you mean, boy?" Lady Claire asked.

"Ah, Lady Claire," Sebastian said looking upon that earnest face, "for all your age and worldliness, you are still an innocent."

Lady Claire snorted. "Why do I feel as if I have just been insulted? What reason would Amanda have to wish you away when it was she who brought you here in the first place?"

"Lured me here, perhaps. I am after all, quite wealthy and I am not ill to look upon," Sebastian speculated. "Perhaps she found me to be more elusive quarry than she expected."

"And a man of matchless modesty." Lady Claire rolled her eyes. "The bump on the brainbox must have been worse than we feared."

"Why would a woman as handsome as Mrs. Westford remain unmarried after all these years?" Sebastian persisted. "Surely she has had offers."

"She has, but none that claimed her heart," Lady Claire said, the idea beginning to grow now that her godson had put it in her head. What could be better? "She chose to stay with me."

"As your *companion?*" Sebastian questioned. "Not that

she does not seem to live very well for a woman in her circumstances. A house of her own. She as much as told me that the Vicarage is hers."

"Yes, she owns it now." Lady Claire nodded. The sudden interest in Amanda was most gratifying indeed. "You know that I cannot abide roundaboutation. Is there a point you mean to light on, boy, or are you merely circling aimlessly?"

"I do not blame your Amanda if she is keeping her eye on the main chance," Sebastian said, trying to break it as gently as he could. "After all, the situation of a widow with a crippled child is not an enviable one. I just want you to beware. If she has managed to get the Vicarage from you . . ."

"*Get* the Vicarage?" Lady Claire threw back her head and laughed raucously. "You mean . . . you believe . . . that she is an . . . an adventuress," Lady Claire stammered out between bursts of mirth. "How . . . utterly droll."

"Why is that so preposterous?" Sebastian asked, totally bewildered. The only explanation that came to mind was the onset of senility. Yet, Lady Claire seemed to have all her wits about her. "You were cozened often enough when I was a boy. What of that fellow who got you to invest in that flying machine? Or that ludicrous calculating device that ran on cards with holes?"

"Who has not made a few errors in their finances? You nearly lost everything when you began your distillery," she reminded him. It was a pity that she could not tell him that Amanda was a considerable heiress, but Lady Claire had given the girl her word. Still, Lady Claire felt a touch of hope at his concern over her affairs.

"How do you know about the distillery?" Sebastian asked, startled.

"I have friends everywhere, you ought to know that," Lady Claire said, her chin lifting in a smug smile. "They have kept me informed, even when you have not."

"Wellington would have envied your net of spies, I suspect," Sebastian commented drily. So Mrs. Westford's accusations were to be taken in full seriousness. There was no denying the knowledge in the old woman's eyes. Just how much did she know? he wondered, his face growing suddenly hot.

"Actually, the Iron Duke owes me any number of favors

for assistance rendered," Lady Claire said, her eyes twinkling as she guessed at the thoughts behind Sebastian's guilty expression. "I have helped him a time or twice during my travels, it happens."

"And do you *happen* to know anything regarding a mysterious last-minute investment?" His eyes narrowed suspiciously. "An anonymous one that saved my hide?"

"I? Invest in a rum manufactory?" Lady Claire gave an airy wave. "I, who never touch spirits?"

The prevarication was more transparent than an outright falsehood, but Sebastian saw no use in pushing her to admit her involvement. If Lady Claire had indeed been his nameless benefactor, then she had gotten a more than adequate return for her money. Nonetheless, it was unsettling to know that she had been there, watching over his shoulder when he had thought himself utterly alone.

"You are trying to turn the subject," Sebastian said, his hands bunching the sheets as he tried to contain his frustration. "I am merely attempting to warn you."

"Unnecessarily," Lady Claire said, trying not to enjoy his discomfiture too much. Just listening to the sound of his voice made her heart glad. She perused that beloved face, finding the boy she once loved beneath that self-possessed facade. The gestures, the facial expressions were much the same as she remembered and she committed them to memory, like a cherished poem, to keep against the time when he would leave her again.

"Ah, look. Peggoty has arrived with more of Mrs. Peggoty's lovely gruel," she said. "You may leave it with me. I shall make sure that Sebastian finishes it all."

"Aye," Peggoty said, casting a doubtful look upon Sebastian. "That'd be best, it would, if he know what's good for him. Mrs. Westford's talkin' of calf's-foot glue with the woman right now. I'd as soon be drawn an' quartered."

"It will be gone by the time you return," Lady Claire promised, waiting until the door closed behind the old sailor. She slipped from the chair and opened the window. Ceremoniously, she tipped the bowl. "Like old times," she said, pulling the panes closed.

"I am beginning to remember now. . . ." Sebastian said, putting his worries about Mrs. Westford temporarily to the side. There seemed no merit in belaboring the point. "I was feeling quite miserable and very sorry for myself. You taught me to play cards. You won every toy that I owned."

"It distracted you from your ailment, did it not?" Lady Claire asked, pulling the second bun from her pocket and handing it to him. "You applied yourself to the cards after that, until you gained back every single one of your possessions."

"I have always suspected that you let me win," Sebastian said, wolfing it down with relish.

"Do you accuse me of being a cheat, Sebastian?" Lady Claire challenged, her mouth turning up at the corner.

"Yes," he said bluntly.

"Learning to lose is the first exercise of gaming," Lady Claire said, resisting an impulse to wipe a crumb of cake from the top of his lip. He was a little boy no longer, much as she might wish it so. "Having taught you what you needed, I saw no reason to take your things from you. It would be far more gentlemanly to call it a 'lesson' than 'cheating.' "

"And you of all people know, Lady Claire, that I am no *gentleman,*" Sebastian said, his voice bitter.

"Is that the reason you cast me loose then?" Lady Claire asked softly. "Because I know the truth?"

Two pairs of blue eyes met.

There was no bitterness or accusation in that rheumy look, only an abiding sorrow and, much as Sebastian would have denied it, love. Mrs. Westford had been correct; for some reason that he could not fathom, this old woman loved him. And although he had hurt her deeply, that affection had survived.

"I feared that you would reject me for that reason," Lady Claire said, the years suddenly weighing heavily upon her. She had lost him once. How could she bear it if he were to cut her off again? "Ah, boy, you know full well that it never made the least bit of difference in my feelings for you. Kinship is more than ties of blood. From the moment I first set eyes on you, I recognized that we were of a kind. You know that I would gladly have taken you into my home, given you every advantage. But you could not forgive my silence."

"How could I have stayed?" Sebastian asked, remembering the anger, the tearing pain as if the very heart was being ripped from him. "The people that I had loved most in the world were gone. You were all that I had left and then I found that even *you* had lied to me. All that I had believed in was all at once untrue. Even the very blood in my veins was suddenly alien. I had no heritage, no family, none of the keys that open the doors of this world. Everything runs upon connections, Lady Claire, in every sphere."

"Yet *you* prospered, advanced in the army on your *own* merit," Lady Claire countered. "Surely you realize that it does not take noble blood to be a noble man."

Sebastian regarded her intently, remembering the slights and indignities that he had suffered, the compromises and ultimate costs of the success that he had achieved. She had been born into the privileged strata and, therefore, could never understand the struggles that he had endured. "I once thought that honor could balance the scales and compensate for my birth, but I soon lost my naïveté. Sometimes honor is a commodity that only the wealthy may afford."

She shook her head in disbelief. "There is no justification for the intemperate life you have come to lead, boy."

"Tell me, Lady Claire, what woman of good family would wed a man of my background?" Sebastian asked, trying to control the anger that welled up within him. "I am not so lost to sensibility that I would keep the truth from my wife. Is it any wonder that I seek the company of Cyprians when there is nothing better available?"

Her eyes fell before that steady gaze. There was nothing that she could say to him that would be more than a lie. "I had no right to rebuke you, Sebastian," she said, at last. "Somehow I had thought that all those years of affection would be able to hold you in good stead. Celia and Nathan Armitage loved you dearly, you must believe that."

"Then why did they lie to me?" he asked, the anguished question coming from the heart. "Why did they not tell me the truth?"

"You were their son in every way that mattered, boy," she said, her bony hand reaching out to grasp his. "Every pregnancy that Celia conceived ended in the graveyard, poor dear. She thought that you were a blessing from Heaven itself."

"A curse you mean," Sebastian said. "Someone's bastard, dropped carelessly upon a stranger's threshold."

"No," Lady Claire said, shaking her head vehemently. "Not carelessly. From what Celia told me, I have little doubt that the woman who birthed you was quite selective when she chose the Armitages."

"Just what did my mother tell you?" Sebastian asked, wondering if Lady Claire knew more than she was saying. "If anyone alive knows the circumstances surrounding my adoption, it is you. You were Mama's dearest friend."

"I doubt that I could add anything to your knowledge," Lady Claire said cautiously. "They were living in Kent at the time. Celia told me of how Nathan found you in the vestry. There was no note, just you wrapped in a basket. It was market day. The town was filled with strangers coming and going. There were no clues to your identity to be found."

"Ah, but there were," Sebastian said. "Apparently there was a Miriam hiding among the bulrushes to see what became of her baby Moses."

"Whatever do you mean?" Lady Claire asked uneasily.

"I suppose the biblical allusions are the natural consequence of being raised by a churchman," Sebastian said with a small smile. "Miriam kept watch over her brother by the riverside, if you recall. Well, a carter saw a young girl, waiting outside the church on that day."

"How did you determine that?" Lady Claire asked, trying to keep the quaver from her voice.

"I have hired Bow Street to locate my mother," Sebastian said. "If anyone can find her, most likely the Robin Redbreasts can. In fact, that was the only stop that I made in London, other than your town house. I gave them my direction with instructions to send me any new information that they may uncover. They are speaking to midwives in the area."

"The Runners?" Lady Claire forced the words out though they stuck like gravel in her throat. "But why, Sebastian? Why can you not simply accept the Armitages as your parents? Nathan left his pulpit in Kent for your sake, you know. It was far more prestigious and lucrative than the living that I offered him at the Mills. But he came to Cheshire so that you would be fully accepted as their child and for the most part they succeeded. The Armitages made great sacrifices for you, and would have made more if they had been given life."

"And I would have lived a lie. Do you think that they ever would have let me know the truth?" Sebastian asked, staring blindly at the Stubbs print.

"Who can say?" Lady Claire asked, her eyes glistening. "Certainly they did not expect to be taken so soon. Are you so ungrateful for the love that they gave you, that you still hold that against them? Is that why you insist on this foolishness?"

"It is not a matter of gratitude," Sebastian asserted, his hands balling into fists. "It is a *need,* a need that I feel deep in my bones as much as weariness or hunger."

"And you have allowed it to become consuming," Lady Claire said angrily. "To deny all the good that you were given for the sake of a wild quest. It has been over two-and-thirty years. How can you expect to find someone who has deliberately hidden her connection to you for so long?"

"In my experience, there is always some fool who will break a trust and reveal a confidence," Sebastian said, his eyes blazing. "Information can always be found—at a price, and I am both willing and able to spend the blunt. I will find the answers."

"Answers?" Lady Claire asked finding the anguish in his countenance almost too difficult to bear. "And pray what are the questions?"

"My parents, Lady Claire; who are they? Even if the woman who bore me threw me away, I would at least know the reason why; I would know whose blood runs in my veins, albeit my forebears were likely thieves and whores. And I will find out," he said, renewing his oath to himself. "One day, I will know who I am."

7

"**B**reakfast," Mr. Peggoty announced, bearing a tray and setting it on the table with a flourish. "Waitin' on what the surgeon had to say, we was. The gruel was at the ready too, it was, but a fair wind was with you this mornin'."

"It was quite apparent that Howell was disappointed with me," Sebastian said, tucking up the sleeve of his nightshirt. "I imagine that he hoped to find me languishing in unspeakable agony."

"Aye, lookin' in on milady now, he is, hopin' to get a double fee from one visit, I'd wager," the old sailor laughed. "Like barnacles and hulls, that man is to gold, is he. Just as soon bleed you as give you the time o' day that 'un, but if you ain't got the shot, give you neither, he will. Why, when young Marcus had the pleurisy, he wouldn't bestir himself till Lady Claire herself assured him that his charge would be paid even if the lad didn't pull through."

"I take it, then, that Mrs. Westford is not particularly well-to-do?" Sebastian queried.

"Well," Peggoty said, scratching his head. "Wouldn'ta said she was flush with the ready before, but now . . ."

"Her circumstances have improved?" Sebastian suggested.

"Aye . . . say as much, I would," Peggoty ventured. "And if milady has Abernathy to do with it, wouldn't surprise me. 'Twas Mrs. Westford, not the leech, who's owed the thanks for Lady Claire's gettin' well, though Howell took the fee and would as like take the credit, too, I'd say. With her day and night, Mrs. Westford was; spoonin' gruel and physic down milady's gullet. Kept the old woman goin' when th' surgeon was ready to have her measured for a shroud. So if milady is bein' gratitudeful, I don't begrudge it, sir. 'Tis as much as

114

Mrs. Westford deserves, is my reckoning." He took the cover from the tray. "Eat hearty now."

Sebastian inhaled, with pleasure, savoring the aroma of thick sliced ham, mounds of fresh eggs, bread still hot from the oven, and more. He lifted his fork and began to dig in, chewing over the food for thought that Peggoty had given him along with the substantial fare. If Lady Claire had chosen to reward her companion, what right had he to quibble? *Where did the boundary between gratitude and greed lie?* he thought as he cleared the tray of its contents.

With any luck, he would be able to find out a bit more about the mysterious Mrs. Westford and satisfy himself as to her motives. He had secretly spent part of the night trying his foot. If he went gently on it, he found that he could get about, but he decided to conceal his partial recovery as yet. It always was of benefit to allow the opponent to underestimate your resources. "Can I get a bit more of the bread, Peggoty?" he asked. "And can you see about getting me some books? The doctor gave leave for me to read."

"Aye, aye, sir. Another loaf in the oven, the missus says. Be up with another helping quick as a whistle and I'll see about sommat t'read, I will," he said, detouring around Marcus at the doorway.

"Are you feeling any better, Mr. Armitage?" Marcus asked hesitantly, half-in, half-out of the room.

"Far better now that I have some real food in me," Sebastian confessed. "Come visit, if you wish. It is your chamber that I am taking from you, after all."

"And your foot, sir?" Marcus inquired, his anxiety apparent in the troubled look on his face. "Is it healing well?"

"Very well," Sebastian said, flattered by the child's obvious concern.

Marcus brightened. "And you won't be left with a limp then? I wouldn't want you to have to go about with a stick for the rest of your life. I asked Dr. Howell, but he told me it was none of my affair."

The pompous ass, Sebastian thought. *It would have cost him naught but a few words to relieve the boy's fears.* "No," he said firmly, "there was no permanent damage at all. I suspect that I shall be on my feet in a matter of days."

"But he told Lady Claire that it may be some weeks."

"Betwixt the two of us, Marcus," Sebastian said, beckoning the boy closer, "I believe that Dr. Howell just wishes for an excuse to continue to come here."

"You are rich, aren't you?" Marcus asked, leaning his crutch on the chair.

Amused, Sebastian confirmed the speculation with a nod.

"That explains it," Marcus said wisely. "Why, when we were staying with Lady Claire, he came to call every day and some days, even twice, until Lady Claire told him to . . ." Marcus hung his head. "I ought not to repeat such things."

"I can quite imagine what my godmother said." Sebastian grinned, imagining Lady Claire ripping a strip off the physician's hide with the rough side of her tongue. " 'Tis kind of you to come visit me, but I am sure that you are anxious to be off on such a beautiful morning." Sebastian gestured at the window. "I vow, I envy you, to be out and about on a day like this. When I lived here, autumn was my favorite time of year. There is something about the sound of leaves crackling, watching your breath rise on a crisp morning after a good bruising ride, or climbing up in Kendall's orchard for a nice crisp apple."

"But I can't ride, sir," Marcus said wistfully. "Or climb trees."

"Why not?" Sebastian asked in surprise.

"Just can't," he said simply, picking up his crutch pointedly. "If I am pestering you, sir, I shall leave. You need not hint at it."

"It was not my intention to chase you out, lad," Sebastian said gruffly. "I just cannot understand why you have not been taught to ride or why you have not tried for the treetops."

"How can I climb?" Marcus frowned. "Or ride, with a leg like mine."

"And I repeat, why not?" Sebastian said, trying to banish the skeptical look on the child's face. "Your lameness might hamper you somewhat, it's true, but I see no reason that you cannot learn to do either. An acquaintance of mine by the name of George has a problem similar to yours."

"Did he climb trees?" Marcus asked.

"Not in the brief time that I knew him," Sebastian said with a smile as he pictured the poet up in a tree, "although I would wager he did when he was a boy. George is a bruising rider, a great swimmer, an excellent athlete even though he is lame."

"Was he always lame?" Marcus asked.

"He was born with a club foot," Sebastian replied.

"Like mine?" Marcus asked.

"Quite probably. He once told me that his mama had searched desperately for cures, taking him from doctor to doctor."

"And did the doctors put squeezing things on his foot?" Marcus questioned, cocking his head to one side. "Things that costed lots of money and hurt, but he didn't cry because it would make his mama sad."

Sebastian hesitated a moment, aching for the child who was so familiar with the ways of pain. "Yes, from what Byron described, it was much like that."

"But I thought his name is George?" Marcus asked.

"It is. George Gordon, Lord Byron. He is also a famous poet."

"Rhymes." Marcus imbued the word with all the force of childish contempt. "But scribbling is all that one is fit for, I suppose, with such a leg." He sighed.

Sebastian bit back his laughter in the face of the boy's obvious disappointment. "I would not underestimate the power of poets, lad," he said. "A skilled pen can do far more than the most ably wielded sword."

"I suppose," Marcus said, with polite disbelief as he yielded to adult opinion. "It is just that I had thought that if this Byron fellow could do all of those things he might even be a soldier. But that is impossible, isn't it?"

"I suspect that Byron would make an excellent soldier, if he chose to be one," Sebastian said. "He can hit the keyhole of a door with his pistol, or any other target that you might care to name. George is also quite handy with his fives."

"Is he?" Marcus asked excitedly. "Did he thrash the boys in his village, do you think, when they called him names?"

"He might have," Sebastian conceded, his heart aching for the child. "But he has no need to thrash people now. George just outdoes them all. Why, I recall when he and Lieutenant Eckenhead attempted to swim the Hellespont."

"Like Leander?" Marcus's eyes opened wide. "Lady Claire

told me that story. I did not know that there really is a Hellespont."

"Indeed there is," Sebastian assured him. "And George swam it on the second attempt. Made it across in an hour and ten minutes, beating Eckenhead by a full five minutes."

"He beat a *soldier?*" the boy asked.

"Indeed he did," Sebastian chuckled at the boy's open astonishment, as if a soldier was the epitome of manhood and valor. But then, Sebastian had once thought so himself.

"If this George fellow could do it . . ." Marcus began, his brow knitting in thought.

"Now do not go attempting to swim any rivers," Sebastian warned, beginning to feel a trifle uneasy.

"Of course not," Marcus said, sensibly. "I've got to learn how first. And I will learn . . . I will."

"Ah, Marcus, there you are," Amanda said as she walked in with the refilled tray in her hands. "I have been searching for you. It is time for you to do your lessons. The grammar is on the library table."

"Please, Mama," Marcus begged, his eyes sparkling with excitement. "May I stay a few moments more? Mr. Armitage was telling me about his friend George, with the long funny name, who writes poems and has a club foot like mine and he swimmed the Hellespont—"

Amanda looked at Sebastian, her eyes narrowing as her son spoke on like a tight spring unwinding.

"—and he rides," Marcus continued. "And the bestest part is he's so strong that he beat a soldier when he swimmed, Mama. A full five minutes. Do you think that I can swim, and learn to ride and to shoot and to climb trees like this George Byron does?" Marcus finished at last, breathing like a spent runner.

"We will talk of it later, Marcus," she said tightly. "When you come back for your game of soldiers. *If* Mr. Armitage is up to it."

From her threatening look, Sebastian feared that he might not be up to anything when she got through with him.

"But Mama, this George Gordon fellow could be a soldier if he wanted, like Papa," Marcus said.

"Downstairs, Marcus," Amanda repeated, putting the tray by the bedside. "And close the door behind you, please."

"I think that my head is beginning to ache," Sebastian said. Sometimes the better part of valor was a strategic retreat. Mrs. Westford's expression was ominous.

"If it is not yet aching, it soon may well be," Amanda threatened. "What right have you to cast Lord Byron in the figure of a hero in Marcus's eyes? From all accounts, the poet is a vain, selfish womanizer who loves only himself. And his verse reflects the mirror image of a proud, petty man. His rhymes are poor stuff designed to befuddle weak-headed females."

"On the contrary," Sebastian disagreed. "I find his verse most excellent. I have yet to find a match to 'She walks in beauty, like the night—' "

"You make my point, Mr. Armitage," Amanda said, recalling how Marcus's father had often quoted Byron's verses, whispering in her ear when no one else could hear. "The very lines you choose would appeal to the more foolish members of my sex, but then, what else could one expect—"

"From a man like me?" Sebastian finished. "I see that there is nothing that can change your ill sentiments. You do flatter me, madam, by classing me with Byron. However, George, being something of a stickler, might be somewhat offended by my inclusion with him in the pantheon of rogues and knaves. Gazetted rake though I may be, my accomplishments are somewhat modest, compared to his."

"Give yourself time, Mr. Armitage, from what I have heard of you, your infamous career is still young," Amanda said bitingly.

Sebastian inclined his head in mocking acknowledgment, the copper lights in his hair glinting in a red-gold shimmer. "I must say, the idea of his poetry being irresistible is novel, certainly a far less expensive means of seduction than the jewels and fripperies that most of your sex demands for their favors. According to your theorem a mere line of *Don Juan* and the ladies ought to fall like ripe plums into my lap. Or would it take something more for a woman of your moral stature? Perhaps a canto of *Childe Harolde?*"

Amanda blushed and Sebastian watched as the line of red crept from her cheek on down to the bodice of her gown. "Yes, indeed." Sebastian pressed the advantage that her discomfiture gave him. "I suppose it might even take more than one canto of that heady stuff to befuddle you. Alas, that puts you beyond the reach of an illiterate rake like me, for I must confess that more than one canto of Byron's work sends me to sleep straightaway."

"Do not mock me, Mr. Armitage, and do not make light of my concerns," Amanda said, her voice tight and controlled.

"A little mockery, Mrs. Westford, is justifiable when you condemn me solely on the basis of a little boy's garbled version of a conversation," he said quietly. "And as for lightness, I believe that you could do with a bit of that too, if only for your son's sake. Marcus is far too earthbound for a child his age. He ought to be dreaming of climbing toward the sky, yet he feels himself incapable of even reaching for the lowest limbs of a tree."

" 'Tis easy for you to venture advice, when you know nothing of his history," Amanda retorted. She would have said no more, but he regarded her steadily; his countenance entirely earnest. For some reason this man really did care for Marcus. Startled by the discovery, she sank wearily into the chair beside the bed, deciding to try and explain. She did not expect him to understand, no one could. "I fought for my son's life from the moment of his birth, Mr. Armitage. The sound that greeted Marcus's arrival in this world was not one of joy, but the midwife's horrified shriek when she saw his misshapen leg. The woman all but threw him into Lady Claire's arms and ran from the room. It was left to your godmother to cut the cord," Amanda said, the memory of those first moments still painfully fresh.

Sebastian felt an unreasoning anger at the unfairness of it, at the midwife who had condemned a child for an accident of birth. "I can imagine . . ." he began.

"No," Amanda said. "I doubt you could, to look at the child you had carried under your heart for nine months . . . it was your godmother who first held Marcus, first loved him, hushed his cries, for I confess I found it difficult."

"Certainly it would be hard, to see your baby and not feel pained," Sebastian said, as his hand found hers. He wanted to comfort her, but he did not know how. He had never felt the need to console before.

"Not pain, Mr. Armitage," Amanda confessed, knowing that she ought to pull her hand away. But she could not; just as she was powerless to stem the flow of words that spilled from her tongue. "I was so consumed with fear and hate for my circumstances that there was no room for love. It was guilt that I felt when I first saw Marcus."

"But you love your son," Sebastian protested, his fingers tightening around her palm. "You put yourself in front of a charging horse for his sake."

"I love Marcus . . . now," Amanda agreed, "and would gladly lay down my life for him if it came to that. But in the months that I carried him, I was so alone, no husband, no family. If Lady Claire had not sought me out, not found me . . ." She shook her head, unable to bear the thought of what ultimately might have been. "And all my disappointment was focused on the child growing inside of me. Perhaps that is why Marcus's leg is . . . a punishment for my sins, for all those twisted thoughts." Amanda choked out the words, giving voice to the long-held convictions that she had never expressed aloud. "But when Lady Claire put Marcus in my arms and he opened his eyes and looked at me, I saw myself and I knew that to deny him would be to deny myself."

"The Reverend would have said, that the Creator is not cruel, but his creations sometimes are," Sebastian said, the long-forgotten words coming to his tongue with difficulty. In truth he himself had found precious few consolations for the cruelties of the world, but he felt that he had to try. "He believed that with all his heart, Mrs. Westford, as much as he held that everything that occurs is for a purpose."

"And is that *your* belief, sir?" Amanda asked cynically. "Was there a purpose to Marcus's many illnesses? He was a sickly child from the start, and I knew there were many who whispered that I was a fool to suckle a hell-spawn, a babe with the devil's sign upon him. But we battled for Marcus, Lady Claire and I." She touched the arm of the chair. "I have sat in this place more times than I care to count, wondering if my son would live to see the dawn with me." *Why must Marcus bear my burden?* she asked silently, but there was still no answer to that unspoken question. There never was. "Was there a reason for that?"

"My father would have given you an emphatic 'yes,' " Sebastian answered. "However, I . . . I have not followed the paths of his beliefs for quite some time. When I was a boy,

I was very certain of heaven's purpose and my place in the world. Now . . ." He shook his head. "I suspect that my faith was very fragile."

"As is my son," Amanda said, appalled at herself. She had never revealed those feelings before, not even to Lady Claire, feelings that ought to shock even a hardened rakehell; yet, he had not condemned her. "Marcus is still quite frail, Mr. Armitage, far more weak than you realize."

"I think that you have made him stronger than you care to recognize. He is a boy and wishes to do the things that other boys do," Sebastian countered.

Amanda's gray eyes were bleak. "I know," she said. "I have seen him sometimes, looking at the other children with envy. But there is naught that can be done. They taunt him when they think that I cannot hear, blame him for an imperfection that is no fault of his. And their parents are just as bad. I have seen them make superstitious signs, as if he was an evil spirit of some kind. He has been hurt so much." *It is your responsibility,* the voice within her whispered. *You have not told him the whole of it else Mr. Armitage would agree that you are to blame.*

"He is a fine boy, Mrs. Westford. Even a miscreant like myself can see that; others will, in time. But you must let him try," Sebastian pleaded with a passion that surprised even himself. "Let him stumble and grow or he will never forgive you."

"On what do you base this judgment, sir?" Amanda asked, her voice acid with sarcasm. "Is it your vast experience with child-rearing?"

"Other than having been a boy once myself, I claim to know little," Sebastian admitted. "But I did know a man with an infirmity like your son's. I realize that you abhor the mention of his name, but I did have some acquaintance with Byron."

"Like to like," she said, her eyes steely as daggers.

"There is some truth to that," Sebastian said. "Disparate people are often drawn together by common threads."

"Two rakes."

"Two men who had no one, no purpose, who believed themselves to be standing at the edge of the void, utterly alone," he recalled, wondering why he was telling this to her.

He had never mentioned it to another living soul, but it was for the boy's sake, he told himself. "We met in Italy, some years ago."

His frank admission silenced her. His eyes were far away, as if he saw that other time and place.

"Byron was in exile by then, reviled by the very people who had once lauded him. Perhaps it was because I was the only countryman in a foreign place that he confided in me. Perhaps he somehow knew that I would not stand in judgment, or it may even be as you said, like is often drawn to like." He looked at her, trying to find the words to make her understand. "George talked to me about his childhood; his foot was clubbed, much as your son's. He was made to feel less than a man, that he could never achieve a normal life." Sebastian paused, letting the point sink in, before he continued. "I have come to believe that Byron has spent much of his existence attempting to prove that he is as much a man as any, a better man in fact."

"You think that I am not doing everything within my power for Marcus?" Amanda asked.

"Let him do whatever is in *his* power, Mrs. Westford," Sebastian said. "He may surprise you."

"As you have, Mr. Armitage," Amanda said, looking at him curiously. "I believe that you spoke from the heart."

"But that is impossible," Sebastian said, the corner of his mouth quirking. "As you know, rakes are heartless."

"Mrs. Westford?" It was Peggoty's voice at the door. "Is it in there you are?

"Come in, Mr. Peggoty," Amanda said, hastily, not wishing the servant to think that anything worth hiding was occurring behind the closed door.

" 'Tis Lady Claire, ma'am," the servant said, putting a pile of books down on the night table. "Bringin' up some readin' like Mr. Armitage asked me, when I was walking past milady's door. Couldn't help but hear it. Talks to milady like she's deaf as a stone, the doctor does, yellin' at her."

"Get to the point, Peggoty," Amanda demanded, rising from the chair.

"He's wanting to bleed her, is what I heard. Says she's seeming poorly, and can't say he's wrong about the look of her phiz neither, to my mind, but knowin' how you feel about bloodlettin' and all . . ."

"Excuse me," Amanda said, leading the sailor out the door. "I have never met a man so bloodthirsty as Howell."

"Tell me how she fares," Sebastian called after them.

"I will keep you informed," Amanda promised.

Sebastian returned his attention to his second helping of breakfast, but somehow, his appetite had waned considerably.

"Mrs. Westford." Dr. Howell acknowledged Amanda's presence with the barest pretense of civility.

"Amanda," Lady Claire said, her voice barely above a whisper, "will you kindly tell this fool to put his knife away?"

Dr. Howell lifted his chin and gave Amanda a superior look. "She needs to be bled immediately, else I will not answer for the consequences."

Amanda looked at Lady Claire with concern. The elderly lady's face was rather pale and drawn and her skewed nightcap gave her a frail, forlorn look.

"Get away from me, you pill-peddler," the elderly woman said, shooting the doctor a malevolent look.

"An abundance of bile as well," Dr. Howell observed, reaching for the thinly veined wrist. "A little blood."

"Put the knife any closer and we shall see what color *your* blood is, sir!" Lady Claire said, shaking her fist.

"I do not think that there will be any need," Amanda said, relieved that Lady Claire was beginning to act more like herself. Nonetheless, below the nightcap, her face looked haggard, as if sleep had entirely eluded her. Perhaps she was just tired.

"*You* do not think?" Dr. Howell sputtered. "*You* do not think? I do not recall asking you for your thoughts, Madame."

Amanda looked at the doctor's choleric face, stunned.

"I have suffered your insolence, but no longer, Madame, no longer." He turned and walked out the door, down the hall to Sebastian's door, with Amanda following close on his heels. "Mr. Armitage!" Howell exclaimed. "If you value your godmother's continued existence, I suggest that you remove her from beneath this . . . this . . . *woman's* roof."

"And why should I do that, pray?" Sebastian asked.

"She has questioned my judgment, countermanded my orders, obstructed proper treatment, and . . ."

"And from what Mr. Peggoty has told me, my godmother is likely alive today because she did, Dr. Howell," Sebastian said coldly.

"You would take the word of a *servant?*" The doctor was taken aback, but only for a moment. "She is turning Lady Claire's mind—"

"It is my studied opinion, sir, that Lady Claire has more wits at seventy and five than most individuals of half her years," Sebastian said, his eyes meeting Amanda's. She was plainly astonished.

"You will regret this, mark my words," the physician warned with an angry glare.

"I doubt it," Sebastian said with a shrug. "I trust my godmother's judgment, Dr. Howell. If she places her faith in Mrs. Westford, I suppose that I may as well." Despite his doubts, if it came to a choice between Howell and his godmother's companion, his preference was clear.

"I shall send my bill," Dr. Howell muttered darkly as he took his leave.

"I was sure that you would," Sebastian retorted.

"He is the only physician between here and Chester," Amanda said, looking at Howell's retreating back worriedly.

"I would as soon send to Chester and take my chances of expiring in the interim," Sebastian said.

"Thank you, Mr. Armitage," Amanda said, her eyes glowing with silver lights.

"For what?" Sebastian asked.

"For defending my honor," she answered, "for believing in me."

"Hush!" he said in a mock whisper. "If word gets around, it could utterly destroy my reputation."

"I am rapidly becoming convinced that you are a poor excuse for a rake," Amanda said, her voice husky with emotion.

"You misjudge me, Madame," Sebastian said, putting on his most lascivious expression. "I am a most capable rake."

Despite herself Amanda shivered. The look in his eyes made her feel eminently desirable, as if she were his one passion, his only need.

He was the prisoner of his own spell, caught in a quicksilver pool, drowning in longing. Never before had he been caught this way, trapped in another's eyes.

"I will cast no more aspersions," she said, breaking the spell with a shaky laugh. "I surrender, sir."

"Would you?" he asked softly.

His voice was like a caress, sensuous and filled with the promise of unspoken pleasures. "Yes, you are most definitely a rake," she said finally. "However, I cannot linger so that you may practice the rest of your wiles. Lady Claire needs me." She hurried from the room.

Still somewhat bewildered, Sebastian reached over to the night table and began to sort through the titles that Peggoty had brought him. It was obvious that the illiterate sailor had been the one who chose the volumes. To him, one book was as good as another. There was a Latin text as well as a treatise on herb lore. Pressed between the pages was a dried sprig of rosemary that crumbled in Sebastian's hand, leaving a faint smell on his fingertips. For the first time in many years, Sebastian allowed himself to remember the woman whom he had called 'mother.' The lithe movements of her hands as they pummeled and pounded bread, the sound of her voice singing hymns off-key as she weeded her garden. His eyes misted, he closed the book and set it aside.

There was no title on the plainly bound spine of the next volume in the pile. The cracking leather and yellowing corners of the pages showed it to be of inferior quality. Sebastian opened it gingerly, yet the first page came away in his hand. He would have set the book aside had the date not caught his eye, October 1, 1798. The handwriting was faded and, therefore, he had not immediately recognized the Reverend Armitage's fine script. But for the quality of the hand, the aged ink would have been entirely illegible.

"Sebastian was thrown from his horse this afternoon. Celia was beside herself with worry, but to hear of it from Lady Claire's groom, the lad simply dusted himself off and was back in the saddle immediately. Dear Celia is so protective of the child, sometimes too much so, I fear."

Sebastian read on, the journal recalling incidents long-forgotten. When he looked up at last, the waning sun cast shadows of the old oak limbs against the walls. In almost every entry there was some mention of him, the milestones and bon mots that make up the life of a child, the words replete with a father's love. *Why?* he asked himself ... *Why didn't you tell me, Papa? Surely you knew that someday the truth would come out?* Despite all the affection contained within that diary, Sebastian could not bring himself to forgive that sin of omission.

Even so, he could not keep himself from reaching on in the fading light. Time was distilled into its essence and the days passed quickly upon the pages, summer slipped away into fall once again, and fall withered into winter.

"Sebastian continues to delight us with his fine intelligence," the Reverend wrote proudly. "His Latin is progressing well beyond my expectations for a boy his age, and I suspect that his mathematical skills will someday surpass mine. I have written to his Mother to inform her of his progress and ..." Hurriedly, Sebastian turned the page seeking the rest of the entry, but it was gone, the tattered remains of the leaf revealing nothing more of value.

Seventeen ninety-nine ... that would have put his age at about ten at the time that those words had been written, Sebastian thought with growing excitement. "I have written to his Mother ..." Why would his father have been required to *write* the news ... unless, it was not Celia Armitage who was the recipient of the letter. It was to "his Mother ..." Sebastian's mother, someone other than the Reverend's wife. Except for that fatal trip to Bath, Celia Armitage had never left the cozy little world of the Vicarage.

Sebastian racked his memory, trying to recollect if Celia Armitage had ever absented herself from home for any length of time, but he could remember no such event. Surely he would have recalled so significant an occurrence at the age of ten. "... his Mother ..." yes; that was decidedly odd. Eagerly, Sebastian thumbed his way through the rest of the journal. It was as he expected. There were no other mentions of the impersonal-sounding "his Mother," although there were numerous loving references to "Celia" and "my dearest Celia." The singular use of the word "Mother" was obviously important in its peculiarity.

Ruefully, Sebastian thought of all the money that he had wasted on hiring investigators. He would post a letter first thing in the morning informing the Runners of his find. The answers to the questions that had troubled him for sixteen years might very well be found in the library downstairs among the remaining journals. It appeared that the Reverend had been in correspondence with Sebastian's natural mother.

8

The wind outside was mournful, its low keening like a ghostly sob. Sebastian had never believed in ghosts or spirits, yet the memories of his past were more haunting and vivid than any phantasm. Sebastian allowed his thoughts to drift as the candle by the bedside sputtered and died. He lay back on the pillow, hoping to somehow find sleep, but rest was elusive. There were far too many questions chasing round in his head, old conundrums and new riddles vying for his attention as the shadows shifted along the walls. Other than the crackle of logs, the house was quiet. Everyone else had gone to bed long before he had finished the last page. According to the chronology there were several volumes absent and Sebastian was half-tempted to try the stair and search for them himself.

He wondered if there was something that he had missed in the journals that were at hand, some vital clue, perhaps, that had eluded him? With a sigh, he reached for the tinderbox to light another candle, but it went skittering to the floor. He was just about to go and retrieve it when he heard the creak of the floorboard in the hall. Quickly, he tucked himself back under the covers.

"Mr. Armitage?"

It was Mrs. Westford's anxious whisper. She had opened the door to peer in.

"Is everything all right?" she asked, rubbing her eyes with one hand as she set the candlestick down. "I heard a noise."

"I could not sleep," Sebastian said, trying to keep from gaping as she stood in the door. "And thought to read a bit, but the tinderbox seems to have gotten away from me. I am sorry for waking you." He never would have guessed. It seemed that the sensible Mrs. Westford had a few less than practical whimsies. The night rail that she wore was a dreamy confection of shimmering silk and lace, the fabric clinging to her body in a way that whetted the imagination.

Once more, Sebastian recognized the touch of an expensive modiste. Were it not for his suspicions that his godmother was footing the bill, he would have reckoned the peignoir well worth the price, the woven sheen catching the lambent glow of candlelight. Her hair had been tamed into two plain plaits, yet the contrast between the simple style and the gown's sophistication added a piquant charm. She floated forward, bending to pick up the fallen tinderbox. It was only after she handed it to him that she seemed to realize her state of dishabille. Belatedly, she pulled her wrapper tight around her.

"No, you did not wake me, not at all," she confessed, using her candle to light the one by his bedside. "I was tossing and turning myself. I shall bid you a good-night, Mr. Armitage."

He did not want her to depart leaving him alone with his thoughts once again. "Perhaps a glass of warm milk might do us both some good," he suggested.

"Warm milk, Mr. Armitage?" Amanda asked, her lip twitching in amusement. "Is that your customary remedy for sleeplessness? Rather odd for 'The Demon Rum' to be seeking such bland soporifics."

"Shh!" Sebastian said, putting a cautioning finger to his lips. "Not so loud, Mrs. Westford. I have already done enough damage to my reputation today."

"I daresay. It would quite destroy your image, but your secret shall be safe with me," Amanda said, starting for the door. "Are you sure that it is milk you want?" she asked, pausing at the doorway to pick up the candlestick.

No, it was not the warmth of milk that he wanted, he thought as he looked at her, touched by the nimbus of soft light. The almost-teasing look in her eye, the scarcely hidden smile caused a tension in him that could not be so easily assuaged. He looked away, worried that he could not mask his growing desire. "Milk," he asserted, his throat suddenly dry.

Amanda picked up the taper that she had left on the hall table and quietly made her way down to the darkened kitchen. *A puzzle of a man,* she thought as she added fuel to the stove. Perhaps it was her unfamiliarity with the ways of the opposite gender that was causing her difficulty. Certainly, she met few enough men here in Cheshire. Nonetheless, she had easily been able to place them in various categories, to depress their pretensions. She was long practiced in the art of quelling stares and icy responses, yet Lady Claire's godson easily reduced her to a blushing ninnyhammer.

She dipped some milk from the pail into the pot, stirring to keep the liquid from scalding as she tried to discern the whys and wherefores of her feelings. This curious response almost caused Amanda to long for the obtrusively lewd behavior he had exhibited by the roadside. She knew what he was; he himself made no bones about it. Every instinct warned her to treat him warily, keep him at a distance. Why then did his merest touch sear her to the core? Was it only the longings of her twisted imagination that made him into a smoldering inferno, radiating this fatal heat, drawing her to him, like a foolish fluttering moth? Was this another manifestation of the same disastrous flaw of character that had caused her to singe her wings years ago?

In the late-night silence, he could hear the clatter from the kitchen, a familiar comforting sound that conjured up so many memories. *Think of something else,* he told himself, as the images of bedtime conversations, of the reflection of candlelight on his father's spectacles, of his mother's nightcap gleaming white and frilly in the firelight all crowded into his mind. The journals had brought it all to the fore, everything that he had locked away so long ago. Deliberately, he returned his thoughts to the conundrum of Mrs. Westford. *Is her seeming lack of guile the result of practiced art?* he wondered. Mrs. Westford had obviously benefited from her association with his godmother. But was it as Peggoty claimed, a well-deserved reward?

Mrs. Westford's mode of dress was beyond the norm—he would bet that at least a year's wages were on her back. And Lady Claire had likely been footing the bill for some rather costly care from the leeches, according to the boy. Then there was a pianoforte, an expensive acquisition, surely. There had been none in the parlor when he was a lad.

Additionally, there had been the matter of the Vicarage itself. How could a mere companion afford to purchase the large cottage? If her late husband had left her that well-to-do, why was Mrs. Westford serving in a menial position? Or had Lady Claire given it away outright? Yet, if it was his god-mother's choice to be generous, he could not blame Mrs. Westford for accepting that largesse. What right did he have to begrudge Lady Claire's beneficence? A curious situation indeed, Sebastian thought, staring at the sword on the wall.

The sword . . . as the firelight sparkled upon the cast or-molu, there was something about the weapon that struck him as odd. It was more work of art than weapon. The scabbard was leather, its casing ornamented with trophies of arms. Light danced on the gilded hilt, from which a gray tassel hung. It had the look of a Teed. Only the famous London swordsmith could produce a blade so beautiful, yet, if need be, so utterly deadly.

Sebastian had once thought of having one commissioned for himself, but at the time it had been far too expensive for a soldier living solely on an officer's pay. Lady Claire had of-fered at intervals to supplement his income, but he had been too proud to be any more in her debt. He had felt that he owed her far too much already.

If he recalled correctly, at the time, even the cheapest va-riety of Teed's ornamental swords had been in the realm of thirty pounds, well beyond his means. The example on the wall had likely been one of the smith's dearer bits of work, one of those made only for higher-ranked officers. What rank had Marcus stated that his father held? Lieutenant? Sebastian would wager that that beauty had cost at least one hundred pounds or more. Strange . . . it did not have the look of a mere lieutenant's sword.

Try though he might, Sebastian could recall no Westford among the officers that he had known. In truth, Sebastian had kept much to himself, separated from the rest of the brother-hood of officers by the invisible barriers of birth and wealth, as well as those walls which he himself had constructed. Nonetheless, as he had risen through a series of battlefield promotions, Sebastian had gotten to know most of the senior army staff. Curious that the name would be entirely unfamil-iar. Perhaps Westford had been brought in from another field of command just prior to the battle? It was not unheard of.

After all, an enormous mass of men had been gathered in that final push to Paris.

Sebastian craned his neck, focusing on the sword once again, trying to discern any identifying marks. But from the distance it was difficult to distinguish the intricate symbols of the ormolu onlay.

Gingerly, he pulled aside the covers and slid his legs round to the edge of the bed. Cushioned by layers of bandages, his ankle gave him surprisingly little difficulty as he shifted some of his weight to it. It was foolish, he knew, to risk discovery. He had no wish for anyone to know just yet that he was able to walk. Judging from the sounds issuing from the kitchen, though, he still had some time left before Mrs. Westford's return. Slowly, he rose, putting most of his bulk on his good leg and propping himself with the bedpost. He reached out and grasped the back of a chair, using the furnishing to aid him as he made his way toward the wall. Bit by bit, he edged forward, until the hearth was within reach. Holding on to the mantel, he reached up, and slipped the sword from its mounting. He leaned against the wall as he examined the scabbard. Frowning, he examined the design of the insignia. Just as he had suspected, it was not the symbol of the Third Division.

Taking care to keep the metal from making noise, he slipped the blade from its sheath, examining the hilt closely. There, inscribed in the base, were three initials—R.S.B.; he held it up to the firelight, scrutinizing it once again, but there was no mistaking the lettering.

The milk gave a warning hiss and Amanda pulled the pot from the fire just as it boiled over. Luckily, nothing had burned. She added a pinch of ground vanilla bean and nutmeg as she usually did, before pouring the liquid into cups and placing them upon the tray. As she set foot on the stairs, she made a decision. She would give him his milk and leave before temptation followed.

The sounds from the kitchen had ceased and he heard the sound of light footsteps on the stair. Hurriedly, Sebastian returned the sword to its casing, reaching up and replacing it, but as he brought his hands down, he lost his balance. It was only by dint of quick reflex that Sebastian was able to keep himself from tumbling. Unfortunately, in his grab for the mantelpiece, he knocked down one of Marcus's wooden toys, sending it to the floor with a clatter.

Startled by the noise, Amanda nearly dropped the tray. Hastily she found her balance and hurried up the remaining stairs, setting the tray down as she entered the room. "Mr. Armitage, what in the world? You ought not to be on your feet."

Sebastian scrambled for an excuse. "The chamber pot," he said, his eyes lighting on the earthenware bowl in the corner.

"Why did you not call someone? You could exacerbate your injury," she scolded, hurrying to his side to support him. "I could have gotten Peggoty to help you. 'Tis the height of foolishness to try to get to it yourself."

"I suppose so," he said, simulating a sheepish grin. "Especially since the need seems to have disappeared. I only fear that I might wake the house with my racketing about." With his arm around her shoulders, he could feel warmth radiating from her, the touch of silk at her neck smooth and soft beneath his hand. There was a growing hunger deep within him, a desire that had nothing to do with lack of food. His hand strayed to the pulse at her neck, the steady beating rhythm a slow counterpoint to the pounding of his own blood. The smell of soap and roses filling his nostrils, the sight of that dark hair waiting to be unbound was a feast for the senses, yet honor demanded that he abstain.

Honor . . . once it had been so clear, but now the path was fraught with confusion. It was a long time since he had felt an obligation to conform to the code of behavior he had learned as a child. This room, this house was the symbol of everything that the Armitages had held dear; home, family, God, and country. Although he had violated most of the commandments and trampled upon many of those values, anything less than adherence to those long-ago absolutes would seem like sacrilege in this place. Sebastian duly added hypocrisy to the list of his sins.

But was she owed the same protection as an honest woman? He was now certain that she was deceiving him. Was Mrs. Westford what she seemed, or even who she seemed? Yet he was taking shelter under her roof, or was it a roof that she had inveigled from his godmother? And even if the worst was true, did he have the right to judge? To condemn? But among all the questions came the aching realization that she was a liar. She had committed the most unforgivable sin and yet, he still wanted her. Wanted her very badly indeed. As she helped him settle into bed, Sebastian found himself grateful for the voluminous concealment of Peggoty's nightshirt.

" 'Tis a lucky thing for you I arrived when I did," Amanda said, pulling the covers about him. "Else you might have come to grief."

"Yes, very lucky," Sebastian said, enjoying the sensation of being tucked in. One of her braids caressed his cheek as she bent close and his confused sense of honor was sorely assailed by that light touch. "I am sorry to trouble you. You must be utterly exhausted considering all you have done for me in these past days."

"When needs must," Amanda said, her voice deliberately brusque. Yes, he was to blame for her weariness, in more ways than he knew. She had lain awake thinking about him. She had never known before that she could share laughter with a man, feel so much at ease and at the same time, so entirely conscious of his presence. It was almost as startling as the touch of his tongue on her wrist. "There now, you are all set, Mr. Armitage. If you have any more need for ... er ... relief, please call. Now here is your milk." She went and got the cup from the tray. "Is there anything else that you need?"

There was an impatience in her question, a desire to be gone and quickly. He had to make her stay. "You know, Mrs. Westford, your son is mistaken."

Amanda shook her head in bewilderment.

"There are actually seventy-two cracks in the ceiling," Sebastian said. "Your son has missed the count by at least five thus far."

"I shall inform Marcus," Amanda said, with a smile. "Nonetheless, you ought not to hold it against him, we have been away from the Vicarage for the most part of nigh onto two months."

"Lady Claire's illness, I presume," Sebastian asked.

Amanda nodded as she put the cup within reach. "We almost despaired of her," she said simply. "That is why I wrote to you."

"Peggoty told me that you were with her constantly," he said, watching her reaction carefully. It was like a game of cards, and he was determined to find out what she held. But in order to make her tip her hand she would have to believe in him. "He said that he sincerely doubts that my godmother would have survived were it not for your care."

"Mr. Peggoty is not known for his discretion," Amanda said, heat rising to her face. "He exaggerates my part in her recovery."

"I think not," Sebastian said softly, wondering why she did not pick up the opportunity that he had discarded before her and snatch the credit. If she could paint those blushes upon her cheek at will, Mrs. Westford was entirely wasted as a companion in the backwaters of Cheshire. She would have done well to try her luck on the boards in London.

"I was only doing my duty, as *a paid companion,*" Amanda said stiffly, setting the cup within his reach with a dull clunk, nearly spilling some of the steaming contents.

"Can you forgive me for that remark, Mrs. Westford?" Sebastian asked, bringing all his considerable charm to the fore, all the while wondering where the truth ended and the lies began. Was it possible that she did not know that the sword had not belonged to Lieutenant Edward Westford, and it had not been at the battle of Toulouse? He knew that he was scrambling for excuses, but for some unknown reason, he wanted to give her the benefit of the doubt, wanted to believe in her. "I know now that you were entirely correct in your judgment. Lady Claire does care about me, far more than I had ever imagined, though I cannot say why. How is she, by the by?"

"Sleeping soundly, I hope," Amanda said with a fond smile. "She was all for getting out of bed to come speak with you this afternoon, but I would not allow it. This has been very wearing upon her, but then again, I think your arrival was just the medicine that she required."

"How so?" Sebastian asked, his head cocking to one side as he waited for her response. Would she resort to flattery?

"As you can see for yourself, your godmother is getting old. Although she was recovering from her illness, I was beginning to fear that Lady Claire was ready to lie back and give up. She had lost the zest, if you will, the ability that she has to relish life. She is fighting again and I believe it is due to you, Mr. Armitage."

"Sebastian," he said, "I'd be pleased if you would call me 'Sebastian.' Can we call it 'pax,' Mrs. Westford?"

Amanda smiled at the schoolboy expression. "Pax . . . Sebastian," she agreed, picking up the tray with the one remaining cup, "and you may call me 'Amanda.' I bid you good-night."

"Can we not seal our new accord, Amanda?" Sebastian appealed, raising his milk in the gesture of a toast.

She knew that she ought not to stay, but there was an entreaty in his expression that caused her to set the tray down and lift her own cup. "What does one say when toasting with milk?" she asked.

"This is rather new to me as well, in all honesty," Sebastian said, his brow wrinkling in thought. "Shall we drink to honesty then? 'Honest friendship.' "

Was there an unusual undertone to his words? she wondered, but there seemed nothing but pleasure in his puckish grin. " 'To honest friendship,' then," Amanda agreed, gently touching her cup to his and sitting back in the chair beside the bed.

"Honest friendship," Sebastian repeated, bringing the cup to his lips and taking a sip, letting the warmth slide soothingly down his throat. The smell, the long-forgotten taste worked its own peculiar magic, recalling the simple joy of being cared for, fussed over . . . loved.

"Be careful of your tongue. It is very hot," a voice said softly.

With a start, he realized that it was Amanda who had been speaking. "My mother always used to say that," Sebastian recalled. *Fool . . . do not let your emotions obscure your reason. Keep your cards close to your vest,* he told himself. "Whenever I was up at night with illness, she would bring me warm milk, just like this in fact. What did you put in it?"

"It is actually your mother's recipe," Amanda admitted. "I found a book of her receipts and simples in the library downstairs. She had many excellent remedies and poultices. In fact, I make the rose perfume that I wear according to her instructions."

No wonder the scent had been so familiar, Sebastian

thought, catching a whiff of the subtle fragrance. His throat grew tight as the flood of memories washed through him. "Sometimes Father would come and read to me, but mostly, it was Mama who stayed until I was asleep."

"You were quite lucky, Mr. . . . Sebastian," Amanda said, the glisten in the corner of his eye washing away her barriers. "Not everyone is so blessed."

"Yes," Sebastian said, slowly, watching her face, weighing every word for truth. "I suppose that I was, but then again, that is the lot of parents, is it not?"

"Bearing a child does not always mean loving it," Amanda said, her own parents coming to mind. "There are those for whom a child is a cross to bear, a constant reminder of past mistakes."

"Yet, you came to love Marcus," Sebastian reminded her. That much was definitely true. He wondered what it would be like to be loved with such fierce devotion.

"Yes, but that is not always the case," Amanda said, her lashes veiling her thoughts.

"You speak from experience?" he asked, quick to catch the nuance in her voice.

Perhaps it was the open sympathy in his look, or maybe the combination of warm milk, exhaustion, and the lateness of the hour that dulled her sense of discretion. "Unfortunately I was a burden even before my birth," Amanda admitted, trying to keep her tone light. "And my mama made sure that I knew it. It was my entry into the world that was the cause of Mama's poor health, my fault for the constant bickering and brawling that was my parents' marriage. With such a model it was no wonder that I was a fool for the first—" she cut herself off abruptly, realizing the direction in which her words were taking her.

"Marcus's father?" Sebastian guessed. "Your late husband?"

"I should not . . ." she whispered, aghast at herself.

This too, had the sincere ring of veracity. "Your secret will be safe with me," Sebastian said, echoing her earlier assertion.

Amanda nodded. There was an invitation in that bright blue gaze, bidding her to set down her burdens, to share her thoughts. Although Lady Claire knew the tale, Amanda had never felt it fair to encumber the elderly woman with the weight of guilt, the welter of emotion. "He never saw his son," she said, her voice choking on the words. "Perhaps it is a sin, but I have counted that as a blessing. He would never have been able to deal with Marcus's disfigurement. I would have been condemned to relive my parents' misery, and perhaps, in time, come to hate my son as the symbol of my suffering."

"People survive unhappy marriages," Sebastian said, his eyebrow arching as he drew her out.

"Is mere survival enough?" Amanda asked, setting her cup back on the tray. "Is that all that one should hope for, to pass each day without hope or joy? At least my son knows that he is loved. I have no illusions that his future may be difficult, but when I am no longer here to care for him, I hope that he will be able to reach back in his mind and unearth love when he has need."

Sebastian shook his head. "I do not quite understand."

She gave a shy smile. "Perhaps you might think me fanciful, but I have always imagined that we wrap our memories away in our heads, like the souvenirs that Lady Claire has stored in the attic. And when we have a need, we go up and unwrap those remembrances so that the love that we have collected in our lifetimes is with us always."

The talk of family and children was wearing at his patience, but nonetheless, he let her continue to expose her own weakness.

" 'Tis like your recollections of your mother and father," she added. "I am sure that you will always recall how they stayed up with you during your illnesses. And perhaps when you have children of your own, you will tell them about their grandparents and how much they loved you."

"I doubt it, Amanda," Sebastian said, putting his cup down heavily, staring past her toward the sword, glittering in the firelight. Her face was open . . . vulnerable. It was time to lay down his ace and watch her reaction.

"I think that love is the only part of us that really endures," she said, looking down into the dregs of her cup.

"What about truth, Amanda, does that not surmount time as well?" Sometimes it was best to discard with a flourish.

His tone of voice brought her up short. The compassion in

his eyes had all but disappeared and he was staring at her coldly. His jaw had set into a hard line.

"What do you mean, Sebastian?" Amanda asked, edging back in her chair.

"We were talking of philosophy, I take it. How do you feel about truth? I know that I have little patience for deception."

"State your meaning plain, sir," Amanda said, the remnants of milk suddenly souring on her tongue. "*I* have little patience for cat's-paw."

Sebastian laughed. It was not a pleasant sound. "The sword of Damocles, Amanda, and the cutting edge of truth," he said, pointing to the mounted scabbard. "A Teed sword, but you would know that, would you not, since it was made special for your husband."

"I know very little of swords," Amanda said cautiously.

"Then let me inform you," Sebastian said, the flames giving his eyes a dangerous glitter. "Teed is a master craftsman. The blades that he makes are often as individual as the men that carry them." He could see her eyes darkening and knew that he had her at point non plus. But instead of satisfaction, he felt a curious sinking feeling as he continued. "Shall I tell you about the sword that you display so proudly, Madame? Your *husband*'s sword. Made for a home regiment of dandies with nothing better to do than parade about in uniform. Fashionable fribbles who never saw a drop of bloodshed unless they nicked themselves on their own blades."

She closed her eyes and breathed deeply, hoping that this was a nightmare. But the voice went on.

"The initials on the blade are not those of Edward Westford, nor does the quality of the sword match his supposed rank," Sebastian said hoarsely, driving the point home. He waited for her to say something, to deny his accusations.

"I do not know how—" she began. She had never expected this, never bothered to formulate a ready fabrication and spontaneous falsehood had never been one of her talents.

She was lying to him. He could see it in her eyes, hear it in the hesitation of her voice. The way she held her head, the way she looked down, away, everywhere but at him screamed "liar." He had been willing to make excuses for her, to give her the benefit of the doubt, but this was beyond forgiveness.

"Oh you know . . ." Sebastian said. "You know full well. The question in my mind is, what else are you hiding?"

"Marcus . . ." she whispered hoarsely, daring to look at him at last.

There was a momentary softening of his expression, but it was gone in an instant. "He is not aware?"

She shook her head. "No . . . he believes . . ."

"In his father, the hero, Lieutenant Edward Westford," he spit the words sarcastically. "So you are lying to your son as well. Who else are you lying to, *Mrs. Westford,* if that is truly your name?" He reached out and grabbed her by the wrist. "Is it?" he asked. The fear in her eyes was answer enough. There was no question of honor here. She had none.

This was the man that she had met on the roadside. Hard, cold, and utterly without scruple. He pulled her closer. Her surprise was such that there was no chance to resist. She found herself clasped against his chest, her feet dangling awkwardly off the bed. His other arm closed about her, making escape impossible.

"You are fond of memories, Amanda?" he asked, watching her eyes widen. He would teach her a lesson, one that she would not soon forget. Her lips trembled and her eyes grew dark as the North Sea during a storm. He only meant to brush his lips against hers, to frighten her into confession. But the simple touch deepened into something more, a caress that was in truth a punishment, a sweet torture. His anger melted in the heat of flesh against flesh, his intentions, his fears forgotten in a kiss that had somehow become a communion.

It was the realization of dreams—and nightmares. She told herself that she ought to scream, ought to fight, but she knew that she would not. His hair glowed red-gold in the firelight as he bent his head, his lips claiming hers. She was lost in a maelstrom of sensation, the wild thud of his heartbeat pulsing, his chest hard beneath a rough woven nightshirt as he pulled her closer. Her arms crept round his neck in a breathless wonder that reached deep within her to long-forgotten hopes. A part of her that she had thought dead and buried was miraculously resurrected—only to die once more as she recalled herself to reality.

"No," she whispered, opening her eyes and staring into those azure depths. "No!" she repeated, loathing herself and her weakness. She pulled back her hands, trying to push herself away from him. Only a second more and she would have been utterly lost, willing to sacrifice herself to an illusion, a vision woven entirely of her own fantasies.

"Amanda ..." How could he explain what had just happened? He had always prided himself on his ability to maintain control, to remain absolutely detached.

"Let me go," she said, struggling against the arms that still locked her in their embrace.

He loosened his hold and she slipped to her feet, backing away from him like a wounded animal, her eyes wary. "I ... I ..." He groped helplessly for words, but could find no adequate expression. Tears were streaming down her cheeks as she regarded him silently, accusingly, waiting for him to speak.

Amanda tried to interpret the look in his eyes. Was "whore" now to be added to "liar"? What other conclusion could he possibly draw? A virtuous woman would have remained aloof and rigid, suffering his embrace without any response. Surely, he had felt her arms go around him, pulling him closer, felt the terrible need that had consumed her, urging her to fill the overwhelming emptiness with the passion that he had ignited. Nine years ... years without a lover's touch. But those long-ago caresses were nothing compared to these. It was shaming to realize that she had gone into the arms of a known rake like a woman famished. Never mind that what he set before her was tainted, corrupt, that it could destroy her.

"I owe you an apology, Amanda," Sebastian said at last, wishing that he could somehow undo the last few moments, erase that dark pain from her eyes. Deceiver though she might be, she had not deserved to bear the brunt of his anger, his frustration.

"You may keep your apology, for all that it is worth," she said, gathering the shards of her shattered dignity about her. She wiped her lips as if something foul had touched them. "I would have wished though, for a line or two of Byron in advance warning, but I suppose that all is fair in lust and whore."

"Amanda," he said, stricken by the bitterness that seemed directed as much at herself as at him.

"You may call me Mrs. Westford," she corrected. "Or whatever else you choose, but not by my given name anymore, *Mr.* Armitage. Though I find it difficult, I am trying to remember that you saved my life and my son's. I am responsible for your presence here. For that, I owe you the hospitality of my roof until you are restored. But once that is done, you will have no claim on me, no right to question my honesty, no opportunity to assail my virtue. I will pay my debts, but no more . . . no more, you bastard."

Only he was able to appreciate the cold irony in that epithet.

9

Sebastian awoke in a fog, wondering if his door was being assailed by a battering ram. The demanding thump came again.

"Sebastian Armitage. I am coming in," the querulous voice warned him. "Do not think you can hide yourself beneath the covers, as you used to, boy, for I intend to have my say."

He opened his eyes with a groan and stared at the unfinished cups of milk on the tray by the bedside. So, he had not dreamed it all. It was true. How was he going to break the news to Lady Claire?

The door swung open, caroming against the wall with an angry thud. Lady Claire stood in the hallway frowning with every line in her wizened face. The hinges gave a loud squeak of protest as she entered and then slammed the door shut behind her. Sebastian pulled himself up against the headboard to face the coming onslaught. Her cane beat a battle tattoo as she hobbled toward the bed, plumes waving like a defiant standard.

"Good morning, Lady Claire," he said.

"What is good about it?" she snapped. "Amanda is walking about the house as if the world has come to an end."

"What has that to do with me?" Sebastian asked, his expression bland.

"Do not play your games with *me,* boy," she said, poking her cane as if she were half-minded to spit him upon it. "Amanda was weeping. I have not seen her cry since—" she broke off abruptly. "What did you do to her? A poor chaperone, I have proven to be. I know full well she was in here last night; sleep does not come easily at my age, especially in a strange bed. I know what you have become, but I had never dreamed that you would . . ."

"Is that her game then?" Sebastian said, his eyes narrowing in anger. "Is she crying 'compromised' in the hopes of catching me in the parson's mousetrap? Well, I will not have it! I will not be shackled for life because of a mere kiss."

"You *kissed* her?" Lady Claire asked in surprise. "Sounds like more than a 'mere kiss,' to me if that is why her lips are so swollen. I had thought that she had been biting them as she usually does when she is upset. But that is besides the point."

"What is the point then?" Sebastian asked in growing confusion. "Just what has she accused me of in order to trap me into marriage?"

"My boy, at present, she would not wed you if you were Noah, and the Ark were about to leave the dock," Lady Claire said caustically. " 'Tis Marcus that is the concern here. Do you intend to tell the boy what you have discovered?"

"You know?" Sebastian asked in disbelief.

" 'Twas I who purchased the sword," Lady Claire said, with a sigh of regret. "Paid dearly for it too, but it was a beautiful thing. A sword that a boy could look at and be proud of."

"You were a part of this fabrication?" Sebastian asked in amazement.

"Not just part," Lady Claire said wearily. "The entire Banbury tale was my misbegotten idea. I own that Amanda was against it from the start and now, it seems, she was correct."

"And Lieutenant Westford . . . ?" Sebastian queried.

Lady Claire gave a sad shake of her head. "I can say no more. The story is not mine to tell."

"Lady Claire?" Amanda's voice came anxiously from behind the door. "I know that you are in there."

"Come in, child," Lady Claire called.

"You should not be about, Lady Claire," Amanda said as she entered the room, ignoring Sebastian's presence.

"I was just explaining to Sebastian," she said, drawing the chair closer. "About—"

"About me?" Amanda asked, gently, helping the old woman to seat herself. "There is no need to fight my battles for me anymore, dear friend."

"He is asking about Lieutenant Westford, Amanda," Lady Claire said, her feathers drooping forlornly.

"If you have any questions, Mr. Armitage, you may direct them at me," Amanda said, facing Sebastian squarely. "As you can see, your godmother is badly upset by this whole matter."

Her voice was calm, but the desolation in her eyes was a rebuke. How was it that she managed to make him feel that the fault for this situation was somehow his? "I only wished to protect Lady Claire. I do not wish to see her hurt, or taken advantage of."

"Is that what you say to yourself?" she asked, fighting to keep her emotions in tight rein. She would not break down before him, would never let him see how much he had hurt her. "I will tell you whatever you wish to know, Mr. Armitage. But you must swear to me that you will reveal this to no one, especially my son."

"I would not betray a confidence, Amanda," Sebastian said. "Please believe that."

"I want your oath upon it," Amanda said, her tones tinged with scorn. "Though why I would put credence in the word of a man such as yourself is beyond me."

Her skepticism was no less than he deserved; he had given her precious little reason to trust him. "You have my oath," he said, "and though you think it worthless, I have never gone back on my sworn word."

"You need not tell him anything, my dear," Lady Claire said, grasping Amanda's hand in support. "There is no reason to fear for my welfare, Sebastian," she said, lifting her chin proudly. "I have known Amanda since the cradle. She is the granddaughter of a dear friend of mine; can we just leave it at that?"

"No, he has opened Pandora's box, Lady Claire, and he will not rest until he sees what it contains. If it is your welfare that he truly cares for," she said, unable to keep the doubt from her timbre, "then I cannot gainsay his right to know something of the truth. And if it is mere curiosity, then he will continue to dig anyway. Surely that would be more harmful." She turned to face Sebastian. "Ask what you will, Mr. Armitage, and be damned."

On the surface, she seemed totally controlled, but beneath her composure there was fire amidst the gray of those adamantine eyes, like seething molten rock. Any righteousness that he might have felt disappeared beneath her unsettling gaze. Was it for Lady Claire's sake that he sought the truth, or for his own? Mrs. Westford had thrown him a gauntlet, and now he was strangely reluctant to pick it up.

"You wished to know about Lieutenant Westford, Mr. Armitage?" Amanda prodded. *Think of it as a story,* she told herself, *a tale about someone else.* "We chose the name of a Sergeant Edward Westford from the casualty lists of Toulouse, Lady Claire and I. The rank, we changed. This way, if Marcus by chance encountered anyone who knew the *real* Edward Westford, it would be a credible coincidence. So many men were gathered on that field, that the likelihood is plausible."

"And Marcus's father?" Sebastian was unable to keep himself from asking the question.

Amanda held up her hand and slipped the gold band from her finger. She threw it to the table where it spun on its rim, falling at last with a wobbling clatter. "Lady Claire purchased my widowhood for me at the same place where she found the pawned sword," Amanda said.

"One more woman in black weeds among so many thousands would not be remarked upon," Lady Claire explained. "Although the widow's guise has not done what I had hoped, my dear. You never did marry," she added, looking at Amanda sadly.

"What man would have accepted me knowing that I had borne another man's bastard?" Amanda asked Lady Claire in anguish. "The lie was necessary to protect Marcus—"

Sebastian felt like an intruder. It seemed almost as if the two women had forgotten his presence entirely and were speaking words that each had kept closed in the heart.

"But you would not play someone false for your own happiness," Lady Claire concluded sadly. "I should have realized that from the start."

"Perhaps I have just never met a man worth baring my soul for," Amanda said, ruefully. "If I learned anything from Marcus's father, it was that. I had not had many friends in my life and I was so lonely."

"So vulnerable," Lady Claire added, defending Amanda when Amanda herself would not. "You were only seventeen, child."

"He was so kind to me, willing to listen," Amanda continued, walking to the window. She had not forgotten Sebastian, but she could not bear to face him, to see the contempt that was certain to be in his eyes. It was so much easier to pretend that she was unburdening herself to Lady Claire. "But it was all a facade, a scheme to extract what he wanted from me. When Marcus's father found out that I was with child, I was left to fend for myself." She looked out onto the bare Cheshire landscape, recalling that bitter London winter.

"Have you ever fought urchins for the offal that the well-to-do toss away, Mr. Armitage?" she asked, turning and addressing herself directly to Sebastian once more. "I have. Have you ever looked into the black waters of the Thames from the height of London Bridge and wished yourself over the rail and into the depths? I have done that, too. Have you ever been so hungry that you were on the verge of selling your body for a morsel of food? Well, I was perilously close to that point when Lady Claire returned from her visit to Africa and came to seek me."

"Will you ever forgive me, dear?" Lady Claire asked. "I should have known."

"As I have told you so many times, there is nothing to forgive," she said, coming to the old woman's side and clasping those small, bony hands between her own. "You are not to blame for what happened."

The look exchanged between them went well beyond warmth. Amanda's eyes sent Lady Claire an assurance of unconditional love that filled Sebastian with envy, but when she focused upon him once again, they held only the bleak gray of despair.

"I am a fallen female, Mr. Armitage," Amanda admitted, her contempt turning inward, her face afire with shame. "And there are many who would tell you that my son bears the mark of my sin. I am indeed the 'wicked woman' that you once named me in jest, but in truth I have claim to neither virtue nor honor. But quite certainly you have already sensed that; your treatment of me last night told me as much." She heard Lady Claire's horrified gasp and hastened to reassure her. "Nothing happened, Lady Claire, nothing more than a stolen kiss. It was of no consequence."

The last of his doubts were dispelled; Amanda was exonerating him. It was plain that she had no intention of trapping him into marriage. *A stolen kiss . . . of no consequence . . .* Sebastian felt an ache in his chest as the words whispered in his head. The memory of that kiss had kept him awake till well after dawn. Now, just as he was beginning to acknowledge the import of that touch, she dismissed it as having no consequence. "Amanda . . ." Naked pain stared him in the face, seared him with the knowledge that he had torn open long-ago wounds. And they were bleeding afresh because of him. Pity for her injured innocence mixed with rage at the man who had done this to her, who had taken a young girl's trust and love and thrown them away. But it was more than anger, more than sympathy that moved him, tripping his tongue, as he sought for a way to express feelings he only half understood. He tried to find healing words; and all he could muster was inadequate regret. "Can you forgive me?"

She shrugged. She could not allow him to matter. It was nothing more than words that he gave her, a rogue's stock-in-trade. How had she dared to believe that Sebastian was anything more than what he had always professed to be? Yet, a part of her cried. A small piece of her soul still wanted to believe in him. Ruthlessly, she silenced that small persistent voice. She was wounded but her injured heart had healed before and likely that foolish organ would survive this onslaught as well. But she dared not lose sight of what was most important. "What is of consequence now is Marcus. Will you tell my son that he is a bastard?"

There was an eloquence in her posture that spoke far more strongly than tears or accusations. In a gesture, she rejected his apology—and him. Her concern was reserved for her son and his godmother; he no longer signified to her. Although he had expected no less, the force of her rebuff hit him like a physical blow. The circle of love had closed and once more, he remained outside, but this time, the fault was his own. "I will say nothing to Marcus," Sebastian promised. "You have my word."

Amanda realized that she had been holding her breath. "Thank you," she said softly.

Lady Claire gave a nod of approval. "I knew that you would see reason, boy."

"*You* should be the one to tell him, Amanda," Sebastian

said, knowing that by speaking the truth, he might lose any chance at reconciliation with her. "He has a right to know the truth and it ought to come from his mother."

"Are you mad?" Lady Claire asked, her cane clattering to the ground.

"What happens when someone chips away at the fictitious edifice that you have built?" Sebastian asked, addressing himself to Amanda. "When the entire weight of your falsehood comes crashing down upon your son's head? If I have managed to penetrate your deception, surely someone else will."

"How can I tell Marcus?" Amanda asked. "It would destroy him."

"What will happen when he discovers what I have discovered? Will that not be far worse?" Sebastian countered, his voice resonant with emotion. He closed his eyes and pictured the man he had called uncle, fingering his parent's few possessions with covetous hands, taking his father's watch from him and slipping it into his own pocket, assessing his mother's gold locket with avaricious eyes, reclaiming every last object of value and leaving Sebastian with nothing, not even memories. *Why are you weeping . . . surely they told you that they were not really your mother and father . . . not really your mother and father.*

"It will not happen," Amanda said, with the vehemence of a vow. "I will not allow it."

"Can you prevent it?" Sebastian asked, regarding her steadily. "Are you so certain that you would take that risk?"

His question encompassed all her fears, both spoken and unspoken, the foreboding conviction that someday Marcus would throw the truth in her face and hate her for it. Was she willing to take that chance? But was it fair to lay yet another burden upon the child? The cocoon of safety that she had woven had begun to unravel and she was starting to realize that it could never be made whole again. Amanda opened her mouth to reply, but found that she could say nothing. With a cry of anguish, she rushed from the room.

"Amanda!" He tried to call her back, but she could not or would not hear him. He thrust the covers aside and would have tried to follow.

Lady Claire grasped his wrist. "Leave her be," she said,

her eyes glittering. "She must puzzle this out for herself. I doubt that there is anything you might say to calm her now."

"Yes, there is," Sebastian disagreed with vehemence. "There is a great deal that I should have said. I fully intend to tell her about how Marcus might feel one day if she chooses to pursue her present course. I know how *I* felt."

Lady Claire's plumes fluttered as she shook her head in astonishment. "You would reveal your history to her?"

"If need be," Sebastian said, feeling more than a little amazed at himself. His former so-called uncle was long dead; and other than Lady Claire and O'Shea, the secret of his birth was known to no one. "I understand what it is to find out that everyone around you has deceived you, that you are living an enormous lie. I would not see the boy hurt as I was."

"You would believe it better to tell Marcus of his real father?" Lady Claire asked, her voice shaking. "That he grow up with the onus of 'bastard' upon him? To know that his sire threw his mother out upon the streets because of his existence? I cannot see *that* as preferable. Leave it alone, Sebastian; every child deserves to dream."

"As I did?" Sebastian said, his fists curling with rage.

"Aye! As you did," Lady Claire retorted, her eyes ablaze. "I am sick unto the death of your self-pity. *Poor* Sebastian! For sixteen years, you were secure and happy, never wanting for anything. Yet, you have chosen to ignore that fact and instead concentrate on the unfortunate woman who gave you up. The joys of your childhood are all a humbug, or so you have convinced yourself. Deep within, you are still a child, hurting and alone, denying the truth."

"And what is that truth?" Sebastian sneered.

"You had sixteen years of love, boy," Lady Claire said, tears slipping down her wrinkled cheek. "And that is a damned sight more than many of us receive in a lifetime. My mother died when I was but three. My father thought me a disappointment when he thought of me at all, too ugly to be of any worth on the Marriage Mart and a bluestocking to boot. The only thing I felt toward him was a sense of duty while he lived and relief when he died. So do not whine to me about the ill your mother did in casting you off. She cast you into loving arms, though it likely tore her heart out to do it."

"Amanda kept Marcus," Sebastian said. "She, more than most, would have had reason to give her son away."

"And she would have done so, if she had thought it best for him. And that decision would have been no less courageous than the one she ultimately made. To spend the rest of her life wondering what he looks like, if he is well; crying on his birthday because of the emptiness." Lady Claire shook her head at her godson's adamant expression. He could never comprehend the bitter choices that had been made, difficult decisions that hovered between heartbreak and despair. "I had helped her to make arrangements for Marcus's adoption. There was a fine childless family in Cornwall who would have loved him as their own. If all had gone as planned, Marcus would be with them today. But when Amanda saw his leg, she knew that she had no choice but to rear him herself. Only she could give him the love that he needed, you see. But even with all the affection that a mother may give, a boy needs a father."

"So you gave him an illusion."

"Pah!" Lady Claire said in disgust as she slipped down from her chair and bent to find her cane. " 'Tis clear that you understand nothing, nothing but your own bitterness. Hold your acrimony to your bosom, Sebastian. A cold companion you will find it, and its only fruit is regret." She hobbled toward the door.

"And deception, Lady Claire, is doomed to eventual discovery," Sebastian said, picking up a journal from the bedside table and waving it aloft. "The woman who bore me was not as circumspect as I believed. Apparently, she kept up a correspondence of a kind with my father."

"How did you determine this?" Lady Claire asked, halting in midstep and turning slowly.

He readily turned the pages to the words he had scanned half-a-hundred times and read the significant paragraph once more. "He refers to her as 'his mother,' " he explained, pointing to the scrawled line. "Yet when making any allusion to his wife, Celia, he uses her given name. It must be my natural mother that he speaks of. If the dates are any indication, there must be at least a dozen other volumes in the library."

"Perhaps there are no others," Lady Claire said, at last. "Celia's brother may have taken them."

"Heaven knows that they had no intrinsic value; the library was largely left intact as I recall," Sebastian countered. " 'Tis more than likely that the journals were left behind. Certainly, some other clues must exist; perhaps there is some fragment of my father's correspondence remaining as well. My ankle is far better than I could have hoped for. I think that I could go and get them."

"Then why are you not out the door and down the stair?" she asked, her voice quavering.

"As soon as I am on my feet, Amanda will likely make me leave," Sebastian said. "I cannot go, not with this hanging unsettled between us."

"And matters with Amanda concern you more than this quest of yours?" Lady Claire asked, searching his face.

Sebastian weighed the question, and the answer he found surprised him. "Yes, although I could not tell you why," he replied at last. "I confess that I am more than a little confused. I have never felt quite this way before."

Lady Claire's wrinkles rearranged themselves into a shadow of a smile. "That is the best of signs in a man of fixed notions—a bit of befuddlement. Means that you are finally breaking out of the box that you have made for yourself."

"Can you get her to come back and talk to me, Lady Claire?" Sebastian asked. "I must speak to her, make her understand."

"I believe you do care for her, boy," the old woman said, discerning something in his eyes, a suspicious glimmer like melting ice. She had long ago lost her belief in miracles, but that glimpse of dawning emotion gave her hope. "I only pray that you have not found that out too late."

The sword pursued her, held by an unseen hand. It swooped in a silver arc, the glittering blade naked . . . cold . . . deadly. The truth, Amanda, a voice whispered. I know the truth. Ahead, Sebastian stepped from the shadows. She ran to him . . . He folded her in his arms, but the feeling of safety was brief. The music began and they whirled into the darkness, but the sword wielder was dancing with them. She did not have to see his face, she knew who he was . . . Mama! Marcus was calling . . . he was limping toward the blade, fas-

*cination in his eyes. "The sword of Damocles," Sebastian
whispered, holding her fast. She could not stop the boy as the
honed edge rose, poised to strike.*

Amanda sat bolt upright in her bed, gasping for air. Her
pulse was pounding as she attempted to anchor herself to reality. It was a dream . . . only a dream.

Hands trembling, she lit a candle. Marcus stirred in the
nearby trundle bed and she sat for a few moments, listening
to the sound of his breathing. He was safe, she assured herself. *But for how long?* a little voice within asked. *How long?*

There was no longer any possibility of sleep. Amanda
slipped from the room. The floorboard squeaked noisily as
she paused a moment at the head of the stairs. A glimmer of
light spilled from the crack beneath Marcus's bedroom door.
Apparently rest was eluding Sebastian as well.

She pulled her wrapper tightly about her and walked quietly down the stairs to the library. Perhaps a book would help
her to nod off? To her surprise, the room was already occupied. Lady Claire was kneeling by the grate, staring into the
flames.

"Lady Claire!" Amanda asked. "What are you doing up?"

With a start, Lady Claire attempted to rise and Amanda
rushed to help her. It was then that the younger woman noticed the pile of books at her friend's side, and the peculiar
smell from the fire, as if something other than wood was
burning. She glanced into the hearth and saw the charred remains of a vellum cover.

"Help me, Amanda," Lady Claire whispered, her rheumy
eyes filled with guilt and fear. "Or it will all have been for
nothing. All those years of anguish . . . for nothing."

"What is wrong?" Amanda asked, helping the old woman
to her feet.

"The journals . . . How could Nathan have been so
careless? . . . But then he could not have known that he and
Celia were going to die, could he? Did he intend to tell the
boy all, I wonder?" Lady Claire asked. "But not without asking me, surely? He really should have asked me if he was going to tell."

"Hush my dear," Amanda said, trying to calm her friend's
patent agitation. "Sit down."

"No, I cannot," Lady Claire said, brushing Amanda's hand

away and heaving the pile into the flames. The dried flaking pages caught like tinder. "Not until I have gotten rid of these cursed volumes. He will never forgive . . ." All at once, she gasped, sagging with a sigh of breath like one of Sadler's balloons.

Amanda was barely able to keep her from falling to the floor. For a woman of such diminutive size, Lady Claire was surprisingly heavy. All at once, the burning heap of books teetered, banging the flue shut and sending forth a shower of sparks as it fell out of the grate and past the tile-protected part of the floor.

"Help!" Amanda cried, as she dragged her friend from the room. "Fire! Fire!" She left Lady Claire at the doorway and grabbed the bucket of sand from the near the settle, smothering the spreading flames. The smoke was thick, choking her as she pulled a blanket from the chair and attempted to beat out the licking tongues of flame that were headed toward the laden shelves.

Sebastian came down the stairs as fast as he dared and bent by Lady Claire.

"Amanda," she whimpered weakly. "Library."

Smoke poured from the room and he heard a choking sound. There was a thump from the landing above as Peggoty ran down the stairs. "See to Lady Claire," Sebastian commanded, as he disappeared into the blinding cloud of smoke.

"Amanda," he called. "Where are you?" He followed the sound of her coughing, keeping the trailing sleeve of his nightshirt to cover his mouth and eyes.

"Mrs. Peggoty! Man the pumps!" Peggoty yelled from the hall. "Marcus, get Lady Claire out to the kitchen and make ready to abandon ship if she goes to blazes."

"Amanda!" Sebastian cried, feeling his way around the room. It was by chance that his bare toes found the yielding flesh of her body, collapsed behind the settle. He pulled her up by the arms. She was half-conscious and the two staggered toward the door. "Peggoty . . ." Sebastian choked. "Give us a hand!"

The sailor saw the figures emerging from the billowing cloud and quickly helped Sebastian get Amanda to the bench near the open kitchen door. Peggoty covered his mouth with a wet rag and rushed back to the library, a bucket in his other hand.

Sebastian seated himself beside her, pulling Amanda onto his lap in an effort to keep her from sliding to the floor. Her breathing was ragged, punctuated by intermittent coughing as she cleared the smoke from her lungs. It had been a near thing, he realized as he brushed back the hair from Amanda's soot-covered face. The edges of her jet eyebrows were singed. It was said that at the edge of oblivion, one's life marched past in review. Amanda was the one who had been within a flame's kiss of death, yet it was Sebastian's mind that filled with images. He saw Amanda looking up at him, shielding Marcus with her frail frame; Amanda in the rain, urging him to take the next step up the path. He remembered the determined look on her face as she had guided her knife steadily to save his leg; laughing over the gruel, her eyes bright as new-minted shillings; blushing in the candlelight— then in his arms and, lately, in his dreams; and Amanda, as he had last seen her, after he had shattered her carefully constructed world, and she had been filled with fear for her son.

The rambling thoughts that had kept him from sleep began to coalesce, to make a curious sort of sense as he looked at the woman in his arms. Understanding dawned and with it, a strange sort of peace. Precisely when he had fallen in love with her was a question that he knew he'd never be able to answer. How such strong feelings could come into being within the space of a few days was a question for which no reasonable explanation could be found. As for the whys and wherefores, the more that Sebastian tried to analyze them, the more confused he became. One thing, however, was beyond doubt, he had never felt anything so strong and true, never believed in anyone with such absolute certitude.

She stirred in his arms and he held her closer, suddenly afraid. The burden of his past weighed like a millstone around his neck, pulling him down. But it was not his birth that pressed upon him; he knew that she might look beyond that. The path that he himself had chosen, all of his past unsavory deeds and dealings, piled one upon the other to attain the stature of an unscalable wall. And Amanda was on the other side.

She, too, had a history, but she had dealt with adversity

with far more courage than he ever had. Would he have had the strength of spirit to keep a babe that many might have cast away, even under the best of circumstances? How much easier it would have been for her to give Marcus up, to pretend that he had never existed. Sebastian wondered if he would have been able to feel affection for an imperfect child as she had, a hurtful token of the past, who would forever bar her from respectability? The recognition that he might have failed that test of love was humbling.

A cough from the chimney corner diverted his attention. As Lady Claire rose from her seat, he realized guiltily that he had forgotten about her entirely.

"Is she ... all right, Sebastian?" Lady Claire asked. The look in his eyes told her far more than he realized and a frisson of fear touched her. Surely heaven would not be so unfair.

"She has inhaled a great deal of smoke," Sebastian rasped, his own throat raw. The feeling of helplessness was almost unbearable, yet there was nothing for it but to wait.

It was safe here. She could feel strong arms around her, holding her close and warm. The rough linen felt good against her cheek and the deep rumble in her ear was soothing. But her chest ached, as if gripped by a steel band. Dimly she began to remember—Lady Claire ... the books ... the fire. ... She was choking, could not breathe.

She felt the comforting strength of Sebastian's arms as the cough racked her. "Good girl," he encouraged. "Get it out of your lungs."

Her bones ached as she hacked away, sucking in breath between paroxysms. Her eyes flickered open, confused and frightened. "Lady Claire," she moaned. "Where is she? The smoke ... could not find my way out ... Marcus?"

"I am ... here ... my dear," Lady Claire said. "Marcus helped me from the hall."

"Marcus?" Amanda said in disbelief and concern. "Where ... ?" She made a move to get up, but Sebastian held her back.

Lady Claire coughed. "He is assisting Mrs. Peggoty at the pump," she said. "Oh, Amanda. I am so sorry ... This

is all ... my fault. I have nearly burned down your house
... around your ears."

"Mama, Mama!" Marcus came in the door, his hair
smeared with the dark effects of the fumes. "We have gotten
it all out. Peggoty says that I was a great help, wasn't I,
Peggoty?"

"Aye, lad, kept the buckets comin', you did, got strong
arms," Peggoty said, ruffling the child's head proudly as he
set his bucket down. "Mostly smoke it was, Mrs. Westford.
Flue got closed somehow and the stuff had noways t'go but
in."

"And the books," Sebastian asked suddenly. "Did the fire
catch the books?"

Amanda felt him stiffen. His hands gripped her tighter.

"If it had, sir, 'twouldn't be here we're sittin'," Peggoty
said gravely. "Place woulda gone up like a tinderbox. There
be some damage, but not much. My Missus is doin' a bit of
cleanup now."

Amanda felt his hold relax slightly. Of what import was
the library to him? And why had Lady Claire been burning
those books? She could see the anxious look upon her old
friend's face. As gray eyes met blue, there was no need for
words to be exchanged. Lady Claire was silently begging her
to say nothing. Amanda gave an almost imperceptible nod.
There would be time later for explanations. Shameful though
it was, she wanted to stay here in Sebastian's arms. She
closed her eyes and slipped into the darkness of her dreams.

10

Marcus and Lady Claire were surrounded ... walled in by a ring of flames. Amanda felt herself choking as she tried to get to them ... the heat ... the smoke was blinding her ... She could hear Marcus crying and felt her own hot, wet tears.... "Amanda ..." It was Sebastian's whisper.... "Amanda ..." Strong arms gathered her ...

"Lady Claire ... Marcus ..." she mumbled.

Sebastian could barely make out the muffled names as he tightened his grasp and breathed deeply of her smoky scent. It was wrong, he knew, to embrace her thus unawares, but he found himself in need of the reassurance that could only be given by touching her, holding her, and feeling the rise and fall of her breath. And, he told himself, she obviously needed some comfort as well; the nightmare cries abated and she rested peacefully in his arms. Gently, reluctantly, he put her back against the pillows. Mrs. Peggoty would likely return any moment and she had been uneasy about allowing him to stay without her watchful attendance.

Amanda crossed the bridge into consciousness. Yet when she saw Sebastian looking down at her, she wondered if she were still hovering in dreams. There was an inexplicable tenderness in his eyes, a softness that found its echo in the smile that lit his face.

"I thought that you were going to sleep the day away," he said, almost wishing that she had. It would have given him time to make plans, but then the whole night had not been time enough as he had discarded one possible approach after another.

"Strange nightmare," she whispered hoarsely, not quite awake enough to wonder at his presence. "Fire ... smoke." She sniffed, the unmistakable scent of soot strong in her nostrils. Her eyes widened. "Not a dream!" she exclaimed, sitting bolt upright as she recalled the events of the night.

"Everyone is fine, Amanda," Sebastian said, trying to soothe her. "Peggoty says that the damage was minor, although you will have the awful smell hanging about for some time to come."

"What are you . . . doing in here?" she asked, suspicion replacing confusion. "In my room." Unconsciously, she edged away from him, memory inciting the need for caution. Once before a man had invaded her bedchamber, taking a kiss for an invitation for more. The mistaken belief that she had loved him was even less of an excuse now than it had been before. For she knew now that she had never truly been in love with Marcus's father. And Sebastian knows, Amanda remembered, her heart falling. *He knows what you are, what you have been.*

The fear in her eyes was a warning. She had been badly used, deeply hurt, he reminded himself. "Mrs. Peggoty stepped out to look in on Lady Claire," he said, rising from his seat. He limped to the door. "Perhaps this will reassure you that my intentions are honorable ones." He pulled it wide open. "Unfortunately," he added with a cough, "you will have to choose between the air of decency or the decency of air. There is still a heavy residue of smoke and a substantial draft from the hall." He shivered dramatically as he looked at her, a question in his eyes. *Is there any chance of trust between us? Can you have faith in me, Amanda?*

"Close the door, Mr. Armitage," Amanda said with a sigh.

"And you will allow me to remain on this side of it?" he asked hesitantly, unwilling to take anything for granted. He could not afford to put his foot wrongly, not with so much at stake. "If you call me Mr. Armitage, I shall go, but if it is Sebastian, I shall stay."

Amanda was disarmed by his uncertainty and the fact that he gave her the choice. She took a painful breath. "Sebastian," she said, wondering if she would ever cease to be a fool, "you may stay, if you wish."

He brightened like a little boy who had expected a spanking but gotten a pat on the head instead. Something about him had changed. The attitude of arrogance that had been as much a part of his aspect as his hair or the cleft in his chin had all but disappeared. Peggoty's nightshirt puffed about him like a sooty cloud. "You can walk," she commented, for lack of anything better to say.

"After a fashion," he admitted. "My foot is still a bit sore, but not enough to signify. I suspect that I may travel to the Mills safely enough."

"I would not have thought it could heal so quickly, considering the appearance of your ankle but a few days ago," Amanda commented, feeling a ridiculous sense of regret. She ought to be dancing and singing hosannas.

"Lady Claire always said that I was lucky to be a quick healer, considering the amount of bruising I took as a boy," he said.

"How is Lady Claire?" Amanda asked, trying to turn the subject to something safer. She had no wish to think of him as a boy, to recall Lady Claire's stories about the child he had been. Perhaps that was the cause of her problems. It was almost as if she had come to know him far too well through her elderly friend's tales. A proper sense of wariness, a deserved degree of distance was difficult to maintain when the image of a hardened rake was replaced with the picture of a red-haired boy, pulling the stops from the fox dens. "Imagine," she recalled Lady Claire laughing. "Sebastian said that the cubs were his kins, since they both wore red hair. And the master of the hunt replied, 'Then you shall both have red tails.' And he made good on his word." Amanda could only hope that once Sebastian was gone, her life would regain its equilibrium, but the more she thought of it, the more remote that hope seemed. He would leave a gaping void, one that she knew would never be filled.

"She was sleeping peacefully when last I saw her," Sebastian said. "Mrs. Peggoty is with her now."

"Do you think we ought to send for the doctor?" Amanda asked, gnawing at her lower lip. "I would even apologize to Howell, for Lady Claire's sake."

"I asked Lady Claire," Sebastian told Amanda. "She said that she would just as soon be attended by the devil." Amanda smiled, as he had hoped, but the silence stretched, until it seemed to take on a texture, a stifling weight of its own. This would not do, he thought, as he struggled for something to say, but all that would come to mind was a ba-

nality. Damned if he would discuss the weather when he
wanted to say that he thought himself in love with her. But
how could he expect her to put credence in him if he could
barely believe his own feelings?

She knew that she ought to feign sleepiness, at the very
least, make him leave, but she could not. The quiet length-
ened uncomfortably, broken only by the occasional bark of a
cough. There was something unsettling in his eyes. They
seemed to change from minute to minute, like a pool at the
tide. By the time she caught a glimpse of something, it was
gone with the waves and something new had taken its place.
She nearly jumped when he spoke, at last.

"Amanda," he cleared his throat like a schoolboy about to
recite his lesson. What he was about to say was foolish beyond permission, but pride was a luxury that he could not afford. "Will you marry me?"

It was the preposterous situation, the stuff of absurd
dreams. The question struck like a bolt of lightning from a
cloudless sky. She looked at him in utter disbelief. "You must
still be suffering from a surfeit of smoke," Amanda concluded. "Or you are mad; or you believe that *I* am mad."

"There is yet one more likelihood," Sebastian pointed out.
"I could actually want you as my wife."

"That possibility can be dismissed by a simple question,"
Amanda said, her tongue dry in her throat. "Why? Why
would you want to marry a woman like me? A woman with
a tarnished past and a bastard son."

She gave herself no quarter, nor him, he thought as he
looked at her. He could barely comprehend these new feelings himself. How could he explain them? It would be a challenge to convince her that he had felt the need to possess
before, but never a desire to protect, to cherish. And there
had never been an instance when the merits of novelty palled
before the prospect of a lifetime of familiarity. Until now.

Yet he could think of no reason why she ought to put stock
in the sincerity of a renowned rake. Reaching inward, he
sought for resources he was not sure that he still possessed.
Truth deserved no less than the truth. "You know my reputation, Amanda," he began. "As you yourself have said, it is
less than savory. But I am not what I seem."

"Who is?" she asked, raising her singed brows in amusement. "Are you to tell me now that you are maligned? That you are not truly as bad as they say? Would that not make me all the less deserving?"

"This is no jest," he said, wondering at how difficult it was to come out and say it. "I am all that they say . . . and more. . . . Unfortunately. I . . . I am a foundling, Amanda." He looked down at his bare feet. "The Reverend and Mrs. Armitage were not truly my parents. I am a bastard, of uncertain ancestry, a flaw that few women would deign to overlook."

Amanda blinked rapidly, hoping to hide the glint of tears before he saw them. For one brief shining moment, she had been hoping for those foolish lies that every woman yearns to hear. It was a stupid fantasy, but she had thought that he would claim that he loved her. What kind of rake was he if he did not know when to cloak a courtship in flattery and false protestations? A poor sort of rake indeed, looking like a boy in his father's nightshirt, smeared as if he had just gotten into the bootblacking. There was no sop to romance in that proposal, just an honest statement. He was flawed merchandise, as was she.

It was obvious that he did not know that she was an heiress, deserving of at least some honey-coating. Pride told her that she ought to throw his left-handed suit back in his face. Common sense demanded that she reject a rake as a suitable husband. Yet the pounding of her heart cried "yes!" Looking at his hopeful face, she could only guess what his confession had cost him. He had overcome his pride. So must she.

"No," she said, sadly. "I am honored, Sebastian, but my answer must be no."

"Is it because of Marcus?" he asked, hopefully. "I am quite fond of the boy, if that will make any difference."

She shook her head, avoiding his eyes, unwilling to let him see her pain. He did not love her. Perhaps she might previously have been able to accept a marriage like the one that he proposed. But there was now one insurmountable obstacle. Fool that she was, she had fallen in love with him. Once before, she had given her affections only to find that she had given her love to an illusion. She would never go through that agony again.

"Is it my birth then?" he asked, rising from his chair.

She forced herself to look at him. At least that much, she had to give him. "No, Sebastian, the circumstances of your birth are of no consequence to me. You pay me a great compliment by trusting me with your confidence."

The heartache in her eyes convinced him of her honesty and moved him to make one more plea. "Your past does not matter; I would care for your son as my own. I am a wealthy man," he said abandoning all pretense of pride. "You would lack for nothing."

Except love, she reminded herself, shaking her head in silence.

Sebastian turned away, momentarily defeated. Where had he gone wrong? He marched his words in review, but there was no flaw that he could find in the arguments that he had marshaled in favor of marriage. All of her conceivable objections had been anticipated and countered. Yet she had turned him down flat.

There was only one other possibility that he could muster, the single obstacle that all his logic and all his love could not hope to surmount. Blindly, Sebastian groped for the door-knob. How could he possibly compete with a memory? Obviously, Amanda was still in love with Marcus's father.

Sebastian was so intent on making his exit that he failed to notice Peggoty standing in his way, tray in hand. Though the sailor barely budged, the impact caused Sebastian to ricochet like a rifle shot and the tray and its contents to crash to the floor.

"I am . . . sorry, Peggoty," Sebastian said, trying to catch his breath.

"Fierce on th' eyes, th' smoke is still," Peggoty said with a shake of his grizzled head as he helped Sebastian up. "No wonder, it is at all, you didn't see me, way your peepers is pourin' water. 'Tis sorry I am, t'knock th' wind outter yer sails. Ain't no harm done t'me, but Lady Claire's tea . . ." He knelt to clear the shards of china.

"Peggoty, you seafaring oaf! Is that my Bohea that has come to grief?" came the querulous voice.

"It is my fault entirely and I shall tell Lady Claire so," Sebastian said, an idea dawning. Perhaps his godmother would be able to advise him. Although the outlook was less than promising, she might be able to persuade Amanda to accept his proposal. "I fear that *I* am the oaf who is responsible for the mishap that has befallen your Bohea, Lady Claire," Sebastian said as he entered the room. His godmother rested among the pile of pillows, a frilly nightcap afuss with bows and lace perched on her head.

"Sebastian! Have you been weeping?" Her brow wrinkled in worry. "There is nothing wrong with Amanda, is there? Mrs. Peggoty told me that you would not leave her all the night through. What has happened?"

"Amanda is awake," Sebastian said quickly. "She seems well enough. As for my bleary state, the smoke in the hallway—"

"Cut line, boy," Lady Claire said, her expression intent. "You never could hoax me, not even as a wide-eyed innocent."

"Yes," Sebastian said with a half smile. "You always could tell when I was playing fast and loose with the truth. If you must know, I have asked Amanda to marry me."

The elderly lady clapped her hands in delight. "I was wondering when you would get around to it. Even a dotard could see that you are head over heels. Though I must confess, I had not thought you the type to weep with joy, even though it is a perfect match."

"Amanda does not seem to think so," Sebastian said, folding the voluminous sleeve of Peggoty's nightshirt. "She will not wed me."

"Do not say so!" Lady Claire exclaimed. "But I had thought—"

"—that she would jump at the opportunity," Sebastian finished the sentence ruefully. "So did I. I told her that she need not worry for funds ever again, that I would cherish Marcus as my own. I even told her the truth of my uncertain ancestry."

"Aaand . . .?" Lady Claire queried impatiently.

" 'Aaand' she said 'no,' " Sebastian concluded, slumping into the chair beside the bed. "I suspect that she must still be in love with Marcus's father."

Lady Claire gave a throaty chuckle.

"I see no reason for laughter," Sebastian said indignantly. "If she chooses to waste her affections on a man who treated her like so much trash, there is naught that I can do about it.

I daresay that some females are gluttons for such punishment.
Give a woman a choice between Hades himself and a man
rich as Croesus, as handsome as Apollo . . ."

"And blind as Cupid," Lady Claire added, her blue eyes
alight. "Damme boy, why did you not simply say—" She
stopped abruptly at the knock on the door. "It must be
Peggoty with my tea. Enter."

Peggoty charged into the room, waving a square of vellum.
"Th' man downstairs says he be a'waitin' for your reply, he
will, Mr. Armitage. Looks like a Fielding's man, he does," he
added in concern.

"He is," Sebastian said in amusement, as he broke the seal.
"Although I vow that the Runner believes that he blends with
the scenery; they all think themselves experts at disguise."

"Plain as a landlubber on a riggin', he is." Peggoty snorted.

"Tell him that I shall have his answer shortly," Sebastian
said, smoothing the sheets in his hand.

"A Runner?" Lady Claire gasped, leaning back into the pillows as Peggoty closed the door behind him.

"There is no need for concern," Sebastian said absently, his
attention diverted by the pages before him. "I had mentioned
to you, I believe, that they were pursuing that delicate matter
for me."

"And . . . what . . . have they found?" she stammered as he
scanned the last lines.

"Nothing," he said, softly, rising to stare out the window.
"They have questioned all the midwives in the area. Unfortunately, the most promising prospect, a woman who delivered
more than her share of babes of so-called 'widows,' died well
over a year ago. However, the carter has remembered but one
additional detail about the redheaded girl. The Robin Redbreasts think that it is inconsequential, but I find it highly significant."

"And that is?" Lady Claire quavered.

"She was crying," Sebastian said, his voice catching in his
throat. "That was why the carter remembered her, you see.
Her eyes were swollen and her face streaked with tears." He
seated himself at the escritoire in the corner of the room and
cut a pen.

"Do they believe that they will find her?" Lady Claire
asked when the quill ceased its scratching.

Sebastian sanded the paper and rose. "The Runners are quite confident that they could, given time ... and money. But they will have no more of either as far as I am concerned. Although I suspect I shall wonder about my mother for the rest of my days, I am calling off the hounds, Lady Claire," he said, folding the letter and lighting a candle.

"Why, Sebastian?" she asked in tones of disbelief.

"Why, indeed?" He delved within himself for the answer. "Amanda ... I suppose. In my anger, I pictured some faceless woman, tossing me aside with scarcely a thought. It was all so clear before. I had rehearsed every cutting word that I would say to the woman who bore me; now I am not quite so sure what I would say to her. You see, now, despair has a face ... Amanda's face." He watched the sealing wax drip onto the folded edge of the sheet. "Perhaps one day I will find my mother, but I shall no longer hunt her like a criminal. I am giving the Runners their congé."

He turned to face his godmother and was surprised to see tears running down her furrowed cheeks. "I had thought you would be pleased?" he asked in puzzlement, going to the bedside.

"Aye," she said, her bony hand reaching out to squeeze his fingers. "Your father would be proud, boy. You have grown. We must continue our talk."

"About Amanda," he agreed, eyeing the elderly woman's pale countenance with concern. "Later, perhaps. I shall hand this to the Runner and send him on his way."

"Later," Lady Claire conceded with a teary smile. "There is much that we must talk about."

"There now, sir," Peggoty said as he helped Sebastian on with his jacket. "Sharp as a sixpence is how you're lookin'."

Sebastian adjusted the folds of his cravat with an expert hand. "I vow, it is good to be out of that tent of yours."

" 'Tis a bit small on me, truth be told." Laughter shook the sailor's massive frame as he opened the door. "Missus gave it to you for that reason, she did."

"Well, I thank you for the loan of it, Peggoty," Sebastian said, glancing at the closed door of Amanda's room. She had not been out all day. "Resting," Mrs. Peggoty had claimed, but Sebastian tended to think that Amanda was avoiding him.

He stopped at Lady Claire's door, but heard the sound of Marcus's voice. It would be best to continue his conversation with her later, in private, Sebastian decided. Grasping the stair rail, Sebastian carefully made his way down, followed anxiously by the old sailor. "And my thanks for locating this cane in the attic," Sebastian said, caressing the ebony handle. "I had forgotten that my father had owned this."

"Glad to do it, sir," Peggoty said, his smile genuine. "Hadn't o' been for you t'other night, don't know what woulda happent." He followed Sebastian into the library. "Did a bang-up job, th' Missus did. Shoulda seen it this mornin'."

The draperies and furnishings had been removed for airing, but the smell of smoke was still strong. Otherwise the room was much the same as Sebastian remembered it. The walls were filled with books of varying languages and subjects. "Where were the journals that you found, Peggoty?" he asked at last, taking a volume from his pocket. "The ones like this." Although he had given up his search, Sebastian was still curious to find out whatever he could.

"Over there, I'd say," Peggoty pointed to the south wall, the one farthest from the fireplace. " 'Bout on level with th' eye."

Sebastian searched the shelf indicated and found a huge gap. Clearly something had been removed, but it was impossible to tell how recently.

The door knocker sounded hollowly in the hall. Sebastian absently noted the footman's measured tread and the sound of voices as he looked in vain, above, below, and beyond, but there was no trace of the other journals. "Are you sure it was here, Peggoty?" Sebastian asked.

The sailor scratched his head. "Aye, sworn to it I woulda. Show us again."

Obediently, Sebastian held up the book and the sailor's brow furrowed in thought.

"Wait, I'll be comin' right back," Peggoty said, his weathered face brightening. "May be that I can put my hands on 'em." With no more explanation, he rushed from the room.

"I am sorry, madam," the footman's voice carried from the hall. "But neither Mrs. Westford nor Lady Claire is receiving today."

Sebastian went to the door, observing the pair in the entry-way surreptitiously. Their sophistication of dress declared London; their supercilious manner proclaimed "Ton."

"We have come all the way from Town, my man," the female said, as if no other 'town' existed. "And we shall not be turned away. Go, at once, and tell *Mrs. Westford* that Lord Whittlesea and his mama, Lady Whittlesea, are her to see her."

The footman hurried upstairs.

"Just as that Dr. Howell person told us," Lady Whittlesea said, adjusting her son's cravat. "I cannot fathom how anyone could live here, but then what could one expect from a déclassé female of her sort. Taste is a combination of breeding and upbringing. She is deficient in both."

"Mama, you are speaking of the woman I intend to marry," Lord Whittlesea snickered. "You ought to be glad for her cheeseparing. All the more for us."

There was something about his face that was familiar. When Whittlesea removed his beaver hat to reveal a tawny head of curls, part of the puzzle slipped into place for Sebastian. The resemblance was startling. Except for the color of eyes and the signs of age and dissipation, Lord Whittlesea was the very picture of Marcus. From the spot in which he hid, Sebastian heard the rustle of skirts on the stair.

"Sir, . . . Madame."

The frost in Amanda's voice was chilling. Sebastian could imagine the color of her eyes, cold and gray as a winter's day.

"Amanda, my dear," Lady Whittlesea moved forward, arms outstretched.

"What do you want?" Amanda asked, her words clipped.

Lady Whittlesea was clearly taken aback. She stopped midway across the hall. "Amanda, Arthur and I have come all the way from London to speak with you. It was a long, arduous journey. Perhaps we could repair to some place more private?"

"We have had a fire; and the furnishings have been moved out of doors to air," Amanda said, unwilling to let them settle themselves in. Marcus was upstairs, playing spillikins with Lady Claire. She hoped he would be occupied until she could be rid of the Whittleseas. "Say what you have come to say and then get out of my house."

Sebastian moved to a position that gave him a wider view. Amanda stood on the stair, her gaze a combination of shock and distaste.

Lady Whittlesea stiffened, but she quickly schooled her expression. "We did you a great wrong, Amanda. Arthur and I have come to make amends." She looked speakingly at her son.

"Amanda, my love," Arthur declared, catching his cue. "How I have missed you. All these years, I have been searching for you. Wondering what had become of you. My conscience has been troubling me." He put his hand demonstratively over his breast.

Sebastian tried to read Amanda's face, but it was impassive. Those gray eyes, for once, were unfathomable.

"Has it?" Amanda asked with deceptive calm.

"Alas, yes," Arthur said, warming to his role. Gad, she was pretty, more of a stunner, in fact, than she had been all those years ago. There was an air of sophistication about her that was far more exciting than innocence. "Many's the night I have gone sleepless for thinking of it."

" 'Tis true," Lady Whittlesea added, wringing her hands, "All these years he has not married. Because of you! Oh, if only I had known the truth. Why did you not tell me, Amanda?"

Amanda's mouth rose in mockery of a smile. "But you already knew. It was everyone and anyone, from the butler to the potboy, who got me with child. You claimed that I was sharing my favors with them all. And you," she turned to Arthur, the memories pouring like ice water through her veins, chilling her to the marrow. "You stood silent through it all. Naive idiot that I was, I waited for you to speak ... waited for you to claim me, to tell your mother that you loved me and had promised yourself to me. I waited for you to tell this harpy that you wanted to give me and our child your name. But you said nothing. It was no more than I ought to have expected, considering your reaction when I told you that I was carrying your child."

Arthur's face reddened, his gaze dropping before her frozen stare.

"Yes, *I remember,*" Amanda said bleakly. "You could not meet my eyes then either. You wanted me to rid myself of the babe. But still, I hoped that you truly did love me, that all those promises had not been lies. But I was, as you said, 'a stupid bitch.' "

"You cannot have understood how difficult it was for me not to run to you, to put my arms around you," Arthur declared.

Amanda gave a brittle laugh. "Poor, poor Arthur," she taunted. "So terribly hard for *you* to see the woman you had claimed to love with all your heart called a filthy slut, thrown into the street with neither reference nor a penny of the wages owed. Perhaps it was the excessive agitation of it all that kept you silent? But I cannot claim to be faultless. Those hide-in-the-corner kisses, those embraces in the garden, the honeyed words, the vows that you made had only one possible end. I thought that I loved you. And when you came to my bed half-foxed and forced yourself upon me, I thought that it was my fault—that I had encouraged you. And when you came back, again and again, I convinced myself that I wanted you. What choice did I have but to accept you into my bed, to believe you when you swore that you loved me, that you would marry me? I had to convince myself that I loved you. It was my only excuse. My only hope—I was a fool at seventeen."

"Amanda, I did love you," Arthur said, stepping forward. "You must believe—"

"Must I?" Amanda lashed out, her eyes blazing. "I believe no one anymore, least of all you. I still recall your letter, Arthur, or do you think that I had forgotten?

Arthur clenched his fist, trying to keep his temper. "I had to marry an heiress," he whined. "It was my family's last hope, surely you can understand that? She was a Friday-faced chit with only her purse to recommend her. Her father was a cit, the most common of mushrooms."

"And you were still willing to marry her? How very noble of you," Amanda said, sarcasm giving her words a razor's edge. " 'Do not dare to communicate with me again,' I believe that was your exact statement, 'else I shall have you jailed for attempted blackmail.' "

"My position was precarious," he said. "We were on the verge of Fleet."

"As you are still, no doubt," Amanda said, her eyes narrowing. "Obviously you think that the years have taught me nothing. But I have learned, Arthur, hard lessons all. I have only recently realized what it is to love and I will accept no less than a man who will love me in return. Certainly, I have no intention of accepting the sham that you offer."

In his hiding place, Sebastian felt a spark of hope.

"True love," Arthur sneered, the penitent expression giving way to craft. "You were always quite the romantic. Does he know what you have done, this Romeo of yours? Does he know that you bore me a child?"

"He knows," Amanda said proudly. "And he would marry me despite it. You may have given me a son, Arthur, but you never gave me your heart."

Lady Whittlesea's consternation was plain. Clearly this was not going as she had expected. "What *of* the child? Does not a boy have the right to know its father?"

"A doting grandmama, Lady Whittlesea?" Amanda mocked. "I would not have expected it of you, especially since you have only now learned of his existence. Strange that you were not the least bit curious until now."

"That is all behind us. I am offering you marriage, my love," Arthur coaxed. "You will be Lady Whittlesea and although the boy cannot inherit the title because we were not wed, he shall inherit all else."

"All else? I take it you mean the Hartleigh fortune?" Amanda said, walking to the bottom of the steps to confront him face-to-face. "And I am not 'your love.'"

"The Hartleigh fortune?" Lady Whittlesea asked, her countenance bland. "Why, whatever do you mean?"

"Your theatrics would not even do you credit in Cheltenham, Madame," Amanda said, coolly. "You know full well that my name was Maisson, and that I am the Hartleigh heiress, but you will not get a farthing from me, I vow. I would not marry your son if my life depended upon it."

"What of your son's life?" Arthur asked. "'Twas clear from our conversation with Dr. Howell that you have been posing as a *respectable* widow all these years. Does the boy know that he is a bastard?"

Amanda cursed herself as her blush gave her away.

Arthur laughed unpleasantly. "Marry me, and he will never

know. I shall be his *cher* papa. Or else it would only take a few words in Dr. Howell's ear. For some reason, the man is not fond of you. And then, of course, there is the ton—very unforgiving. It would be a shame to ruin his future."

"Yes, it would," Sebastian said, stepping into the hall. "But then again, the Whittlesea name would be destroyed and so would you."

"Who are you?" Lady Whittlesea asked, peering down her lorgnette.

"A friend of Mrs. Westford's," he said, looking at Amanda reassuringly.

" 'Tis the fellow they call 'The Demon Rum.' Howell mentioned him if you recall, Mama. Said he was injured," Arthur commented, looking him up and down.

"Seems well enough to me," Lady Whittlesea replied, implying all manner of unsavory possibilities with a sniff. "How could you allow such an infamous man under your roof, Amanda?"

"Oh, I admit that my reputation is well deserved," Sebastian said, his eyes meeting Amanda's, asking her for trust. "I am quite ruthless. I have ruined quite a number of men in fact, even a few titled fellows like you, Whittlesea." He smiled companionably. "But I doubt that you would be so foolish as they were. You see, they had already mortgaged their patrimony."

Arthur looked at him in puzzlement.

"If you would allow me to explain my methodology," Sebastian said. "If I wish to destroy someone, it is usually a rather simple matter, particularly if they have a tendency toward the baize or they live above their means."

Suddenly Arthur's collar began to feel tight about his neck, as if a noose were slowly being drawn to a close.

Sebastian limped to Amanda's side as he continued, his hand seeking hers. "With wastrels, it is a rather simple matter of buying up notes, vowels, debts of honor and then," he snapped his fingers, "I call them in."

"You would not," Lady Whittlesea protested, blanching.

"Certainly, Amanda might do it herself, if she chose. She is a considerable heiress." *And I am an utter fool,* Sebastian thought, looking into her eyes, hoping that she would understand the message that he was trying to convey. "However, she is far too kindhearted a creature for such skullduggery. I, on the other hand, would do all that, and more," he promised, daggers in his eyes. "Sully Amanda's reputation and I vow I will make the Whittlesea name stink like the Thames on a hot summer's day."

"Want it for yourself, do you, Armitage?" Arthur sneered.

"Unlike you, Whittlesea, I have no need for a fortune, being already in possession of one," Sebastian said, squeezing Amanda's icy fingers reassuringly.

"Why would she choose you if she could have a title?" Whittlesea continued, ignoring the warning in the other man's eyes. "Are you so anxious to take another man's leavings?"

Sebastian's expression hardened. He took a step forward and brought his fist up, smashing into Whittlesea's jaw with bone-crunching force. Whittlesea fell to the floor with a thud.

"Were I you, milord, I would take extreme care in what I say about the lady," he said, looking down on him, almost itching for Whittlesea to rise so he could strike him again. "I am no gentleman and am, therefore, unbound by your rules of conduct. It would give me uncommon pleasure to rearrange those pretty features of yours on the paltriest excuse."

Lady Whittlesea gave Sebastian a basilisk stare as she helped her son rise to his knees. "You are a brute!"

"And your son, madam, has faulty manners which may need further correction," Sebastian said, brandishing his cane so with quiet menace.

"I would not be so cowardly as to fight with an injured man," Arthur choked out slowly, wincing as he put his fingers to his jaw. "Nor would I soil my honor in a common brawl with a man who is little better than a villain and a cit. Do you know of his reputation, Amanda? What they say of him?"

Sebastian was about to haul him up by the collar and give his lordship another lesson in manners when he felt Amanda's restraining hand on his arm.

"Yes," Amanda said, her chin rising. "I know what Sebastian is. And, moreover, I know what *you* are, Arthur. I know exactly what you are." She took Sebastian's hand and grasped it in hers. "Get out of my house, Arthur," Amanda demanded, drawing strength from the man who stood at her side. "And do not return."

"Mama!" Marcus called from the top of the stair. "Lady Claire lost the game."

"Marcus is a veritable Captain Sharp, my dear," Lady Claire said, as she thumped down the treads, the boy in her wake. "I have never seen ..." Her voice trailed off as she turned the landing and took in the scene spread out before her. "Marcus," she commanded hoarsely. "Go upstairs at once."

"Marcus ..." Arthur called, grasping at the last thread. He scrambled hastily to his feet. "No, Marcus, come here."

The boy peered from behind Lady Claire in confusion, unsure whom he ought to obey.

"Do you not wish to meet your papa?" Lady Whittlesea said in a coaxing voice, any lingering doubts about the boy's parentage dispelled by the uncanny resemblance to her son.

"My papa's dead," Marcus said in bewilderment. "He was killed in the battle of Toulouse."

"No, my dear, your mama was mistaken. Your own dear papa has come back to take you home with him," Arthur said. "I am Lord Whittlesea, your father."

"See how much you are of a face," Lady Whittlesea said, ignoring her son's hiss of pain as she cupped his chin and turned it to show him in profile. "The very image."

Marcus looked on in wonder. "Mama ... why does he appear so much like me?"

Amanda could not speak.

Marcus tugged at Lady Claire's skirt. "Lady Claire, why does that man say he is my papa?"

"Because he *is* your papa!" Lady Whittlesea said triumphantly. "And I am your dear grandmama. We want you to come with us to our great house in London, where we shall buy you all the toys you would wish."

Marcus shook his head in puzzlement. "But you cannot be my papa. My papa is dead. . . ."

"Stop, Arthur, for the love of Heaven, stop. . . ." Amanda begged, finding her voice at last.

"It is within your power, Amanda," Arthur said, massaging his jaw. "All you needs must do is marry me and you will be above reproach. Indeed, we can put it about that we had been secretly wed years ago! A few forged documents and no one will be the wiser. Such things can be done. With that face, who will question that he is my heir? A lord, Amanda, your son will be a peer—if you marry me. Think of it!"

Sebastian felt her fingers tighten, the intake of her breath.

Amanda looked into her son's questioning eyes and then into Arthur's. It was like looking into a distorted mirror, those two images, one after the other. "No," she said. "I will not marry you, Arthur."

Sebastian squeezed her hand. *"Brava,* Amanda," he said only for her, *"brava."*

"Mama!" Marcus moved beyond Lady Claire and limped to Amanda's side, his crutch thumping loudly in his haste. "Is he my papa?"

"A cripple!" Arthur said looking down his nose in disgust. "The little bastard is a cripple."

"It is no more than one could expect," Lady Whittlesea said, her voice pitched high. "Pedigree will tell."

"Get out, you bloody bitch," Lady Claire roared, shaking her cane and her fist. "And take your limp-wristed tulip with you."

Sebastian moved forward menacingly, but Amanda held him back. "Remember what I said, Whittlesea," he warned. "Or you may find yourself swimming in the Thames with a chain around your neck."

"You, sir, are no gentleman," Lady Whittlesea said, as she retreated towards the entrance.

"No, madam, I have the good fortune to be a rich, and rather merciless, bastard," Sebastian said, sketching a mocking bow. "You would do well to remind your son of that . . . when you catch up to him."

"Arthur!" Hastily, she followed him out the door, slamming it behind her with all the force of her venom and disappointment.

"Mama . . . ?"

The fright in that small voice tore at Sebastian's heart, as if the boy were unsure even of Amanda's identity. He knew all too well what Marcus was feeling.

"They were lying, Mama, weren't they? My papa was Edward Westford. He died at the battle of Toulouse and I have his sword on my wall." He recited the words like a prayer as tears slipped down his cheek. "He was a lieutenant,

Mama." He tugged at his mother's skirt, begging her for confirmation.

Amanda shook her head wordlessly as tears blinded her. "Oh, Marcus, my love," she whispered. "I am so very sorry."

" 'Tis my fault," Lady Claire sobbed. "I am all to blame."

Marcus looked from one to the other as the underpinnings to his world crumbled. "I know that I'm a cripple," Marcus whimpered, his lip trembling. "I don't like being one, but it's no less than the truth. But must I be a bastard too?"

Sebastian touched the boy on the shoulder, catching Amanda's eye for permission to speak. "I am a bastard," Sebastian said, "and as my godmama has told me, I have done quite well despite it, with only Lady Claire to love me." He looked at the old woman, silently acknowledging her affection. "You are quite lucky Marcus, to have both your mama and Lady Claire to care for you. I do not know *either* of my parents."

"Not your papa or your mama?" Marcus asked in rising interest.

"No, neither one," Sebastian said with a shake of his head. "You see, my real mama gave me away before I could remember. I used to think that it was a very terrible thing, and I spent a great deal of time hating that unknown woman who was my mother. I was very angry, you see."

"I am *very, very* angry," Marcus sobbed.

"I know ..." Sebastian said softly. "So angry that your stomach is tied into knots."

"And it hurts, way deep inside," Marcus agreed.

"Yes," Sebastian said, realizing there were but small variations in the physical manifestations of pain between eight and sixteen. "I thought that the people who raised me had deliberately deceived me. That was wrong."

"My mama lied!" the boy said, clenching his fists. "She lied!"

"Yes ... she did," Sebastian said, meeting the accusation in Marcus's wide gray eyes, so like his mother's. "But she lied for a reason, Marcus, out of love for you. Perhaps what she did was not right, but she thought it best for you." He looked at Amanda and saw the tears spilling down her cheeks.

"How can a lie be right?" the boy asked stubbornly.

Sebastian reached deep within himself for the answer. "My . . . father and mother . . . lied to me, Marcus. Although I was not really their son, they loved me just the same. They thought it best to keep the truth from me. But they loved me, just as your mama loves you. Your mama wished you to have a papa that you could love, even if he was only imaginary. Surely the papa of your dreams was far superior to the man you met today?"

"I suppose so," Marcus agreed with a sniffle. "He was not a nice man."

"No, he was not," Sebastian agreed solemnly. "Would you have wanted Lord Whittlesea for a papa?"

Marcus shook his head. "He didn't seem the type who would like to play at soldiers."

"Can you forgive me, Marcus?" Amanda asked, slipping to her knees so that she was level with the boy.

The child looked at her doubtfully for a moment, then nodded. "I'm glad you didn't have to marry him, Mama. He creaks." He made a squeaking sound in imitation.

"He was wearing stays," Sebastian interpreted with smile.

Amanda opened her arms hesitantly. With a tremulous smile, Marcus stepped into their shelter, and she hugged him close. Lady Claire touched Amanda's shoulder lightly.

Once more, the charmed circle had closed and Sebastian felt excluded, but then Amanda's eyes met his.

"Thank you," she mouthed the words above her son's tawny head. "Thank you."

With great exaggeration, Lady Claire sniffed the air. "I smell tarts," she declared. "Mrs. Peggoty's raspberry tarts, I vow. Marcus, why do you not go into the kitchen and have some."

"Perhaps we should all have some," Amanda said, rising to her feet and wiping a tear from the corner of her eye.

But Lady Claire gave a minute shake of her head. "Tell Mrs. Peggoty that we shall be along in a moment, Marcus. There is something that I must discuss with your mama and my godson," she said, beckoning the two into the library.

The settle had been scorched, but not burned, and Lady Claire seated herself on the newly cleaned wooden bench. "I vow, I do not know how to begin . . ." she said, her eyes misting as she patted the space on either side of her, motioning for them to sit down. "Do you remember, boy, how we would sometimes sit before this fire and I would tell you stories?"

"Yes, Lady Claire, I recall," he said softly, slipping into his place.

"Well, you told Amanda that she ought to tell her son all, before it was too late . . . you were right, Sebastian." She sighed and stared deep into his eyes for a moment, gathering her courage. "Though it would seem odd, I will tell you a tale now, and perhaps by the end you will know my meaning." She took a deep breath and closed her eyes. "A time ago, there was an ugly princess who had no suitors. The courtiers called her 'The Monkey,' because of her lack of height and her ugliness of face. The princess would laugh and pretend that they did not vex her. But in her soul, she felt pain and, more than anything, she dreamed of a prince, a suitor, who would see beyond her visage. But alas, she grew older and no prince came." Lady Claire swallowed and stared into the fire as if it contained pictures to illustrate the tale.

"When she was two-and-forty, a strange thing happened. A prince from a foreign land came to court and he had eyes only for The Monkey Princess. He danced with her and talked to her and all the courtiers thought him quite foolish, because he could have had his pick of the young and beautiful princesses. But he loved me . . . only me," she whispered, her eyes growing bright. "And the prince and princess secretly pledged their troth, because they wanted a quiet wedding with no mockery from the court. But the prince . . ." She took a breath to ease the pain. "The prince had to return home to settle some family matters in his kingdom. The couple were loath to part and they saw no reason to wait for a pledge in a church when they already shared their hearts. . . ." She shook her head. "The prince departed and weeks passed and the princess found that she was with child. She had never thought that a woman as old as she could conceive. Time passed and no word came from the prince and her joy turned to fear. She thought she had been deceived . . . used." Her voice filled with tears. "It was months before she found that her prince had gone to the guillotine in Paris with her name on his lips."

Lady Claire looked at Sebastian, her eyes filled with trepidation and longing. "The Monkey Princess gave birth to her son in secret, but she had arranged for a nearby family to raise him as their own. All through his youth, she watched over him ... listened to him call another woman 'Mama' ... until ..." She put her face in her hands and wept softly. "Do you hate me, Sebastian?" she whispered. "Do you hate me?"

The resemblance was there, Amanda realized, but only if one searched for it. Sebastian obviously took after his French father, but for the eyes. Lady Claire's had faded, but that blue gaze was still intense and the gray hair beneath her turban had once been the same startling auburn as Sebastian's own. But his heritage was also apparent in his gestures, the tilt of his head as he listened, the humorous quirk of his mouth, the crinkles in the corners of his eyes when he laughed. Amanda had come to love her elderly friend. Now it seemed no wonder at all that she had fallen so hopelessly for Lady Claire's son. *But,* Amanda reminded herself, *he does not love you.*

Tentatively, Sebastian put his arm on Lady Claire's heaving shoulder.

"I shall be outside," Amanda said quietly, wondering if either one of them heard her.

Sebastian found her leaning against the garden gate, her cheeks whipped red by the autumn wind.

"Lady Claire?" Amanda asked hesitantly, as he approached her.

"She is my mother," Sebastian said, his eyes filled with wonder. "All these years ... and I never dreamed."

"She loves you," Amanda said. "Now I know why."

"A man that only a mother could love, eh?" Sebastian said, the corners of his mouth lifting in a smile. There was a startled look in her eyes that gave him confidence. He moved closer, nearly touching her, but not quite. She did not move away. "She loves you too, you know," he said softly. "In fact it was she who sent me out to find you. We had a rather long talk and she has made a few rather interesting suggestions."

"Regarding?"

"You," Sebastian said, his smile turning lopsided. "This morning, I told her that I had sprung the parson's mousetrap, and that you had refused me. Nothing would do, of course, that I would tell her all, every blessed word. And when

I was done, I believe her exact phrase was, 'Boy, for a gazetted rake, you are a veritable looby when it comes to courtship.' "

"I suppose that Lady Claire set you to rights," Amanda
said with a halfhearted laugh. "But the answer will not
change, I am afraid."

"Ah, then the question is clearly at fault," he said enigmat-
ically, offering his arm. "Walk with me, Amanda?" he asked.
"I promise it is safe, avowed roué though I might be, for this
leg will not allow me to chase you if you try to run from
me."

Amanda smiled, taking the proffered arm and they walked
out the garden gate and up the hillside in companionable silence. The valley spread before them in a panorama of red,
gold, and brown. "I had forgotten how glorious the change of
seasons can be," he said. "In Jamaica it is mostly sun and
rain for winter with little else in between. I can barely recall
what snow looks like."

"Are you going to stay long enough to refresh your memory?" Amanda asked, hoping that it would not seem that she
was begging him to stay. It was an unlikely prospect, she
knew, but perhaps, given time, his feelings for her might
deepen.

"I hope that you will want me to; I know that she would
enjoy it. Lady Claire ... I mean, my mother. It is still quite
difficult to accustom myself to the idea," he said, shaking his
head. "She was watching over me all along. Those instances
when I thought that I was being protected by some guardian
angel with a penchant for sinners; I can recall several times
when an investor would appear at a critical juncture, or a
door to an opportunity would suddenly open. Now I suspect
that not a few of those seeming strokes of luck were due to
Lady Claire's intervention. It is somewhat humbling to realize."

"A bit of humility would not do you harm," Amanda said,
with a smile that took the bite from her comment.

"No, I suppose that I deserved to be taken down a peg or
two," Sebastian admitted. "For I certainly had all the pride
that goeth before the fall. In all my hurt and anger, I denied
everything that had been good in my life. Fortunately, the gift

of love that I had been given by my parents stood me in good stead despite myself. Lady Claire chose well."

"They knew whose child you were."

Sebastian nodded, his eyes misting. "It was an act of generosity. Lady Claire believed that she would never see me again. But my father and mother uprooted themselves, abandoned a promising living with the potential for a bishopric for my sake and Lady Claire's. She was in utter despair you see, over the death of my father and the need to give me away. The Reverend and his wife moved to this backwater of England for love of me and her. I never knew quite how much they loved me though, until I read my father's journals. 'Tis a pity that Lady Claire burned the rest of them in fear of my discovering the truth of my parentage. Those pages were filled with affection, all the words that Papa never said aloud. He just assumed I knew how much he cared," Sebastian said.

"Unfortunately, one cannot always make such assumptions," Amanda said with a touch of sadness.

"I know that," Sebastian agreed, looking at her ruefully, "now."

The intensity of his gaze was disconcerting and Amanda decided that the topic of conversation was on a potentially distressing course. "Did Lady Claire tell you anything of your natural father?" she asked gazing out at the vista, but not seeing it at all. She was far too conscious of him, his warmth, the clean scent mixed with the barest hint of smoke. Amanda smiled inwardly, all that was lacking was hellfire and brimstone. For he must be the demon that they named him. Only a demon could be so infernally attractive, disarming every defense of common sense. Only a demon could keep her standing so near to him, despite the fact that comfort was impossible with him so close at hand. Her pulse was pounding, her throat like tanned leather, her knees turning to liquid beneath her. She knew that this was the road to a personal Hell. Yet she did not move away.

"My father was a French *comte*," Sebastian said, allowing himself to be led for the moment, as he surreptitiously searched for the signs that his natural mother had described. Yes; she was most definitely avoiding his eyes, but the glimpse of molten quicksilver in hers made his spirit soar. He gathered his courage. Far easier to face Boney's troops than this woman, who could decide his fate with a single word. "Lady Claire even has a miniature of him at the Mills and swears that it looks exactly like me. I wonder, do all bastards tend to favor their fathers?"

"Only in looks, I hope!" Amanda said.

"I would suspect that the rearing may have something to do with it," Sebastian said, grinning at her vehemence. "So you have little to fear for Marcus, unless he has inherited your rather absurd tendency to blush. That might be rather awkward for a lad."

True to form, she blossomed pink.

"However, on you," he said, his finger brushing her cheek, "on you, it is most becoming. That blush is one of the things that I love about you."

"Love?" Amanda whispered, her cheeks growing hotter.

"Yes, *love,* Amanda. My wise not-quite-spinster mother asked me if I had told you that I love you," he continued, lifting a tendril of her hair and winding it tenderly round his finger. "You might think it strange, but it is rather difficult for me, a gazetted rake, to talk about love."

"And why is that?" she asked, her eyes widening with wonder as his hand strayed to the back of her neck, sending a river of sensation flowing down her spine.

"The rake's code, of course. I have broken most of the rules already—defended a lady's honor, drunk warm milk instead of brandy or rum, and now, worse yet, I have given away the heart that I am not supposed to have," he said, drawing her closer to him. "There is but one remedy to it." He cupped her chin in his hands.

"And what is that?" Amanda asked breathlessly.

"I suppose that I shall have to give it all up," Sebastian said. "Raking, I mean, not love. I intend to love you for the rest of my days, Amanda Maisson. A half-Frenchwoman and half-Frenchman. What could be more *convenable? Ma chérie mon coeur,"* he whispered as his lips came down upon hers.

"Ahoy! Mr. Armitage!" Peggoty called, running up the hill toward them. "Ahoy there!"

"Hell and damnation," Sebastian muttered, as Amanda quickly stepped from his grasp.

"Found 'em, I did!" the old sailor said triumphantly, waving the tattered remains of a journal in his hand. "Knew I had seen 'em. In the ash pit, they was. Curious thing to find 'em in the fireplace like they was. Some ain't but half-burned but the Missus, y'know, when she gets to cleanin'—"

"Peggoty," Sebastian interrupted, putting a restraining hand on the sailor's gesticulating arms. "You can take the journals and—"

"Give them to Lady Claire," Amanda interjected hastily. "She was reading them when they accidentally tipped into the fire."

"Aye, aye, Mrs. Westford," he said, with a smile, " 'tis right to her they'll go. As you were, then."

"As we were, hmm . . ." Sebastian said as the sailor loped out of sight. "I believe my hand was here." He placed his palm in the small of her back. "And your fingers were just starting to roam through my scalp. And as for my other hand . . ."

"Sebastian!" Amanda utttered a cry of surprise.

"Old habits," Sebastian apologized. "Reforming a misbegotten rake is a prolonged process, my love."

"A lifetime at the least," she whispered as her fingers wandered across the ridge of his cheek. "It seems that I have my work cut out for me."

"Then we had best begin the task now," he murmured, brushing a tendril of hair from her forehead. "Shall we start as we intend to go on?"

"By all means," she agreed as his lips touched hers once again.

The two figures on the hilltop merged and Lady Claire twitched the curtain closed.

"How would you like to call me 'Grandmama,' Marcus?" Lady Claire asked, her face aglow.

"I should like that above all things," Marcus said.

"So should I, my dear," Lady Claire said, hugging the boy to her. "So should I."

Avon Regency Romance

SWEET FANCY
by Sally Martin   77398-8/$3.99 US/$4.99 Can

LUCKY IN LOVE
by Rebecca Robbins   77485-2/$3.99 US/$4.99 Can

A SCANDALOUS COURTSHIP
by Barbara Reeves   72151-1/$3.99 US/$4.99 Can

THE DUTIFUL DUKE
by Joan Overfield   77400-3/$3.99 US/$4.99 Can

TOURNAMENT OF HEARTS
by Cathleen Clare   77432-1/$3.99 US/$4.99 Can

DEIRDRE AND DON JUAN
by Jo Beverley   77281-7/$3.99 US/$4.99 Can

THE UNMATCHABLE MISS MIRABELLA
by Gillian Grey   77399-6/$3.99 US/$4.99 Can

FAIR SCHEMER
by Sally Martin   77397-X/$3.99 US/$4.99 Can

THE MUCH MALIGNED LORD
by Barbara Reeves   77332-5/$3.99 US/$4.99 Can

THE MISCHIEVOUS MAID
by Rebecca Robbins   77336-8/$3.99 US/$4.99Can

Buy these books at your local bookstore or use this coupon for ordering:

Mail to: Avon Books, Dept BP, Box 767, Rte 2, Dresden, TN 38225   C
Please send me the book(s) I have checked above.
❏ My check or money order— no cash or CODs please— for $_____is enclosed
(please add $1.50 to cover postage and handling for each book ordered— Canadian residents
add 7% GST).
❏ Charge my VISA/MC Acct#_____Exp Date_____
Minimum credit card order is two books or $6.00 (please add postage and handling charge of
$1.50 per book — Canadian residents add 7% GST). For faster service, call
1-800-762-0779. Residents of Tennessee, please call 1-800-633-1607. Prices and numbers
are subject to change without notice. Please allow six to eight weeks for delivery.

Name_____
Address_____
City_____State/Zip_____
Telephone No._____   REG 0494

If you enjoyed this book, take advantage of this special offer. Subscribe now and get a

FREE
Historical Romance

No Obligation (a $4.50 value)

Each month the editors of True Value select the four *very best* novels from America's leading publishers of romantic fiction. Preview them in your home *Free* for 10 days. With the first four books you receive, we'll send you a FREE book as our introductory gift. No Obligation!

If for any reason you decide not to keep them, just return them and owe nothing. If you like them as much as we think you will, you'll pay just $4.00 each and save at *least* $.50 each off the cover price. (Your savings are *guaranteed* to be at least $2.00 each month.) There is NO postage and handling – or other hidden charges. There are no minimum number of books to buy and you may cancel at any time.

Send in the Coupon Below

To get your FREE historical romance fill out the coupon below and mail it today. As soon as we receive it we'll send you your FREE Book along with your first month's selections.
